VOX

Christina Dalcher

ONE PLACE. MANY STORIES

HQ
An imprint of HarperCollins*Publishers* Ltd
1 London Bridge Street
London SE1 9GF

This edition 2018

1

First published in Great Britain by
HQ, an imprint of HarperCollins*Publishers* Ltd 2018

ISBN: HB: 978-0-00-830063-0
TPB: 978-0-00-830064-7

MIX
Paper from
responsible sources
FSC™ C007454

This book is produced from independently certified FSC™ paper
to ensure responsible forest management.

For more information visit: www.harpercollins.co.uk/green

Printed and bound in Great Britain by
CPI Group (UK) Ltd, Croydon, CR0 4YY

In memory of Charlie Jones
linguist, professor, friend

ONE

If anyone told me I could bring down the president, and the Pure Movement, and that incompetent little shit Morgan LeBron in a week's time, I wouldn't believe them. But I wouldn't argue. I wouldn't say a thing.

I've become a woman of few words.

Tonight at supper, before I speak my final syllables of the day, Patrick reaches over and taps the silver-toned device around my left wrist. It's a light touch, as if he were sharing the pain, or perhaps reminding me to stay quiet until the counter resets itself at midnight. This magic will happen while I sleep, and I'll begin Tuesday with a virgin slate. My daughter, Sonia's, counter will do the same.

My boys do not wear word counters.

Over dinner, they are all engaged in the usual chatter about school.

Sonia also attends school, although she never wastes words discussing her days. At supper, between bites of a simple stew I made from memory, Patrick questions her about her progress in home economics, physical fitness, and a new course titled Simple Accounting for Households. Is she obeying the teachers? Will she earn high marks this term? He knows exactly the type of questions to ask: closed-ended, requiring only a nod or a shake of the head.

I watch and listen, my nails carving half-moons into the flesh of my palms. Sonia nods when appropriate, wrinkles her nose when my young twins, not understanding the importance of yes/no interrogatives and finite answer sets, ask their sister to tell them what the teachers are like, how the classes are, which subject she likes best. So many open-ended questions. I refuse to think they do understand, that they're baiting her, teasing out words. But at eleven, they're old enough to know. And they've seen what happens when we overuse words.

Sonia's lips quiver as she looks from one brother to another, the pink of her tongue trembling on the edge of her teeth or the plump of her lower lip, a body part with a mind of its own, undulating. Steven, my eldest, extends a hand and touches his forefinger to her mouth.

I could tell them what they want to know: All men at the front of the classrooms now. One-way system. Teachers talk. Students listen. It would cost me sixteen words.

I have five left.

"How is her vocabulary?" Patrick asks, knocking his chin my way. He rephrases. "Is she learning?"

I shrug. By six, Sonia should have an army of ten thousand lexemes, individual troops that assemble and come to attention and obey the orders her small, still-plastic brain issues. Should have, if the three R's weren't now reduced to one: simple arithmetic. After all, one day my daughter will be expected to shop and to run a household, to be a devoted and dutiful wife. You need math for that, but not spelling. Not literature. Not a voice.

"You're the cognitive linguist," Patrick says, gathering empty plates, urging Steven to do the same.

"Was."

"Are."

In spite of my year of practice, the extra words leak out before I can stop them: *"No. I'm. Not."*

Patrick watches the counter tick off another three entries. I feel the pressure of each on my pulse like an ominous drum. "That's enough, Jean," he says.

The boys exchange worried looks, the kind of worry that comes from knowing what occurs if the counter surpasses those three digits. One, zero, zero. This is when I say my last Monday word. To my daughter. The whispered "Goodnight" has barely escaped when Patrick's eyes meet mine, pleading.

I scoop her up and carry her off to bed. She's heavier now, almost too much girl to be hoisted up, and I need both arms.

Sonia smiles at me when I tuck her under the sheets. As usual, there's no bedtime story, no exploring Dora, no Pooh and Piglet, no Peter Rabbit and his misadventures in Mr. McGregor's lettuce patch. It's frightening what she's grown to accept as normal.

I hum her to sleep with a song about mockingbirds and billy goats, the verses still and quiet pictures in my mind's eye.

Patrick watches from the door. His shoulders, once broad and strong, slump in a downward-facing V; his forehead is creased in matching lines. Everything about him seems to be pointing down.

T W O

In my bedroom, as on all other nights, I wrap myself in a quilt of invisible words, pretending to read, allowing my eyes to dance over imagined pages of Shakespeare. If I'm feeling fancy, my preferred text might be Dante in his original, static Italian. So little of Dante's language has changed through the centuries, but tonight I find myself slogging through a forgotten lexicon. I wonder how the Italian women might fare with the new ways if our domestic efforts ever go international.

Perhaps they'll talk more with their hands.

But the chances of our sickness moving overseas are slim. Before television became a federalized monopoly, before the counters went on our wrists, I saw newscasts. Al Jazeera, the BBC, Italy's three RAI networks, and others used to occasionally broadcast talk shows. Patrick, Steven, and I watched them after the kids were in bed.

"Do we have to?" Steven groaned. He was slouched in his usual chair, one hand in a bowl of popcorn, the other texting on his phone.

I turned up the volume. "No. We don't have to. But we can." Who knew how much longer that would be true? Patrick was already talking about the cable privileges, how they were hanging on a frayed thread. "Not everyone gets this, Steven." What I didn't say was, *Enjoy it while you can.*

Except there wasn't much to enjoy.

Every single show was the same. One after another, they laughed at us. Al Jazeera called us "the New Extremism." I might have smiled if I hadn't seen the truth in it. Britain's political pundits shook their heads as if to say, *Oh, those daffy Yanks. What are they doing now?* The Italian experts, introduced by underdressed and overly made-up sexpots, shouted and pointed and laughed.

They laughed at us. They told us we needed to relax before we ended up wearing kerchiefs and long, shapeless skirts. On one of the Italian channels, a bawdy skit showed two men dressed as Puritans engaging in sodomy. Was this really how they saw the United States?

I don't know. I haven't been back since before Sonia was born, and there's no chance of going now.

Our passports went before our words did.

I should clarify: some of our passports went.

I found this out through the most mundane of circumstances. In December, I realized Steven's and the twins' passports had expired, and I went online to download three renewal applications. Sonia, who'd never had any documentation other than her birth certificate and a booklet of vaccination records, needed a different form.

The boys' renewals were easy, the same as Patrick's and mine had always been. When I clicked the new-passport-application link, it took me to a page I hadn't seen before, a single-line questionnaire: **Is the applicant male or female?**

I glanced over at Sonia, playing with a set of colored blocks on the carpet in my makeshift home office, and checked the box marked **female**.

"Red!" she yelped, looking up at the screen.

"Yes, honey," I said. "Red. Very good. Or?"

"Scarlet!"

"Even better."

Without prompting, she went on. "Crimson! Cherry!"

"You got it, baby. Keep up the good work," I said, patting her and tossing another set of blocks onto the carpet. "Try the blue ones now."

Back at my computer, I realized Sonia was right the first time. The screen was just red. Red as fucking blood.

Please contact us at the number below. Alternatively, you can send us an e-mail at applications.state.gov. Thank you!

I tried the number a dozen times before resorting to e-mail, and then I waited a dozen days before receiving a response. Or a sort of response. A week and a half later, the message in my in-box instructed me to visit my local passport application center.

"Help you, ma'am?" the clerk said when I showed up with Sonia's birth certificate.

"You can if you do passport applications." I shoved the paperwork through the slot in the plexiglass screen.

The clerk, who looked all of nineteen, snatched it up and told me to wait. "Oh," he said, scurrying back to the window, "I'll need your passport for a minute. Just to make a copy."

Sonia's passport would take a few weeks, I was told. What I was not told was that my passport had been invalidated.

I found that out much later. And Sonia never got her passport.

At the beginning, a few people managed to get out. Some crossed the border into Canada; others left on boats for Cuba, Mexico, the islands. It didn't take long for the authorities to set up checkpoints, and the wall separating Southern California, Arizona, New Mexico, and Texas from Mexico itself had already been built, so the egress stopped fairly quickly.

"We can't have our citizens, our families, our mothers and fathers, fleeing," the president said in one of his early addresses.

I still think we could have made it if it had been only Patrick and me. But with four kids, one who didn't know enough not to bounce in her car seat and chirp "Canada!" to the border guards—no way.

So I'm not feeling fancy tonight, not after thinking about how easily they kept us prisoners in our own country, not after Patrick took me in his arms and told me to try not to dwell on what used to be.

Used to.

Here's what used to be: We used to stay up late talking. We used to linger in bed on weekend mornings, putting off chores and reading the Sunday paper. We used to have cocktail parties and dinner parties and summer barbecues when the weather turned. We used to play games— first, spades and bridge; later, when the boys were old enough to tell a six from a five, war and go fish.

As for me, on my own, I used to have girlfriends. "Hen parties," Patrick called my nights out with the girls, but I know he didn't mean it unkindly. It was just one of those things guys said. That's what I tell myself, anyway.

We used to have book clubs and coffee chats; we debated politics in wine bars, later in basements—our version of reading *Lolita* in Tehran. Patrick never seemed to mind my weekly escapes, although he'd joke about us sometimes, before there wasn't anything left to joke about. We were, in his words, the voices that couldn't be hushed.

Well. So much for the infallibility of Patrick.

THREE

When it started, before any of us could see what the future held, there was one woman in particular, one of the louder sorts. Her name was Jackie Juarez.

I don't want to think of Jackie, but all of a sudden, it's a year and a half ago, not long after the inauguration, and I'm sitting in the den with the kids, hushing their laughter so Sonia doesn't wake up.

The woman on the television is hysterical, Steven points out when he returns to the den with three bowls of ice cream.

Hysterical. I hate that word. "What?" I say.

"Women are crazy," he continues. "It's not like it's news, Mom. You know that saying about hysterical women and fits of the mother."

"What?" I say again. "Where'd you hear that?"

"Learned it in school today. Some dude named Cooke or something." Steven hands out the dessert. "Crap. One bowl's smaller. Mom, you want the smaller one or the bigger one?"

"Smaller." I'd been fighting to keep the weight down ever since my last pregnancy.

He rolls his eyes.

"Yeah. Wait till your metabolism hits forty-something. And when did you start reading Crooke? I didn't think *Description of the Body of Man* had made it into must-read high school fodder." I scoop up the first of what looks like three mouse-sized bites of rocky road. "Even for AP Lit."

"Try AP Religious Studies, Mom," Steven says. "Anyway, Cooke, Crooke. What's the diff?"

"An *r*, kiddo." I turn back to the irate woman on the TV.

She's been on before, ranting about pay inequity and impenetrable glass ceilings, always inserting plugs for her latest book. This one bears the uplifting, doomsday-preaching title of *They Will Shut Us Up*. Subtitle: *What You Need to Know About the Patriarchy and Your Voice*. On the cover, a series of dolls—everything from Kewpies to Barbies to Raggedy Anns—stares out in full Technicolor, each doll's mouth photoshopped with a ball gag.

"Creepy," I say to Patrick.

"Over the top, don't you think?" He looks, a bit too longingly, at my melting ice cream. "You gonna eat that?"

I hand him the bowl, not turning from the TV. Something about the ball gags bothers me—even more than a Raggedy Ann with a red ball strapped to her face should bother me. It's the straps, I think. The black *X* with the bloodred center crossing out each doll's face. They look like half-assed veils, obliterating every feature but the eyes. Maybe that's the point.

Jackie Juarez is the author of this and a half dozen other books, all with similarly nails-on-chalkboard titles like *Shut Up and Sit Down*, *Barefoot and Pregnant: What the Religious Right Wants You to Be*, and Patrick and Steven's favorite, *The Walking Uterus*. The artwork on that one is gruesome.

Now she's screaming at the interviewer, who probably shouldn't have said "Feminazi." "You know what you get if you take the feminist out of Feminazi?" Jackie doesn't wait for an answer. "Nazi. That's what you get. You like that better?"

The interviewer is nonplussed.

Jackie ignores him and bores her mascaraed eyes, crazed eyes, into the camera so it seems she's looking right at me. "You have no idea, ladies. No goddamned idea. We're on a slippery slide to prehistory, girls. Think about it. Think about where you'll be—where your daughters will be—when the courts turn back the clock. Think about words like 'spousal permission' and 'paternal consent.' Think about waking up one morning and finding you don't have a voice in anything." She pauses after each of these last few words, her teeth clenched.

Patrick kisses me goodnight. "Gotta be up at the butt crack of dawn, babe. Breakfast meeting with the big guy in you know where. 'Night."

"'Night, hon."

"She needs to pop a chill pill," Steven says, still watching the screen. He's now got a bag of Doritos on his lap and is crunching his way through them, five at a time, a reminder that adolescence isn't all bad.

"Rocky road and Doritos, kiddo?" I say. "You'll ruin your face."

"Dessert of champions, Mom. Hey, can we watch something else? This chick is a real downer."

"Sure." I hand him the remote, and Jackie Juarez goes quiet, only to be replaced by a rerun of *Duck Dynasty*.

"Really, Steve?" I say, watching one bearded, camo-clad mountain man after another wax philosophical on the state of politics.

"Yeah. They're a fucking riot."

"They're insane. And watch your language."

"It's just a joke, Mom. Jeez. There aren't really people like that."

"Ever been to Louisiana?" I take the bag of chips from him. "Your dad ate all my ice cream."

"Mardi Gras two years ago. Mom, I'm starting to worry about your memory."

"New Orleans isn't Louisiana."

Or maybe it is, I think. When you get down to it, what's the difference between some backwater asshole's advising men to marry teenage girls and a bunch of costumed drunks flinging beads to anyone who shows her tits on St. Charles Avenue?

Probably not much.

And here's the country in five-minute sound bites: Jackie Juarez in her city suit and Bobbi Brown makeup preaching fear; the duck people preaching hate. Or maybe it's the other way around. At least the duck people don't stare out at me from the screen and make accusations.

Steven, now on his second can of Coke and second bowl of rocky road—an inaccurate picture, because he's forgone the bowl and is spooning the last bits of ice cream directly from the container—announces he's going to bed. "Test tomorrow in AP Religious Studies."

When did sophomores start taking AP classes? And why isn't he doing something useful, like biology or history? I ask him about both.

"The religious studies course is new. They offered it to everyone, even the frosh babies. I think they're phasing it into the regular curriculum next year. Anyway," he says from the kitchen, "that means no time for bio or history this year."

"So what is it? Comparative theology? I guess I can tolerate that—even in a public school."

He comes back into the den with a brownie. His nightcap. "Nah. More like, I don't know, philosophy of Christianity. Anyway, 'night, Mom. Love ya." He plants a kiss on my cheek and disappears down the hall.

I turn Jackie Juarez back on.

She was much prettier in person, and it's impossible to know whether she's gained weight since grad school or whether the camera has added its proverbial ten pounds. Underneath the professional makeup and hair jobs, Jackie looks tired, as if twenty years of anger have drawn themselves on her face, one line at a time.

I crunch another Dorito and lick the salty chemicals off my fingers before rolling up the bag and setting it out of reach.

Jackie stares at me with those cold eyes that haven't changed, accusing.

I don't need her accusations. I didn't need them twenty years ago, and I don't need them now, but I still remember the day they started. The day my friendship with Jackie started going south.

"You're coming to the march, right, Jean?" Jackie stood, braless and makeupless, at the door to my room, where I lay sprawled among half the library's neurolinguistics collection.

"Can't. Busy."

"For fuck's sake, Jean, this is more important than some stupid aphasia study. How about you focus on the people who are still around?"

I looked at her, letting my head drop to the right in a silent question.

"Okay. Okay." She threw up her hands. "They're still around. Sorry. I'm just saying that what's going on with the Supreme Court thing is, well, it's *now*." Jackie always called political situations—elections, nominations, confirmations, speeches, whatever—"things." That court thing. That speech thing. That election thing. It drove me insane. You'd think a sociolinguist would take the time to work on her vocabulary every once in a while.

"Anyway," she said, "I'm going out there. You can thank me later when the Senate confirms Grace Murray's seat on the bench. The only female now, in case you're interested." She started in again on "those misogynistic fuckwits on the hearing committee two years ago."

"Thanks, Jackie." I couldn't hide the smile in my voice.

She wasn't smiling, though.

"Right." I pushed a notebook aside and shoved my pencil through my ponytail. "Would you quit giving me shit? I mean, this neurosci class is killing me. It's Professor Wu this term and she's not taking any prisoners. Joe dropped. Mark dropped. Hannah dropped. Those two chicks from New Delhi, the ones who always go around arm in arm and have their butt imprints on next-door library carrels, dropped. It's not like we're sitting around trading anecdotes about angry husbands and sad wives and sharing our vision for how teenage text-talk is the wave of the future every Tuesday."

Jackie picked up one of the borrowed library books from my bed and opened it, glanced at the title at the top of the page. "'Etiology of Stroke in Patients with Wernicke's Aphasia.' Riveting, Jean." She dropped it onto the comforter, and it landed with a dull thud.

"It is."

"Fine. You stay here in your little lab bubble while the rest of us go." Jackie picked up the text, scribbled two lines inside the back cover, and let it fall again. "Just in case you can find a spare minute to call your senators, Bubble Girl."

"I like my bubble," I said. "And that's a library book."

Jackie didn't seem to give a shit whether she'd just tagged the Rosetta stone with a can of spray paint. "Yeah. Sure you do, you and the rest of the white feminists. I hope someone never comes along and pops it." With that, she was out the door, a mountain of colored signs in her arms.

When our lease was up, Jackie said she didn't want to renew. She and a few other women had decided on a place up in Adams Morgan.

"I like the vibe better there," she told me. "Happy birthday, by the way. You'll be a quarter of a century next year. Like Marilyn Monroe said, it makes a girl think. You stay cool, now. And think about what you need to do to stay free."

The present she left was an assortment of related trifles, a themed gift pack. Enclosed inside bubble wrap was a bag of bubble gum, the kind with the idiotic cartoons inside each individually papered brick; a pink bottle of soap with a plastic wand attached to its cap; bathroom cleaner—you can guess which brand; a split of Californian sparkling wine; and a pack of twenty-five balloons.

That night, I drank the sparkling wine straight from the bottle and popped every bubble in the wrap. All the rest went into the garbage.

I never spoke to Jackie again. On nights like this, I wish I had. Maybe things—the election thing, the nomination thing, the confirmation thing, the executive order thing—wouldn't have turned out the way they did.

F O U R

Sometimes, I trace invisible letters on my palm. While Patrick and the boys talk with their tongues outside, I talk with my fingers. I scream and whine and curse about what, in Patrick's words, "used to be."

This is how things are now: We have allotments of one hundred words a day. My books, even the old copies of Julia Child and—here's irony—the tattered red-and-white-checked *Better Homes and Gardens* a friend decided would be a cute joke for a wedding gift, are locked in cupboards so Sonia can't get at them. Which means I can't get at them either. Patrick carries the keys around like a weight, and sometimes I think it's the heaviness of this burden that makes him look older.

It's the little stuff I miss most: jars of pens and pencils tucked into the corners of every room, notepads wedged in between cookbooks, the dry-erase shopping list on the wall next to the spice cabinet. Even my old refrigerator poetry magnets, the ones Steven used to concoct ridiculous Italo-English sentences with, laughing himself to pieces. Gone, gone, gone. Like my e-mail account.

Like everything.

Some of life's little sillinesses remain the same. I still drive, hit the grocery store on Tuesdays and Fridays, shop for new dresses and handbags, get my hair done once a month down at Iannuzzi's. Not that I've changed the cut—I'd need too many precious words to tell Stefano how much to take off here and how much to leave there. My leisure reading limits itself to billboards advertising the latest energy drink, ingredients lists on ketchup bottles, washing instructions on clothing tags: *Do not bleach.*

Riveting material, all of it.

Sundays, we take the kids to a movie and buy popcorn and soda, those little rectangular boxes of chocolates with the white nonpareils on top, the kind you find only in movie theaters, never in the shops. Sonia always laughs at the cartoons that play while the audience files in. The films are a distraction, the only time I hear female voices unconstrained and unlimited. Actresses are allowed a special dispensation while they're on the job. Their lines, of course, are written by men.

During the first months, I did sneak a peek at a book now and again, scratch a quick note on the back of a cereal box or an egg carton, write a love note to Patrick in lipstick on our bathroom mirror. I had good reasons, very good ones—*Don't think about them, Jean; don't think about the women you saw in the grocery store*—to keep note writing inside the house. Then Sonia came in one morning, caught the lipsticked message she couldn't read, and yelped, "Letters! Bad!"

I kept communication inside me from that point, only writing a few words to Patrick in the evenings after the kids were in bed, burning the paper scraps in a tin can. With Steven the way he is now, I don't even risk that.

Patrick and the boys, out on the back porch close to my window, are swapping stories about school, politics, the news, while crickets buzz in the dark around our bungalow. They make so much noise, those boys and those crickets. Deafening.

All my words ricochet in my head as I listen, emerge from my throat in a heavy, meaningless sigh. And all I can think about are Jackie's last words to me.

Think about what you need to do to stay free.

Well, doing more than fuck all might have been a good place to start.

None of this is Patrick's fault. That's what I tell myself tonight.

He tried to speak up when the concept first bounced around the concave walls of a blue office in a white building on Pennsylvania Avenue. I know he did. The apology in his eyes is hard to miss, but speaking up has never been Patrick's strong suit.

And Patrick wasn't the man who showered votes on Sam Myers before the last election, the same man who promised even more votes the next time Myers ran. The man who, years ago, Jackie liked to call Saint Carl.

All the president had to do was listen, take instruction, and sign shit—a small price to pay for eight years as the most powerful man in the world. By the time he was elected, though, there wasn't that much left to sign. Every devilish detail had already been seen to.

Somewhere along the line, what was known as the Bible Belt, that swath of Southern states where religion ruled, started expanding. It morphed from belt to corset, covering all but the country's limbs—the democratic utopias of California, New England, the Pacific Northwest, DC, the southern jurisdictions of Texas and Florida—places so far on the blue end of the spectrum they seemed untouchable. But the corset turned into a full bodysuit, eventually reaching all the way to Hawaii.

And we never saw it coming.

Women like Jackie did. She even led a march of the ten-member Atheists for Anarchy group around campus, yelling out ludicrous prophecies like *Alabama now, Vermont next!* and *Not your body—a PURE body!* She didn't give a shit that people laughed at her.

"You watch, Jeanie," she told me. "Twenty-one women were in the Senate last year. Now we've got fifteen of our own in that fucking holy of holies." She held up a hand and started ticking off fingers, one by one. "West Virginia. Not reelected. Tick. Iowa. Not reelected. Tick. North Dakota. Not reelected. Tick. Missouri, Minnesota, and Arkansas stepped down 'for unknown reasons.' Tick, tick, tick. That's twenty-one percent down to fifteen percent representation in no time at all. And there's word Nebraska and Wisconsin are leaning toward candidates with—and I quote—'the country's best interests in mind.'"

Before I could stop her, she ran the numbers for the House of Representatives. "Nineteen percent down to ten percent, and that's only because of California, New York, and Florida." Jackie paused to make sure I was still listening. "Texas? Gone. Ohio? Gone. All the Southern states? Gone with the fucking wind, that's what. And you think it's some kind of blip? I mean, we're gonna be back in the early nineties after the next midterms. Cut the representation in half again, and we're headed into the dark ages of 1970-something."

"Honestly, Jacko. You're getting hysterical about it."

Her words flew at me like poisoned arrows. "Well, someone needs to be hysterical around here."

The worst part of it all was that Jackie was wrong. We didn't squeeze down from twenty percent female representation in Congress to five percent. Over the next fifteen years, we squeezed down to almost nothing.

By this last election, we reached even that unthinkable goal, and Jackie's prediction of being *back in the early nineties* seemed solid—if one was referring to the early 1890s. Congress had all the diversity of a bowl of vanilla ice cream, and the two women who still held cabinet positions were quickly replaced with men who, in Jackie's words, "had the country's best interests in mind."

The Bible Belt had expanded and spread and grown into an iron maiden.

What it needed, though, was an iron fist, an enforcement arm. Again, Jackie seemed clairvoyant.

"You wait, Jeanie," she said as we smoked cheap clove cigarettes out the single window of our apartment. She pointed to five neat lines of undergraduates marching in lockstep. "See those ROTC kids?"

"Yeah," I said, exhaling smoke out the window, Lysol can at the ready in case our landlady showed up. "So?"

"Fifteen percent is some flavor of Baptist. Twenty percent, Catholic—the Roman variety. Almost another fifth says it's nondenominational Christian—whatever that means." She tried a few smoke rings, watching them dance out the window.

"So? That leaves what? Almost half doing the agnostic dance."

Jackie laughed. "Have you run out of brain room, Jeanie? I haven't even mentioned the LDS people or the Methodists or the Lutherans or the Tioga River Christian Conference."

"The Tioga what? How many of them are there?"

"One. I think he's in the air force."

My turn to laugh now. I choked on a long draw of clove smoke, stubbed it, and sprayed myself with Lysol. "So not a big deal."

"He isn't. But the other ones, yeah. It's a religion-heavy organization." Jackie leaned out the window to get a better look. "And it's mostly

CHRISTINA DALCHER

men. Conservative men who love their God and their country." She sighed. "Women, not so much."

"That's ridiculous," I said, leaving her to burn the other lung with a second cigarette. "They don't hate women."

"You, kiddo, need to get out more. Which states do you think have the highest enlistment rates? Hint: they ain't in fucking New England. They're good old boys."

"So what?" I was exasperating her, and I knew it, but I couldn't see the connection Jackie was trying to make.

"So they're conservative, that's what. Mostly white. Mostly straight." Jackie stubbed out the half-smoked clove, wrapped it in a plastic baggie, and faced me, arms crossed. "Who do you think is angriest right now? In our country, I mean."

I shrugged. "African Americans?"

She made a buzzing noise, a sort of you're-out-but-we've-got-some-lovely-consolation-prizes-backstage kind of a sound. "Guess again."

"Gays?"

"No, you dope. The straight white dude. He's angry as shit. He feels emasculated."

"Honestly, Jacko."

"Of course he does." Jackie pointed a purple fingernail at me. "You just wait. It's gonna be a different world in a few years if we don't do something to change it. Expanding Bible Belt, shit-ass representation in Congress, and a pack of power-hungry little boys who are tired of being told they gotta be more sensitive." She laughed then, a wicked laugh that shook her whole body. "And don't think they'll all be men. The Becky Homeckies will be on their side."

"The who?"

Jackie nodded at my sweats and bed-matted hair, at the pile of yesterday's dishes in the sink, and finally at her own outfit. It was one of the more interesting fashion creations I'd seen on her in a while—paisley leggings, an oversized crocheted sweater that used to be beige but had now taken on the color of various other articles of clothing, and purple stiletto boots. "The Susie Homemakers. Those girls in matching skirts and sweaters and sensible shoes going for their Mrs. degrees. You think they like our sort? Think again."

"Come on, Jackie," I said.

"Just wait, Jeanie."

So I did. Everything turned out pretty much as Jackie thought it would. And worse. They came at us from so many vectors, and so quietly, we never had the chance to assemble ranks.

One thing I learned from Jackie: you can't protest what you don't see coming.

I learned other things a year ago. I learned how difficult it is to write a letter to my congressman without a pen, or to mail a letter without a stamp. I learned how easy it is for the man at the office supply store to say, "I'm sorry, ma'am. I can't sell you that," or for the postal worker to shake his head when anyone without a Y chromosome asks for stamps. I learned how quickly a cell phone account can be canceled, and how efficient young enlisted men can be at installing cameras.

I learned that once a plan is in place, everything can happen overnight.

SIX

P atrick is feeling frisky tonight, even if I'm not. Either that, or he's looking for stress relief before another day in another week at the job that's keeping gas in the car and paying the kids' dentist bills. Even a topped-out government job never seems like enough, not now that I'm no longer working.

The lights on the porch go out, the boys tumble into their beds, and Patrick tumbles into ours.

"Love you, babe," he says. His roaming hands tell me he's not ready for sleep. Not yet. And it has been a while. A few months is my best guess. It might be longer than that.

So we get to business.

I was never one to talk much while making love. Words seemed clumsy; sharp interruptions of a natural rhythm, a basic coupling. And forget about silly porn-style mantras: *Give it to me. Here I come. Fuck me harder. Oh baby, oh baby, oh baby.* They had a place in kitchen flirting or raunchy jokes with the girlfriends, but not in bed. Not with Patrick.

Still, there had been talk between us. Before and afterward. During. An *I love you*, six sounds, diphthongs and glides and liquids with only a single turbulent *v*, a soft consonant in so many ways, appropriate to the setting. Our names, whispered. *Patrick. Jean.*

Tonight, with the children in their beds and Patrick in me, his steady breathing close and heavy in my ear, my eyes shut to the glint of moon refracting off the dresser mirror, I consider what I'd prefer. Would I be happier if he shared my silence? Would it be easier? Or do I need my husband's words to fill the gaps in the room and inside me?

He stops. "What's wrong, babe?" There's concern in his voice, but I think I hear a trace of otherness, a tone I never want to hear again. It sounds like pity.

I reach up, place both palms flat against the sides of his face, and pull his mouth to mine. In the kiss, I talk to him, make assurances, spell out how every little thing is going to be all right. It's a lie, but a fitting lie for the moment, and he doesn't speak again.

Tonight, let it be all quiet. Full silence. A void.

I am now in two places at once. I am here, under Patrick, the weight of him suspended above my skin, part of him and also separate. I am in my other self, fumbling with my prom dress buttons in the back seat of Jimmy Reed's Grand National, a sex car if there ever was one. I'm panting and laughing and high on spiked punch while Jimmy gropes and grabs. Then I'm singing in the glee club, cheering on our no-star football team, giving the valedictory address at college graduation, shouting obscenities at Patrick when he tells me to push and pant *just one more time, babe,* before the baby's head crowns. I'm in a rented cottage, two months ago, lying beneath the body of a man I want desperately to see again, a man whose hands I still feel roaming over my flesh.

Lorenzo, I whisper inside my head, and kick the three delicious syllables away before they hurt too much.

My self is becoming more and more separate.

At times like this, I think about the other women. Dr. Claudia, for instance. Once, in her office, I asked whether gynecologists enjoyed sex more than the rest of us, or whether they got lost in the clinical nature of the act. Did they lie back and think, Oh, now my vagina is expanding and lengthening, now my clitoris is retracting into its hood, now the first third (but only the first third) of my vaginal walls are contracting at the rate of one pulse every eight-tenths of a second.

Dr. Claudia withdrew the speculum in one smooth move and said, "Actually, when I first started medical school, that's exactly what I did. I couldn't help it. Thank god my partner then was another med student; otherwise, I think he would have zipped up and walked out and left me laughing hysterically under the sheets." She tapped my knee and removed one foot, then the other, from the pink-fuzz-covered stirrups. "Now I just enjoy it. Like everyone else."

While I'm thinking about Dr. Claudia and her shiny steel speculum, Patrick orgasms and collapses on me, kissing my ears and throat.

I wonder what the other women do. How they cope. Do they still find something to enjoy? Do they love their husbands in the same way? Do they hate them, just a little bit?

SEVEN

The first time she screams, I think I'm dreaming. Patrick snores beside me; he's always been one to sleep heavily, and his schedule for the past month has run him into the ground. So snore, snore, snore.

My sympathy has already expired. Let them work twelve-hour days to pick up the inevitable slack that canceling almost half of the workforce brought about. Let them bury themselves in paperwork and administrative nonsense and then limp home only to sleep like the dead and get up and do it all over again. What did they expect?

It isn't Patrick's fault. I know this in my heart and in my mind. With four kids, we need the income his job brings in. Still, I'm all dry on sympathy.

She screams again, not a wordless scream, but a blood-curdling waterfall of words.

Mommy, don't let it get me don't let it get me don't let it get me don't let it get me—

I'm out of the bed in a tumble of sheets and quilts, nightdress tangled around my legs. My shin slams into the hard corner of the bedside table, a bull's-eye on my bone. This one will bleed, leave a scar, but I'm not thinking about that. I'm thinking about the scar I'll own if I don't make it to Sonia's bedroom in time to quiet her.

The words continue pouring out, flying through the hall toward me like poisoned darts from a million hostile blowpipes. Each one stings; each one pierces my once-tough skin with the precision of a surgeon's scalpel, driving directly to my gut. How many words has she said? Fifty? Sixty? More?

More.

Oh god.

Now Patrick's up, wide-eyed and pallid, a picture of some silver-screen hero fresh with fright on discovering the monster in the closet. I hear his footsteps quick behind me matching the thrum of blood pulsing through my veins, hear him yell, "Run, Jean! Run!" but I don't turn around. Doors open as I fly past them, first Steve's, then the twins'. Someone—maybe Patrick, maybe me—slaps on the hall light switch, and three blurred faces, pale as ghosts, appear in my peripheral vision. Of course, Sonia's room would be the farthest from my own.

Mommy, please don't let it get me don't let it get me don't—

Sam and Leo start crying. For the smallest of moments, I register a single thought: *lousy mother.* My boys are in distress, and I'm moving past them, uncaring and oblivious. I'll worry about this damage later, if I'm in the condition to worry about anything.

Two steps into Sonia's small room, I vault onto her bed, one hand searching for her mouth, clamping onto it. My free hand gropes under her sheets for the hard metal of the wrist counter.

Sonia moans through my palm, and I catch her nightstand clock out of the corner of my eye. Eleven thirty.

I have no words remaining, not for the next half hour.

"Patrick—," I mouth when he switches the overhead light on. Four pairs of eyes stare at the scene on Sonia's bed. It must look like violence, a grotesque sculpture—my writhing child, her nightgown translucent with sweat; me, lying sprawled on top of her, suffocating her cries and pinning her to the mattress. What a horrible tableau we must make. Infanticide in the flesh.

My counter glows 100 over Sonia's mouth. I turn to Patrick, pleading mutely, knowing that if I speak, if the LED turns over to 101, she'll share the inevitable shock.

Patrick joins me on the bed, pries my hand from Sonia, replaces it with his own. "Shh, baby girl. Shh. Daddy's here. Daddy won't let anything happen to you."

Sam and Leo and Steve come into the room. They jostle for position and all of a sudden there's no more room for me. *Lousy mother* becomes *useless mother*, two words ping-ponging in my head. Thanks, Patrick. Thanks, boys.

I don't hate them. I tell myself I don't hate them.

But sometimes I do.

I hate that the males in my family tell Sonia how pretty she is. I hate that they're the ones who soothe her when she falls off her push-bike, that they make up stories to tell her about princesses and mermaids. I hate having to watch and listen.

It's a trial reminding myself they're not the ones who did this to me. Fuck it.

Sonia has quieted now; the immediate danger has passed. But I note as I slip backward out of her room that her brothers are careful not to touch her. Just in case she has another fit.

In the corner of the living room is our bar, a stout wooden trolley with its bottled assortment of liquid anesthetic. Clear vodka and gin, caramel scotch and bourbon, an inch of cobalt remaining in the curaçao bottle we bought years ago for a Polynesian-themed picnic. Tucked toward the back is what I'm looking for: grappa, also known as Italian moonshine. I pull it out along with a small stemmed glass and take both with me onto the back porch and wait for the clock to chime midnight.

Drinking isn't something I do much of anymore. It's too goddamned depressing to sip an icy gin and tonic and think about summer evenings when Patrick and I would sit shoulder to shoulder on our first apartment's postage stamp of a balcony, talking about my research grants and qualifying papers, about his hellish hours as a resident at Georgetown University Hospital. Also, I'm afraid to get drunk, afraid I might develop too much Dutch courage and forget the rules. Or flout them.

The first shot of grappa goes down like fire; the second is smoother, palliative. I'm on my third when the clock announces today's end and a dull ping on my left wrist gives me another hundred words.

What will I do with them?

I slide back in through the screen door, pad over the living room rug, replace the bottle on the bar. Sonia is sitting up when I enter her room, a glass of milk in her hands, propped up by Patrick's palm. The boys have returned to their own beds, and I sit next to Patrick.

"Everything's all right, darling. Mommy's here."

Sonia smiles up at me.

But this isn't how it happens.

I take my drink out on the lawn, past the roses Mrs. Ray chose with care and planted, out into the dark, sweet-smelling patch of grass where the lilacs bloom. They say you're supposed to talk to plants to make them healthier; if that's true, my garden is moribund. Tonight, though, I don't give a rat's ass about the lilacs or the roses or anything else. My mind's on a different brand of creature.

"You fucking bastards!" I scream. And again.

A light flickers on in the Kings' house, and the vertical blinds twitch and separate. I don't give a damn. I don't care if I wake up the entire subdivision, if they hear me all the way to Capitol Hill. I scream and scream and scream until my throat is dry. Then I take another swig from the grappa bottle, spilling some on my nightgown.

"Jean!" The voice comes from behind me, followed by the slam of a door. "Jean!"

"Fuck off," I say. "Or I'll keep talking." Suddenly, I don't care anymore about the shock or the pain. If I can keep screaming through it, keep up my anger, drown the sensation with booze and words, would the electricity continue to flow? Would it lay me out?

Probably not. They won't kill us for the same reason they won't sanction abortions. We've turned into necessary evils, objects to be fucked and not heard.

Patrick is yelling now. "Jean! Babe, stop. Please stop."

Another light goes on in the Kings' house. A door squeaks open. Footsteps. "What the hell's going on out there, McClellan? People are trying to sleep." It's the husband, of course. Evan. Olivia is still peeking through the blinds at my midnight show.

"Fuck you, Evan," I say.

Evan announces he's calling the cops, although not quite so politely as all that. Then the light in Olivia's window goes dark.

I hear screaming—some my own—then Patrick is on me, wrestling me down to the moist grass, pleading and cajoling, and I can taste tears on his lips when he kisses me quiet. My first thought is whether they teach men these techniques, whether there were pamphlets handed over to husbands and sons and fathers and brothers on the days we became shackled by these shiny steel bracelets. Then I decide they couldn't possibly care that much.

"Let me go." I'm in the grass, nightgown stuck to me like a snakeskin. It's then I realize I'm hissing.

It's also then I realize the pulses are closer together.

Patrick grasps my left wrist, checks the number. "You're out, Jean."

I try to wriggle away from him, an act as empty of hope as my heart. The grass is bitter in my mouth, until I realize I'm chewing on a mouthful of dirt. I know what Patrick's doing; I know he's set on absorbing the shock with me.

So I stay silent and let him lead me back inside as the wail of sirens grows louder.

Patrick can talk to them. I don't have any words left.

EIGHT

Stupid, stupid, stupid.

Sonia's blank stare as I walk her through the rain to the bus stop is the worst reproach, my punishment for last night's grappa-soaked tirade in the backyard. Certainly worse than Officers So-and-So lecturing me on my disturbance of the neighborhood peace.

This is the first time I haven't told her I love her before sending her off to school. I blow a kiss, and immediately regret it when she raises a tiny hand to her lips and starts to blow one back.

The black eye of a camera stares at me from the bus door.

They're everywhere now, the cameras. In supermarkets and schools, hair salons and restaurants, waiting to catch any gesture that might be seen as sign language, even the most rudimentary form of nonverbal communication.

Because, after all, none of the crap they've hit us with has anything to do with speaking.

I think it was a month after the wrist counters went on that it happened. In the produce section of Safeway, of all places. I didn't know the women, but I'd seen them shopping before. Like all the new mothers in the neighborhood, they traveled in pairs or packs, running errands in sync, ready to lend a hand if one of the babies had a meltdown in the checkout aisle. These two, though, they were close-knit, tight. It was that tightness, I understand now, that was the problem.

You can take a lot away from a person—money, job, intellectual stimulation, whatever. You can take her words, even, without changing the essence of her.

Take away camaraderie, though, and we're talking about something different.

I watched them, these women, taking turns to ogle each other's baby, pointing at their hearts and temples in a silent pidgin. I watched them finger spell next to a pyramid of oranges, laughing when they fucked up one of the letters they probably hadn't signed since the sixth grade when they passed messages about Kevin or Tommy or Carlo. I watched them stare in horror as three uniformed men approached, I watched the pyramid of oranges tumble when the women tried to resist, and I watched them being led out of the automatic doors, them and their baby girls, each of the four with a wide metal cuff on her wrist.

I haven't inquired after them, of course. But I don't have to. I've never seen those women or their babies since.

"Bye," Sonia says, and hops onto the bus.

I walk back to the door, shake out the umbrella on the porch, and stand it to dry. The locked mailbox with its single slit of a mouth seems to grin at me. *See what you've done, Jean?*

Our postman's truck stops at the corner and he gets out, swathed in one of those clear plastic raincoats the post office issues for inclement weather. He looks like he's wearing a condom.

My friend Ann Marie and I used to laugh at the mailmen on rainy days, snickering at their shorts and silly pith helmets during summer, at their galoshes slurping through slush in the winter months. Mostly, we laughed at the plastic raincoats because they reminded us of the getups little old ladies wore. Still wear. Some things haven't changed. Although we don't have female postal workers anymore. I suppose that's an enormous change.

"Morning, Mrs. McClellan," he says, sloshing up the walk toward the house. "Lotsa mail today."

I almost never see our mailman. He has a knack for coming when I'm out of the house running errands or inside taking a shower. Occasionally, if I'm in the kitchen, I'll hear the dull metallic thud of the mailbox flap while I'm working my way through a second cup of coffee. I wonder if he plans his timing.

I answer him with a smile and hold my hand out, just to see what he'll do.

"Sorry, ma'am. I gotta put the mail in the mailbox. Rules, you know."

They do have these new rules, except if Patrick is around on Saturday mornings. Then our ever-rule-abiding mailman puts the letters in Patrick's hand. Saves my husband the trouble of having to go hunt for the key, I guess.

I watch the mailbox swallow a stack of envelopes and clank its mouth shut.

"You have a nice day, now, Mrs. McClellan. If you can in this weather."

The automatic reply catches in my throat with seconds to spare.

And then it happens: he blinks three times, each close of his eyes punctuated by an absurdly long pause, like a mechanical batting of lashes. "I have a wife, you know. And three girls." This last emerges in a whisper as the mailman—What was his name? Mr. Powell? Mr. Ramsey? Mr. Banachee? I warm with embarrassment at not knowing even the name of this man who visits our house six days a week.

He does it again, the eye thing, not before checking over my shoulder for the porch camera and lining himself up so I'm eclipsing its lens. Am I the sun or the moon? Probably Pluto, the un-planet.

And I recognize him. My mailman is the son of the woman who should have been the first human to get the anti-aphasia shot, Delilah Ray. It's no wonder he was so worried about my fees last year, which would have amounted to exactly zero if I'd ever reached the trial stage of my Wernicke X-5 serum; he can't be pulling in much as a postal worker.

I liked the man. He had a sensitivity about him when he brought Delilah Ray in to see me, along with a child's sense of wonder at the magic potion I proposed to inject into her brain. Family members of other patients had been awestruck, but this man was the only person who cried when I told him my projections, explained that if the trial went well, the old woman would speak her first coherent words after a year of post-stroke linguistic confusion. In this man's eyes, I wasn't simply another scientist or speech therapist in a long line of diagnosticians and do-gooders. I was a god who could bring back lost voices.

Was.

Now he looks at me questioningly, expectantly, so I do the only thing I can: I raise my left hand to my face, turning the counter outward.

"I'm sorry," he says.

Before he leaves the porch to plod back to his mail truck, I close and open my eyes, three times, as he did.

"We'll talk another time," he says. It's only a whisper. And then he goes.

Off to my right, a door slams, its tinny aluminum double tapping on the frame. Olivia King, hidden by a paisley umbrella, emerges from the shelter of her porch. The scarf around her head is plain pink silk, or polyester. It gives her the air of a grandmother, although Olivia is at least a decade younger than I am. She checks the skies, puts a hand out, and closes the umbrella.

She does not take off the scarf before stepping from the porch and folding herself into the front seat of her car. Weekday mornings are the only times Olivia drives anymore; if her church were closer, she'd walk.

In this moment, Olivia seems small, almost shrunken, a house mouse scuttling from one refuge to another, fearful of what might lie in wait along her trajectory. She's what Jackie would have called a Kool-Aid head, content with her place in the hierarchy: God, man, woman. Olivia had drunk up the poison, every last drop.

My own repertoire of religious doctrine is shit, which is how I like it. But when Steven first came home with his reading from that AP course—an innocent-sounding title, *Fundamentals of Modern Christian Philosophy*, blazoned on the cover, innocuous blue lettering on a white background—I leafed through the book after dinner.

"Pretty lame, isn't it?" Steven said on his second trip to the kitchen's snack cabinet.

"They're mainstreaming this next year? That's what you said, right?" I asked. My eyes didn't stray from the page, a chapter titled "In Search of a Natural Order in the Modern Family." The chapter, like all the others, was preceded by a biblical quote; this one, from Corinthians, informed the reader that "The head of every man is Christ, the head of woman is man, and the head of Christ is God."

Fantastic.

Further along, chapter twenty-seven began with this nugget from the book of Titus: "Be teachers of good things; teach the young women to be sober, to love their husbands, to love their children, to be discreet, chaste, keepers at home, good, obedient to their own husbands." The gist of the text was a call to arms of sorts, a reaching out to older generations of women.

There were chapters on feminism and its insidious deconstruction of Judeo-Christian values (as well as manhood), advice for men on their roles in husbanding and parenting, guidance for children on respecting their elders. Every page screamed extreme-right fundamentalism.

I slammed the book shut. "Tell me this isn't the only required reading."

"That's the book," Steven said after he downed a mason jar of milk and refilled it halfway.

"So the point of this class is, what? Highlighting the pitfalls of conservative Christianity?"

He stared at me blankly, as if I'd just asked the question in Greek. "I don't know. The teacher's cool. And she makes some good points. You know, like about how hard it is on kids when both their parents work, how we've gotten to this place where people forget about simple things."

I put the milk back into the fridge. "How about you save some of this for your brothers' breakfast? And what simple things?" A slide show played in my head: women gardening, women canning peaches, women embroidering pillowcases by candlelight. Shakers abstaining themselves out of existence.

"Like, well, gardening and cooking and stuff like that. Instead of running around working dumb jobs."

"You think I should garden and cook more? You think the work I do is less important than—I don't know—crafts?"

"Not you, Mom. Other women. The ones who just wanna get out of the house and have some kind of identity." He picked up the book and kissed me goodnight. "Anyway, it's just a stupid class."

"I wish you'd drop it," I said.

"No way, José. I need the AP credits for college."

"Why? So you can major in modern Christian thought?"

"No. So I can get into college."

And that was how they did it. Sneaking in a course here, a club there. Anything to lure kids with promises of increasing their competitiveness.

Such a simple thing, really.

NINE

The president's wife is next to him on the screen, a few steps back and to his right, her blond hair covered by a delicate mauve scarf that matches her dress and sets off her eyes.

I don't know why I turn on the television. By the time I've reheated my coffee, the rain has started beating a steady, wet rhythm again, so I don't much feel like going out. Also, it's safer here at home, by myself. No temptation to speak.

She's a beauty, the first lady. Almost a reincarnation of Jackie O, only fair and blue-eyed instead of dark. I remember her from before she married, when she decorated the pages of *Vogue* and *Elle*, almost always modeling low-cut and high-cropped swimwear or lingerie, smiling out from the magazines as if to say, *Go ahead. Touch me.*

Now, watching her stand placidly behind her husband, I'm struck by the change. A metamorphosis, really. She appears shorter, but maybe that's because of a footwear choice. The president is not very tall, and one supposes there's an aesthetic issue at play, as if the photographers decided to even out their frames, smoothing the peaks and valleys of their subjects.

Who am I kidding?

She's never smiling anymore, never wearing anything that falls less than three inches below her knees or that's cut lower than just at the bottom of that concavity on her throat, the one I can never remember the name of. Supra-something notch. Her sleeves are unfailingly three-quarters length, like today, and the counter on her left wrist matches her dress exactly. It looks like a piece of antique jewelry, a gift from a great-grandmother.

The first lady is supposed to be our model, a pure woman, steadfast at her husband's side in all things, at all times.

Of course, she's at his side only during public events. When the cameras click off and the microphones are muted, Anna Myers, née Johansson, is promptly escorted back to her home by a trio of armed Secret Service agents. This is never filmed, but Patrick has been in attendance at more than one of the president's appearances.

The trio stays with her night and day.

In other times, this constant supervision of the first lady would be accepted as routine security for her protection. The truth, however, is in Anna Myers' blue eyes; they have the vacant, lusterless quality of a woman who now sees the world in shades of gray.

There was a girl in my dorm, five doors down on the left, who had Anna's eyes. It seemed the muscles around them never moved, never contracted and stretched to match the smile she wore when we asked if she was okay, if she felt better this morning, if she wanted to talk. I remember when we found her body, eyes open and dull, like country wells or puddles of spilled coffee. If you want to know what depression looks like, all you need to do is look into a depressed person's eyes.

Strange how I can remember the dead girl's eyes but not her name.

Anna Myers lives in a prison with rose gardens and marble bathrooms and two-thousand-thread-count sheets on the bed. Patrick told me about her, after one of his visits as a favor to President Myers, about how the Secret Service men check Anna's bathroom twice a day, how they search her bed for objects that might have migrated unseen from the kitchen, how they hold her prescription meds and dole out pills one at a time. There are no liquor bottles in Anna's home, no locks on the doors except for those of the storage cupboard where the housekeeping supplies are. Nothing in her house is made of glass.

I switch the channel.

We still have cable, more than one hundred choices of sports, garden shows, cooking demos, home restoration, cartoons for the children, some movies. All the movies are PG—no horror, a smattering of light comedy, those four-hour epics about Moses and Jesus. Then there are the other channels, but they're all password protected, viewable only by the head of household and males over eighteen. No one needs much imagination to guess what kinds of shows are on these channels.

Today, I choose golf: pure boredom involving a metal stick and a ball.

When my coffee is cold and the leading player reaches the eighteenth hole, the doorbell rings. It's an unusual occurrence during the day. I mean, what would be the point? The only people who aren't out at work are women, and what would they do? Sit in silence and watch golf? Company only draws attention to what we no longer have.

I realize I'm still wearing my robe when I open the door and find Olivia, pink scarf knotted tightly around her head, not a shred or wisp of curl peeking out.

She checks me over, a slow, disapproving look from my neck to my feet, and holds out a nearly empty sack of sugar and a measuring cup.

I nod. If it weren't still pissing rain, I'd let her wait on the porch while I take the cup into the kitchen and pour sugar into it. Instead, I motion for her to step inside, out of the wet.

Olivia follows me to the kitchen, and the stack of dirty breakfast dishes receives the same frown my bathrobe did at the front door. I'd like to slap her, or at least tell her what I think of her sanctimonious attitude. When I take the measuring cup from her hands, she grasps my wrist. Olivia's hands are cold, moist from the rain.

I expect some sound, some uppity, self-righteous little "Hm," but she says nothing, only regards my counter, its ceaseless blinking of the three-digit number.

She actually smiles, and the smile brings back a memory of another day, another unexpected doorbell ring, another request for a cup of sugar, a half-pint of milk, an egg.

"Mind if I sit a minute?" Olivia said two years ago, not waiting for a yes before she planted her ample bottom on the sofa in the den. I'd left the TV on, tuned to some talk show or another, while I waded through final exam blue books. Jackie Juarez was going head-to-head with three women, each of them dressed like a cross between Donna Reed and an Apollo-era astronaut's wife.

"Oh, isn't she something," she said. It wasn't a question.

"Which one?" I asked, holding out the Rubbermaid container of milk.

"The one in the red suit. The one who looks like Satan."

Jackie was a bit over-the-top, even for Jackie. The red stood out like a suppurating sore amid the other three women, drab and dull in their pastel twinsets. Each wore a strand of pearls, high enough on the neck to look like a collar; Jackie's chunk of pendant—an owl—dangled between her tits, pushed up by the miracle of modern underwire and padding.

"I know her," I said. "Knew her. We were in grad school together."

"Grad school," Olivia repeated. "What did she do?"

"Sociolinguistics."

Olivia snorted but didn't ask me to explain before she turned back toward the quartet of women and the moderator.

As usual, Jackie was ranting. "You actually think women should obey their husbands? In the twenty-first century?"

The woman to her right, the one in the baby blue cardigan, smiled. It was the sort of smile a flustered kindergarten teacher might give to a child throwing a tantrum, a smile full of pity and understanding. *You'll grow out of it,* the smile said. "Let me tell you a few things about the twenty-first century, dear," Ms. Baby Blue Cardigan said. "We don't know who men are or who women are anymore. Our children are growing up confused. The culture of family has broken down. We have increases in traffic, pollution, autism rates, drug use, single parents, obesity, consumer debt, female prison populations, school shootings, erectile dysfunction. That's just to name a few." She waved a stack of manila folders in front of Jackie as the other two seventies-era Barbie dolls—Pure Women, they called themselves—nodded in somber agreement.

Jackie ignored the folders. "I suppose the next thing you'll be telling us is that feminism is at fault for rape?"

"I'm glad you mentioned that, Miss Juarez," Baby Blue Cardigan said.

"Ms."

"Whatever. Do you know how many incidents of violent rape were reported in 1960? In the United States."

"It's interesting you use the word 'reported,'" Jackie began.

"Seventeen thousand. Give or take. We're up to five times that number this year."

Jackie rolled her eyes, and the other two Pure Women went in for the kill. They had the numbers. They had charts and surveys. One of them introduced a collection of simple pie charts—they must have been organized in advance, I thought—while Jackie fought for airtime.

On the sofa next to me, Olivia chewed her lower lip. "I had no idea," she said.

"No idea about what?"

"These numbers." She pointed to one of the charts, now being televised with a prepared voice-over of Baby Blue's voice. She had moved on from rape and was reciting statistics on antidepressant usage. "Jeez. One in six? That's awful."

No one in the studio audience was paying attention to Jackie's claims of skewed statistics, of the correlation-causation fallacy, of the fact that of course no one was taking selective serotonin reuptake inhibitors in 1960, because they didn't exist.

That was how it started. Three women with a stack of pie charts and people like Olivia.

TEN

It took forever to get Olivia out of the house, her and her goddamned cup of sugar. She probably didn't even need it and only barged in to stick her nose around, see what I was up to. Olivia has become the purest of Pure Women, always rocking on her porch with her abridged and annotated Bible, always covering up her curls, always smiling and bowing—actually bowing—to Evan when he pulls their Buick into the driveway.

Bibles are still allowed, if they're the right kind.

Olivia's is pink; Evan's is blue. You never see them switch, never see the blue book in Olivia's hands as she sits in the shade with her glass of sweet tea or drives off to services in their second car. It's a compact, that car, much smaller than the one Evan takes to work.

By two o'clock, I almost wish Olivia were still here.

I take two packages of hamburger from the freezer and set them in a lean-to on the counter to defrost. There aren't enough potatoes for all of us, let alone for three growing boys who seem to be hosting persistent tapeworms, so rice will have to do. Or I could make biscuits, if I can remember the proportions. Automatically, I turn to the bookshelf next to what used to be my desk in the kitchen and reach for the stained copy of *Joy of Cooking* as if I'm expecting it to be there. In its place, and in the place of all the other books, are a few photos of the kids, one of my parents, one of Patrick and me on our last vacation. Sam or Leo took that one, and I'm chopped in half, the right side of my face obscured by the Popsicle-stick frame Sonia made in school. Apparently they still do crafts.

If I move the pictures, the shelf doesn't look so abandoned, so I shuffle the frames around, stick the kitchen timer and scale in the empty spaces, and step back to admire this achievement of the day. With a little imagination, I can persuade myself I've just carved Mount Fucking Rushmore. Start the ticker-tape parade.

Mamma and Papà are now much more prominent than they were before this adventure in interior design. I'm not sure whether I want them to be. They call from Italy, or they Skype Patrick on the laptop he keeps locked in his office, the one with the keystroke logger and the camera and a thousand other custom bells and whistles attached to it. Usually, this happens on Sundays when the kids are home from school and the time difference works out so that they can say hello to the entire family. It's supposed to be joyous, but Mamma ends each call in tears or hands the phone off to Papà before she breaks down.

So. Dinner.

The kids would love biscuits, and I'm pulling on jeans and an old linen blouse, ready to risk a supermarket trip, when Patrick's car roars up the street. I know it's his—if there's one skill I've honed to a point in the past year, it's sound discrimination. Mustang, Corvette, Prius, Mini Cooper. You name the car, I know the sound.

What bugs me as I look out the blinds isn't that Patrick's home early, but that three black SUVs are in a line behind him. I've seen those vehicles before.

I've seen their insides, too.

ELEVEN

*S*hit.

Three cars means at least three men. Something tells me they're not bearing precious gifts. Not today, not after my backyard performance of last night.

There will be a lecture. Maybe more than that.

Mrs. McClellan, you have the right to remain silent—

Okay. Lousy joke.

I let the blinds fall back into place and I return to the kitchen, ready to put on my best Donna Reed face (an apron will have to do) and be the picture of domestic bliss. On the way, I hit the television's remote and change the channel from golf to CNN. CNN isn't what it used to be—nothing is—but Patrick's job might have a better chance of survival if it looks like I've been overdosing on presidential propaganda instead of watching balls fly over manicured courses.

Breaking: President announces—

That's all I get to see before Patrick and his escorts—I was wrong; there are six of them—invade my space.

"Jean McClellan?" says the first suit, a suntanned man who is all angles.

I've seen him before, of course. Everyone has, only he used to wear one of those black-and-white clerical collars instead of a necktie during his public appearances. On Sunday mornings, while Jackie and I chugged coffee to chase away a weekend hangover, he'd be on the TV, the star of his own show. Jackie turned it on as if she were one of the fold; she claimed it got her anger up.

"Listen. Saint Carl's about to start his shtick again," she'd say.

And there he'd be, in his minister's uniform, preaching about the fall of the American family one week, the joy of surrender to God the next. He welcomed anecdotes, real-life experiences, and the bottom few inches of the TV screen always flashed the same toll-free number. After a few years, he added a second number; in more recent years there were Facebook links, then a Twitter account. God had sent him traffic, he said, and he would deal with it by whatever means the Lord provided.

At the time, Jackie and I couldn't imagine more than a few hundred Southern Baptists from Mississippi followed Reverend Carl Corbin.

It sucks to be so wrong.

"Dr. Jean McClellan?"

Now, this is different. I haven't been "Dr." anything since last spring. Also, Patrick is smiling. I nod, because there's nothing I can say.

In the den, on the television, one of the talking heads says two magic words: *brain trauma*.

Those words alone, those three syllables, would be enough to prick up my ears, but the words that surround them hit me like a runaway train. *President. Skiing accident. Brother.*

"Dr. McClellan, we have a problem." It's Reverend Carl again, although he looks less like paste and more like fungus in person than when he's in front of a camera, speaking for the president.

"Great. Fix it," I say. "What am I, fucking Houston?"

No, I don't say this. I don't say anything.

"Jean," Patrick says. Not "babe," not "hon," not any of those sweetie-isms that spouses share. He's all business now. "Jean, something's happened."

On the television, CNN is blaring. In between live footage of some snow-covered mountain, He Who Rules the Free World flashes on and off, a picture of solemnity. Anna stands at his side, lovely in her blue and beige ensemble. It does seem that she's smiling, if only in her eyes.

Reverend Carl motions to one of the others, who steps forward into my kitchen. I don't care for this intrusion; if I'm to be a silent domestic, let me at least keep some domestic sanctuary for my own.

"Go ahead, Thomas," the man in charge says.

And then it happens.

Thomas of the dark suit and dark mien reaches forward for my left hand. I instinctively retract, like a frightened wild dog that knows the pain of a trap, but Patrick comes toward me.

"It's okay, babe. Just let them do this."

With his free hand, Thomas produces a small key. It's like an elevator key, one of those round, single-purpose gizmos that don't seem to have a reason for being except in an elevator, a device that brings to mind all the other silly little inventions: can openers, lemon zesters, melon ballers. Things that do only one thing. We have so many of them.

Where do we get this shit? Bridal shower and wedding gifts, stocking stuffers, spur-of-the-moment purchases at Ikea. They're all so goddamned useless, hidden in the backs of kitchen drawers, taken for granted and never taken out. This is what goes through my mind as Thomas frees me with the high-tech equivalent of a can opener.

"You can speak now, Dr. McClellan." Reverend Carl extends a hand toward my living room, like he's turned magnanimous host.

It isn't the only role reversal today. Everything they want is being broadcast on CNN as the story of the president's brother's skiing accident unfolds. As further details are reported—posterior left hemisphere, alert but uncommunicative, babbling—I know what else Reverend Carl and his crew want.

They want me.

If it were Anna Myers who had skied her way off-piste into a tree, I'd be out the door without a second thought. Although I doubt there would be any SUV-driving men here if it were the president's wife lying in an intensive care unit.

"What do you want me to say?" My words come out slowly, tentatively, while I move out of the kitchen, past the television—which I click off—and over to one of the wing chairs. I don't want to have to share space with any of these people.

"Hot in here," Reverend Carl says, glancing toward the fridge with its built-in water and ice dispensers.

"Yep," I say.

One of the other men, not Thomas, coughs.

I take the cue. "Patrick, why don't you get our guests a glass of water, hon? Since you're right there."

He does, and neither of us misses the slight shake of Reverend Carl's head. I'm the wife. I should be the one serving.

"So?" I say. "Sounds like Bobby Myers might have brain damage. Locus?"

Reverend Carl arranges himself on the love seat opposite my chair. "You're the medical man, Patrick. Show her the reports the hospital faxed over this morning."

My husband, who is on a first-name basis with the individual who single-handedly put that metal cuff on me, comes into the room with a tray of water glasses and a slim folder. He stops in front of me before passing around the drinks. "I think you'll be interested in this, Jean."

And I am. The first page is all text, and on the second line my eyes find the reason for Reverend Carl's unexpected visit: lesion in posterior section of STG. Superior temporal gyrus. Left hemisphere. Patient is right-handed, therefore left-brain dominant.

"Wernicke's area," I say, to no one in particular. As I read on, my left arm feels light, and there's a band of paler skin around my wrist, as if I'd taken off a watch before diving into a pool. One of the Secret Service men—I'm assuming that's what they are, given Carl Corbin's presence—rubs his own wrist. He wears a plain gold ring on the fourth finger of his left hand. So he knows. What camp he's in isn't clear; like Patrick, they're all trained to follow along, rather like puppies.

Reverend Carl nods. "The president is very concerned."

Sure he is. I think Mr. President relies on his older brother quite a bit, and he is going to have one hell of a time getting information either to Bobby or from him. Pieces of future conversations play themselves in my mind:

There's a situation in Afghanistan, Bobby, the president will say.

Bobby's response will sound something like *Nice twinkles for your banana flames.* His speech will be precise and fluid, each syllable articulated perfectly and without hesitation. What comes out will be absolute gibberish: not code, not broken speech, but the ramblings of what we once called an idiot—in the clinical sense of the word.

It's all I can do to keep from smiling. I have to bite the inside of my cheek—hard—to maintain the proper visage of seriousness, of concern, of duty.

I flip through the other pages. The MRIs, or magnetic resonance images, show a substantial lesion exactly where I expect it, in Brodmann area 22. "This was from a skiing accident?" I say. "No indication of prior damage?"

Of course they don't know. Thirty-four-year-old men aren't in the habit of having brain scans, not unless there's cause.

"Did he suffer from headaches?"

Reverend Carl shrugs.

"Is that a yes or a no, Reverend?" I say.

"I don't have that information."

Now I turn to Patrick, but he shakes his head. "You have to understand, Jean, we can't release the president's family's medical history."

"But you want me to help."

"You're the country's leading expert, Dr. McClellan." Reverend Carl has stepped in, or leaned in across the coffee table. His face, all sharp lines, is inches from my own. There's something anime about him, but he's still handsome. He's still wearing his suit jacket, despite the heat, but under the fabric is a solid frame. I wonder if women like Olivia King are secretly in love with him.

The chance to correct his tense is too good to miss. "Was," I say. "I don't need to tell you I haven't worked for the past year."

Reverend Carl doesn't react, only sits back and steeples his hands together, his long fingers forming a perfect isosceles triangle. Maybe he practices this in front of a mirror. "Well, that's why we're here today." He pauses, like he used to do during his televised sermons, a bit of extra razzle-dazzle suspense-building effect.

But I already know what he's going to say. My eyes wander from his to Patrick's to the other men in the room.

"Dr. McClellan, we'd like you on our team."

n our team.

O A hundred responses bubble up inside me, ninety-nine of which would mean forced resignation—or worse—for Patrick. But anything approaching agreement or eagerness will never make its way through my brain to my mouth. Instead of excitement, I feel a gut punch of pain, as if Reverend Carl just reached out with a claw instead of words and bored into me. They might need me, but need is different from want. And I don't trust any of these men.

"Do I have a choice?" I say. It seems safe.

Reverend Carl unsteeples his hands, separating them into a saintlike gesture of prayer. I've seen him do this before, on television, when he's asking for help, for more Pure Women and Pure Men and Pure Families to join his fold, for money. Right now, those hands seem more like the sides of a vise ready to squeeze me until I burst.

"Of course," he says, his voice overgenerous and falsely kind. "I know how you must feel, how leaving your home and your children to go back into the daily grind must be—" He searches for a word as his eyes search my house. There's clutter and mess everywhere: three pairs of my shoes where I kicked them off last week, dust on the windowsills, an old coffee spill on the carpet next to his shoes.

I've never been an ace at housekeeping.

He continues. "We talked to another scientist, Dr. Kwan, in case we need a backup. You know her, I think."

"Yes."

Lin Kwan is the chair of my old department. Or was, until they replaced her with the first man they could find. I don't need to ask why they haven't approached him for this project—if Lin had gotten her way, the guy's funding would have been severed after the first disaster of an experiment. He was that inept.

"So," Reverend Carl says. His hands are down now, and he's no longer looking at me, but at the steel cuff Thomas has been holding for the past twenty minutes. "It's your choice. You can set up a new lab, recommence your research, and move forward. Or—"

"Or?" I say. My eyes find Patrick's.

"Or everything can go back to normal. I'm sure your family would like that." He doesn't look at me while he's talking, but at Patrick, as if he's studying my husband's reaction.

As if anything about our lives in the past year has been normal. Then I get it—Carl Corbin actually believes what he preaches. At first, I'd thought he'd spun the Pure Movement, that his motives for resurrecting the Victorian cult of domesticity and keeping women out of the public sphere were purely misogynistic. In a way, I wish that were true; it's less creepy than the alternative.

Steven was the first to explain it to me, on a Sunday morning two years ago.

"It's sort of traditional, Mom. Like in olden times."

"Olden times? Like what? Greece? Sumer? Babylonia?"

He poured himself a second bowl of cereal, mixed in two bananas, and topped it with half-and-half. By the time Sam and Leo reached fifteen, I'd have to buy futures in Cheerios. "Well, yeah. It was there with the Greeks, the idea of public spheres and private spheres, but it goes back further. Think hunter-gatherer communities. Biologically, we're suited to different things."

"We?" I said.

"Men and women, Mom." He stopped crunching and flexed his right arm. "See this? You could go to the gym every day for a year and you still won't have muscle like I do." He must have seen the look of pure disbelief on my face, because he reversed course. "I don't mean you're weak. Just different."

Christ.

I pointed to my temple. "See this, kiddo? Ten more years of school and you might have one like it. Or you might not. And it has absolutely shit to do with gender." My voice was rising.

"Calm down, Mom."

"Don't tell me to calm down."

"You're getting kind of hysterical. I'm only saying that it makes biological sense to have women do some stuff and men do other stuff. Like, for instance, you're a really great teacher, but you probably wouldn't last more than an hour if you—I dunno—had a job digging ditches."

That was it. "I'm a scientist, Steven, not a kindergarten teacher. And I'm not hysterical."

Well, I sort of was.

I poured my second cup of coffee with shaking hands.

Steven didn't let up. He opened his textbook from that goddamned AP class—Religious Nuttership 101 or whatever they called it—and started reading. "'Woman has no call to the ballot-box, but she has a sphere of her own, of amazing responsibility and importance. She is the divinely appointed guardian of the home. . . . She should more fully realize that her position as wife and mother, and angel of the home, is the holiest, most responsible, and queenlike assigned to mortals; and dismiss all ambition for anything higher, as there is nothing else here so high for mortals.' That's Reverend John Milton Williams. See? You're queenlike."

"Terrific." I needed the coffee but didn't want Steven to see how on edge I was, so I left it on the counter. "I think you should drop this course."

"No way. I'm kinda into it. I mean, there's a crap ton to think about. Even a few of the girls say so."

"I find that hard to believe," I said, not bothering to take the snideness out of my voice.

"Julia King, for instance."

"Julia King isn't exactly representative of the entire female population." *Poor kid,* I thought, wondering what my next-door neighbors had done to brainwash their daughter. "Really, Steven. Drop the course."

"No."

Fifteen years old. The age of defiance. I knew it well, having been there.

Patrick came into the kitchen, emptied the coffeepot into a mug, and stirred in the last of the half-and-half. "What's going on?" he said, tousling Steven's hair and then pecking me on the cheek. "Kinda early for a domestic argument."

"Mom wants me to drop my AP Religion class."

"Why?" Patrick said.

"I dunno. Ask her. I think she doesn't like the textbook."

"The textbook is shit," I said.

Patrick picked it up and flipped the pages like they were an old cartoon. "Doesn't look so bad to me."

"Maybe if you tried reading it, hon."

"Come on, babe. Let him take what he wants. It can't hurt anything."

I think it might have been that moment when I started hating my husband.

Now I'm back in my living room, hating the seven men seated or standing around me, waiting for me to join their ranks. "I need some details," I say. Maybe they won't notice I'm stalling.

Maybe you think I'm crazy for not leaping at the chance to go back to work. I can understand that.

We could use the extra income. There is that. And I've missed my research, my books, the collaboration with Lin and my graduate assistants. I've missed talking.

Most of all, I've missed the hope.

We were so fucking close.

It was Lin's idea to abandon our fledgling work on Broca's aphasia and move on to Wernicke's. I could see her rationale: the Broca's patients stammered and stuttered with a palpable frustration, but they got their words out. For the most part, their language was intact; only the ability to transfer it into speech had been hamstrung by a stroke, a fall down the stairs, a head injury sustained while they waded through some desert country in the uniforms of the free world. They could still comprehend, still hear their wives and daughters and fathers encouraging them on. It was the other victims—the ones with damage farther back in their brains, much like Bobby Myers—who suffered the more sinister loss. Language, for them, had become an inescapable labyrinth of non-meaning. I imagine it must feel like being lost at sea.

So, yes, I want to go back. I want to forge ahead with the serum and—when I'm ready—inject that potion into Mrs. Ray's old veins. I want to hear her tell me about *Quercus virginiana* and *Magnolia stellata* and *Syringa vulgaris* in the way she did when she first came to my home, identifying the live oaks and the giant, starry trees and the lilacs with a scent that no perfumer has been able to match. She considered them God's gifts, and I tolerated that. Whatever might be up there, he or she or it did a crackerjack job with trees and flowers.

But I don't give a shit about the president or his baby brother or, really, any man.

"Well, Dr. McClellan?" Reverend Carl says.

I want to tell him no.

THIRTEEN

Christ, it's hot in here. There must be a leak in the air-conditioning compressor again. Wouldn't that be just our luck?

I get up, jeans sticking to the backs of my legs, and go to the kitchen to refill my glass with water. "Patrick, can you give me a hand for a sec?" I call. He makes the rounds in the living room, collecting empty glasses, and joins me.

While I'm pressing one glass after another into the ice dispenser, he takes hold of my left wrist. "You don't want that back on, do you?"

I shake my head, out of habit.

"You should look at it like a trade, babe. They get something and you get something."

"I should look at it like what it is," I say. "Fucking blackmail."

He sighs like he's been holding the entire universe in his lungs. "Then do it for the kids' sake."

The kids.

Steven doesn't care. He's busy filling out college applications and writing admissions essays and boning up for exams, which are right around the corner. Also, he's been making eyes at Julia King for most of this semester. The twins, only eleven, have soccer and Little League. But there's Sonia. If I'm going to trade my brain for words, I'll do it for her.

The hamster wheel in my head must be making noise, because Patrick stops with the water glasses and turns me toward him. "Do it for Sonia."

"I want more details first."

Back in the living room, I get them.

Reverend Carl has morphed from politician to salesman. "Your wrist counter stays off for the duration of the project, Dr. McClellan. If you agree, of course. You'll have a state-of-the-art lab and all the funding and assistance you need. We can"—he checks the paperwork in another folder—"we can offer you a handsome stipend with a bonus if you find a viable cure within the next ninety days."

"And after that?" I ask, back in my chair with my jeans sticking to me.

"Well—" He turns toward one of the Secret Service men.

The man nods.

"Back to one hundred words a day?" I say.

"Actually, Dr. McClellan—and I'm telling you this in strict confidence, understand?—actually, we'll be increasing the quota at some point in the future. Once everything gets back on course."

Well, this is new. I wait to see what other confidential tidbits he's got up his sleeve.

"Our hope"—Reverend Carl is in full preacher mode now—"is that people will settle down, find their feet in the new rhythm, and we won't need these silly little bracelets any longer." He makes a disdainful gesture with his hand, as if he's talking about a trivial fashion accessory and not a torture device.

Of course, we only feel pain if we flout the rules.

I remember the day when I learned about these rules.

It took only five minutes, there in the bleached white government building office. The men spoke to me, at me, never with me. Patrick would be notified and given instructions; a crew would come to the house—was this evening convenient?—to install cameras at the front and back doors, lock my computer away, and pack up our books, even Sonia's *Baby Learns the Alphabet*. The board games went into cardboard boxes; the cardboard boxes went into a closet in Patrick's office. I was to bring Sonia, barely five years out of my body, to the same place that afternoon so her tiny wrist could be fitted. They showed me a selection, a rainbow of colors I could choose from.

"Pink would be most appropriate for a little girl," they said.

I pointed to silver for myself and blood red for Sonia. A trivial act of defiance.

One of the men left, and returned with the bracelet that would replace my Apple Watch, the one Patrick had surprised me with for Christmas last year. The metal was light, smooth, an alloy of sorts, unfamiliar to my skin.

He trained the counter to my voice, set it to zero, and sent me home.

Naturally, I didn't believe a word of it. Not the sketches they showed me in their book of pictures, not the warnings Patrick read aloud to me over tea at our kitchen table. When Steven and his brothers burst in from school, full with news of soccer practice and exam results, while Sonia ignored her dolls, mesmerized by her new shiny red wristband, I opened the dam. My words flew out, unbridled, automatic. The room filled with hundreds of them, all colors and shapes. Mostly blue and sharp.

The pain knocked me flat.

Our bodies have a mechanism, a way to forget physical trauma. As with my non-memories of the pain of birth, I've blocked everything associated with that afternoon, everything except the tears in Patrick's eyes, the shock—what an appropriate term—on my sons' faces, and Sonia's delighted squeals as she played with the red device. There's another thing I remember, the way my little girl raised that cherry red monster to her lips.

It was as if she were kissing it.

FOURTEEN

Finally, they leave.

Reverend Carl slides into his Range Rover; the Secret Service men and Thomas ride in the other cars. Patrick and I are left in the living room with eight empty glasses of water dripping rings on the coasters beneath them.

Nothing has been decided yet.

He's pacing the length of the room, sweat making his usually gelled-down hair stick in blond clumps around his face. Right now, he looks less like my husband and more like a caged feline. Or maybe a wild dog is the better choice; they're pack animals.

"They won't take off Sonia's counter," I say.

"They will. Eventually. Think how it would look if she turned up at school without that—"

"Don't you dare call it a bracelet."

"Okay. Counter."

I load the tray with glasses, using only my thumb and index finger so I don't touch them more than necessary. Shaking Reverend Carl's hand made me want to scrub myself with lye. "Can't you do something? You're the one who called it a trade, so let's trade. I go to work for the bastards; they let my daughter talk."

"I'll see what I can do."

"Patrick, you're the president's fucking science adviser. You'd better be able to do something."

"Jean."

"Don't 'Jean' me." I slam down the glass I'm holding hard, and it shatters.

Patrick's over like a shot, catching the blood as it leaks from my hand.

"Don't touch me," I say. There's a single sliver of glass wedged in the soft pad of flesh under my thumb. And there's blood. Quite a lot of blood.

As water rolls over the wound, I travel back thirty minutes, back to when Reverend Carl was holding court in my living room, educating me on the plans for the future.

Something was wrong. Maybe it was his eyes, which didn't smile along with his mouth, or the pattern of his sentences. They were too well rehearsed, almost, too practiced in their even cadence and intonation. Even so, the hesitance was audible—a few too many *um*s and *ah*s littered his recital of the president's intended changes, modifications, dispensations.

I couldn't put my finger on exactly the moment when I realized I didn't trust him.

"What if they're playing some game, Patrick?" I called over the running water while he cleaned up the bits of broken glass and dumped them into the trash bin. I didn't turn to look; those pieces of glass looked too much like our marriage.

It wasn't always this way. You don't have four kids by accident.

He joins me at the sink, scrubs his hands as only a doctor can, all the way up to his elbows, and looks a question at me before reaching for my wrist. He's still got that gentle touch. "You want the good news or the bad news first?"

"Good news."

"Okay. The good news is you're not going to die."

"And the bad?"

"I'll get my sewing kit."

Stitches. Shit. "How many?"

"Two or three. Don't worry—it looks worse than it is." When he comes back with his black bag, he pours me a short glass of bourbon. "Here. Drink this. It'll take the sting away." Then he sits me at the kitchen counter and takes the equipment out, ready to play doctor on the gash in my hand.

I take a long swallow of the hard stuff, and the needle slides into my disinfected skin without much pain. Still, I won't look, only hand Patrick the pickup when he asks for it.

"Damn good thing you didn't go into nursing, babe," he says, and there's tenderness again between us.

For a moment.

He makes an expert knot, cuts off the excess thread, and pats my hand. "There you are, Dr. Frankenstein. Good as new."

"Dr. Frankenstein wasn't the one with the zipper neck," I say. "Anyway, what do you think? Are they playing a game, or are they serious about what they said?"

"I don't know, Jean." 'Jean' again. He's pissed.

"Look, if I take this job, how do I know they won't—I don't know—use my research to promote worldwide evil?"

"With an anti-aphasia serum? Come on."

The blood loss and bourbon cocktail have made me light-headed. "I just don't trust these people."

"All right, then." He pours a drink for himself, then slams the bottle on the counter with enough force to hurt my ears. "Don't take the job. We'll deal with the AC when my direct deposit comes through next week, you can put your goddamned bracelet back on, and we'll all go back to exactly the way we were this morning."

"Fuck you."

He's mad, he's hurt, and he's frustrated. None of this justifies the next words out of his mouth, though, the ones he will never be able to take back, the ones that slice deeper than any shard of broken glass and make me bleed all over.

"You know, babe, I wonder if it was better when you didn't talk."

FIFTEEN

E ven without the metal contraption on my wrist, dinner is a quiet affair tonight.

Steven, normally garrulous in between forkfuls of food, hasn't mentioned school or Julia King or soccer. The twins seem confused and shift a little in their chairs. Sonia alternates between staring at her plate and staring at my left wrist, but she's been silent since she got home from school. Another thing—there hasn't been a single fist bump between her and Steven.

As for Patrick, he eats, takes his plate into the kitchen, and escapes to his study with a tumbler of bourbon and a few curt words about having to meet a deadline. It's impossible to tell whom he's more angry with—me, or himself.

"You explain it to them, Jean," he says before shutting the door to that book-lined sanctuary of his.

Well, this is awkward.

I haven't had a real conversation with my kids for more than a year.

What once would have been an animated debate over whether Pokémon Go was a time waster or the cleverest innovation in gaming since Xbox is now four young faces staring in silent expectation. And I'm the main event.

I might as well get it over with.

"So, Steven, what's going on at school these days?" I say.

"Two exams tomorrow." It's as if he's the one with the daily word quota.

"Want me to help you study?"

"Nah. I'm cool." Then, as an afterthought, he adds, "Thanks anyway."

Sam and Leo are slightly more eager, pummeling me with news of their new soccer coach and how they played a trick at practice this morning, each one pretending to be the other. The two of them do most of the talking. I suppose that's what they've grown used to.

Only Sonia watches me with wide eyes, the kind of look that makes me feel as if I'm a new person. Or have grown fur. Or turned into a dragon. She's eaten none of the meat loaf on her plate, and only a few of the potatoes I'd run to the store to buy after the falling-out with Patrick this afternoon.

"Will I have another bad dream?" she asks.

Automatically, I respond with the wrong kind of question. "What makes you think that, honey?" I rephrase. "No. I won't let the bad dreams happen. And I'll tell you a story when I tuck you in, okay?"

She nods. The number on her wrist glows 40. "Scared," she says.

"No reason to be."

Sam and Leo exchange a nervous look, and I shake my head at them. Steven raises one finger to his lips, his silent sign to his baby sister, something normal.

Then Sonia nods again. Her eyes—Patrick's Irish hazel—are glazed over with unfallen tears.

"You're still afraid?" I ask.

Another nod.

"Of the bad dreams?"

Now she shakes her head.

The thing is, Sonia doesn't know what the wrist counters do, other than glow brightly and show her numbers and pulse against her wrist, one time for each word she speaks. We've been careful to keep this secret from her. Maybe it's a foolish thing, but I've never been able to figure out exactly how to describe an electric jolt of pain to a six-year-old. It would be like telling a child about the horrors of the electric chair in order to instill some sense of right and wrong. Grisly, and unnecessary. What parent would enumerate the exact workings of Old Sparky to get their kid not to fib or steal?

When the counters went on our wrists—there was no acclimation period, not even for children—I decided to go about it from the opposite direction. A scoop of ice cream, an extra cookie before bed, hot cocoa with as many marshmallows as would fit in the cup whenever Sonia nodded or shook her head or tugged on my sleeve instead of speaking. Positive reinforcement rather than punishment. I didn't want her to learn the hard way. Not like I had.

Also, I knew something else about the counters. The pain increases with each infraction.

There was no time for me, on that first day, to process the steady surge in charge. Patrick explained, afterward, as he applied cold cream to the scar on my wrist.

"First word over a hundred, and you'll get a slight shock, Jean. Nothing disabling, just a little jolt. A warning. You'll perceive it, but it won't actually hurt."

Terrific, I thought.

"For every ten words after that, the charge augments by a tenth of a microcoulomb. Get to half a microcoulomb, and you'll feel pain. Reach a full microcoulomb and"—he paused and looked away—"and the pain becomes unbearable." He took my left hand in his own and checked the number on the counter. "Whew. One ninety-six. Thank god you didn't keep talking. Another few words and you would have hit one microcoulomb."

Patrick and I had rather different ideas of what "unbearable pain" meant.

He continued while I held a bag of frozen peas to the circular burn and kept my eyes trained on the closed door of Sonia's bedroom. The boys were in there with her, at Patrick's insistence, no doubt making sure she didn't speak. No one wanted a repeat performance of the Electrocuted Female, not when a five-year-old was cast in the lead role.

"I think what happened is this, babe. I think you were going so fast, the device couldn't keep up." There were tears in his eyes now. "I'll go talk to someone about it tomorrow morning. I promise. Christ, I'm so sorry."

It took only a second's worth of imagination to see my little girl blasted from her chair, no idea why she was hurting, to turn my bowels into liquid fire. So I went about it the Pavlovian way, focusing on the reward, as if I were training a dog, all for the greater good, I thought at the time.

Now, in the middle of this odd nonconversation at our dinner table, I realize I needn't have bothered.

Sonia's tears have started, falling into her plate of untouched meat loaf and potatoes like fat raindrops.

"Did something bad happen at school today?"

A single nod. Up once, down once, like an exaggeration. I can fish out of her whatever secret she's holding.

"All right, baby girl. There, there." I'm stroking her curls, trying to get some calm into her while all I want to do is scream. "Did someone say something to you?"

The tiniest of moans escapes her lips.

"One of the other girls?"

Now her head moves right, then left, under my hand. So not one of the students.

"Teacher?" I catch her eye—just a flicker from me to Steven. And I know. "Steven, your turn to clean up, okay?" I say.

He gives me the Look.

"Please," I say.

I don't expect it to work, but a softness comes into my son's eyes, and he picks up the plates, careful not to stack them before they're rinsed. He makes this little bow, an insignificant thing, but I can't help seeing Reverend Carl Corbin and the way he swept out his hand this afternoon, offering me a place to sit down in my very own living room.

Offering, I think, and words tumble around in my head like Scrabble tiles. Officious. Official. Offensive. Off. *Off with her fucking head*.

The twins join Steven's cleanup parade without too much objection, and Sonia and I are left at the table.

"You all right, darling?" I say. Then I place a hand to her forehead. A moment ago, my girl was sweating like a gin and tonic forgotten on a porch in July; now she's settled down a bit. Not sweating, but far from a cool cucumber.

This is the worst of all of it. This, right now, watching Sonia track Steven, watching her grow more calm with every step he takes toward the kitchen. It's the worst, because now I know what Sonia is really afraid of.

I don't speak, only cock my head toward the place where Steven is rinsing bits of ground beef and potato off plates, humming some old tune.

And she nods.

Steven was eleven when his only sister arrived—almost old enough to be a father himself, if only in the biological sense. He had a way with her, kept her distracted and happy, changed the crappy diapers without more than a "Hey, Mom, this is some crappy nappy!" Few tweens learn baby sign language, but my eldest son was one of them. By barely older than a year, Sonia had the signs for her entire world down: eat, drink, sleep, dolly, and—her all-time favorite—go poo. Steven dubbed this particular gesture, often accompanied by the spoken words, a translation of some primitive language, a system so arcane that no one, not even Dr. Jean McClellan, would be able to piece it together.

He launched into a tune so grotesquely bastardized I didn't know what to think. Patrick nearly spilled his morning coffee at the sound of Steven singing.

There were the Police and their doo-doo-doo-da-da-da—or however it goes; there was that Lou Reed piece about how the "colored girls" sing "do-do-do"—ultra-racist now, but it was Lou Reed and he could get away with all kinds of shit back then; there were those Motown bands and those white people who wanted to sound like they were a Motown band and there was every other songwriter in the modern world who stumbled over a lyric and ended up filling the space with something that rhymed with the kiddie word for defecation. And, finally, there was my own son crooning along to the entire musical canon from Brahms to Beyoncé, replacing each and every word with "poo."

The memories make the present doubly hard, but, finally, I say it.

"Did Steven come to your school today?"

A nod.

"Do you want to tell me about it?"

No. She does not.

"Story, then?" I say.

I let her go off to her bedroom, my lackluster reminder to brush her teeth following her from the dining table, down the hall, to the bathroom she has for herself now that the twins are of that age when separate peeing quarters become important. Patrick's door doesn't so much as squeak on its hinges when Sonia runs by it.

I take everything out on Steven. Maybe this isn't the best parenting tactic, but I'm furious.

"What happened at Sonia's school today, Steven?" I say after sending Sam and Leo off to the TV room. They're eager to go, mostly because, without their older brother, they get a few minutes alone with the remote.

Steven shrugs but doesn't turn from the sink.

"I'd like an answer, kiddo," I say, and I press his shoulder, forcing him to turn.

It's only now that I see the small pin on his collar, about a pinkie's worth wide. Inside the silver circle, on a white field, is the single letter *P* in bright blue. I've seen this before.

The first time, it was on television during that ridiculous segment

where three Bible-thumping women in twinsets tore Jackie Juarez to
shreds. Not a week later, I saw it decorating one of Olivia King's church
dresses when she knocked on my door asking if I had an egg to spare.

It's supposed to be a symbol of solidarity, I guess, this quiet blue *P* worn
by both men and women now. Olivia's daughter, Julia, has one, and sometimes I've seen it when I've been at the grocery store or at the dry cleaners
picking up Patrick's shirts. I ran into Dr. Claudia, my former gynecologist,
in the post office, and even she had one, although I suspected her husband
had more to do with Claudia's choice of accessories than she herself did. I
know the *P* stands for "Pure"—Pure Man, Pure Woman, Pure Child.

What I don't know is why my own son is wearing this pin.

"When did you start this?" I say, fingering his collar.

Steven brushes my hand off as if it's an annoying fly and returns
to rinsing plates and loading the dishwasher. "Got it the other day. No
big deal."

"Got it? As in, what? It fell from the sky? You found it in a storm drain?"

No answer.

"You don't just get these, Steven."

He shoulders past me, pours himself a glass of milk from the fridge,
and downs it. "Of course you don't just get them, Mom. You have to
earn them."

"I see. And how does that happen?"

Another glass of milk disappears down Steven's gullet.

"Save some for cereal tomorrow," I say. "You're not the only human
in this house."

"Maybe you should go out and get another carton, then. It's your job,
right?"

My hand flies with a will of its own, makes contact; and a bright
palm print blooms on the right side of Steven's face.

He doesn't flinch, doesn't raise his own hand, doesn't react at all,
except to say, "Nice, Mom. Real nice. One day, that's gonna be a crime."

"You little shit."

He's smug now, which makes everything worse. "I'll tell you how I earned the pin. I got recruited. Recruited, Mom. They needed volunteers from the boys' school to make the rounds to the girls' schools and explain a few things. I accepted. And for the past three days, I've been going out in the field and demonstrating how the bracelets work. Look." He pushes up one sleeve and brandishes the burn mark around his wrist. "We go in pairs, and we take turns. All so girls like Sonia know what will happen." As if to defy me once more, he drains his glass of milk and licks his lips. "By the way, I wouldn't encourage her to pick the sign language back up."

"Why the hell not?" I'm still trying to absorb the fact that my son has purposefully shocked himself "so girls like Sonia know what will happen."

"Mom. Honestly. You of all people should get it." His voice has taken on the timbre of someone much older, someone tired of explaining how things are. "Signing defeats the purpose of what we're trying to do here."

Of course it does.

"Look, I can't tell you the details, but there are people researching the new—you know—devices. They'll be more like gloves. Really, that's all I should say." He straightens, smiling. "Except that I've volunteered to beta test them."

"You what?"

"It's called leadership, Mom. And it's what Pure Men do."

I don't know what to say, so I say the first thing that comes to mind. "You goddamned bastard."

Steven shrugs. "Whatevs." Then he stalks out of the kitchen, leaving the glass on the counter next to a note saying *Buy milk.*

Sam and Leo are in the kitchen doorway, staring at me, so I don't dare cry.

SIXTEEN

After I read Sonia her bedtime story and lie next to her, waiting for the steady breathing that tells me she's asleep, I go to my bedroom. Our bedroom. Tonight, I have it all to myself because Patrick is still in his study, even though it's approaching midnight. Rarely does he stay up so late.

Tonight, I think about men.

When I put the twins to bed, Steven was in the TV room, eating ice cream and watching part of a series of talks by Reverend Carl, who I now believe might be my son's hero. The two of them make a pair, both so steadfast in their ideas of reversion to a former time, an age when men were men and women were women and glory glory fucking hallelujah, *things were so much easier back when we all knew our places.* I can't hate Steven because he believes in something so wrong, even if I hate what he believes.

Other men, though, are different.

Not long after Sonia's fifth birthday, after we were fitted with the counters, I phoned my doctor at home, ready with a precisely worded set of questions, a pidgin of sorts. I pared the phrases down, eliminating copulas and modifiers, getting to the meat as quickly as possible. The recorder would pick up every word, even a whisper.

Who knows what I expected from her, what my doctor of more than ten years could tell me? Maybe I wanted a partner in silence. Maybe I only wanted to hear how pissed off she was.

Dr. Claudia answered, listened; and a low moan escaped before her husband came on the line.

"Whose fault do you think it was?" he said.

I stood in my kitchen, wanting to explain, careful not to, while he told me we'd marched one too many times, written one too many letters, screamed one too many words.

"You women. You need to be taught a lesson," he said, and hung up.

I didn't call her again to ask how they had silenced her, whether they had stormed into her practice or whether they had invaded her kitchen, if they had loaded her into a van along with her daughters and spelled out the future inside a dim gray room before fixing shiny wristbands on each of them and sending them home to cook and clean and be supportive Pure Women. To learn our lesson.

Dr. Claudia would never have put on that collar pin, not without a fight, but I know she's still wearing it. Probably, her daughters are, too, like Julia King next door. I knew Julia when she wore cutoff jeans and halter tops, when she raced her bike down the street with an MP3 player on full volume, singing along to the Dixie Chicks, when she caught me in the garden and told me another story about how weird her mother was acting, rolling her eyes at the ridiculousness of all that Pure crap. When her father caught her talking to me—I guess it was about a year and a half ago, now—he took Julia by the arm and shuttled her through the screen back door.

I still remember what her crying sounded like when Evan beat her.

Patrick's study door squeaks open, and his footsteps move down the hall, away from our bedroom, toward the kitchen. I could go to him, pour us a stiff drink, and tell him what happened with Steven after dinner. I should go; I know it.

But I won't.

Patrick is the third type of man. He's not a believer and he's not a woman-hating asshole; he's just weak. And I'd rather think about men who aren't.

So tonight, when Patrick finally comes to bed, even after he apologizes, I decide to dream of Lorenzo again.

I never know what brings it on, what makes me imagine it's his arm, and not my husband's, curled around my waist during the night. I haven't spoken to Lorenzo since my last day at the university. Well, and that one other time, afterward, which didn't involve an abundance of vocalization.

I wriggle out from the heavy appendage encircling me. It's too much like ownership, that gesture; too possessive. Also, the smoothness of Patrick's skin, his soft doctor's hand and fine hair, they're all getting in the way of my memories, blotting them out.

Lorenzo may have returned to Italy by now. I'm not sure. It's been two months since I followed my heart and libido and went with him. Two months since I risked everything for an afternoon tumble.

Not tumble, Jean—love, I remind myself.

It was his plan, all along, to go back to what we called the Boot, once the visiting professorship had run its course. He missed the cooking and the sea, oranges and peaches fattened on rich volcanic soil until they grew as big as the sun. And his language. Our language.

Patrick stirs beside me, and I slip out of bed. In the kitchen, I get out the old *macchinetta* from a cupboard, press espresso grounds into its tiny perforated cup, and fill the bottom container with water before putting it on a low flame. It's nearly five o'clock, and I won't be sleeping anymore.

Was it the coffee that started things on their trajectory? Or was it the Italian? All of a sudden, I feel cold and warm at the same time.

He kept a hot plate in his office, one of those single-burner electric jobs you find in efficiency apartments and cheap motels. Tucked between it and his semantics texts was a tin of coffee, real coffee, not the ground-up dust they stocked the faculty kitchen with. We'd met to review the progress on lexical recall in my patients with anomia. For some reason, the anomics had me stumped; their inability to conjure up the names of the most common objects while knowing exactly how to describe them had set my research back to ground zero. If I couldn't produce a positive report by the end of the month, I'd be saying goodbye to funding and sayonara to tenure.

Lorenzo set the coffee to percolate, and we walked through the latest brain scans. There, among MRIs and EEGs and Italian coffee, it began.

The first thing I noticed was his hand as it poured thick black espresso into a demitasse. His skin was dark, had none of the scrubbed pinkness of Patrick's hand. One of his nails was chipped, and there were calluses on the tips of his fingers, which were long and thin.

"You play the guitar?" I asked.

"Mandolin," he said. "And some guitar."

"My father played the mandolin. My mother would sing along; we all would. Nothing great, just the usual folk songs. 'Torna a Surriento,' 'Core 'ngrato,' things like that."

He laughed.

"What's funny?"

"An American family singing 'Core 'ngrato.'"

Now it was my turn to laugh. "What makes you think I'm American?" Only I didn't say it that way. I said it in Italian.

We met like that, in his office, where the hot plate and the little coffee maker were. Once I'd put the anomia project to bed, thus securing my somewhat unstable future for another semester, we still met.

"I brought you a bit of Italy," he said one day, not long after he'd returned from visiting family over spring break. Our speech had migrated from half English, half Italian to full-throttle Neapolitan, and

Lorenzo's office became an oasis of continentalisms: *caffè*, music, the crunchy baked *taralli* cookies he brought in on Mondays after slaving all weekend over his grandmother's recipe.

He pushed a newspaper-wrapped object across the desk.

"What is it?" I asked.

"Some music for you, Gianna. Open it."

I did. Inside the paper was a wooden box, inlaid and polished, a five-petaled rose motif around the border. It didn't look much like music until Lorenzo reached over and pushed up the cover with a finger.

I still remember that, how he lifted the hinged top with such care, like a bridegroom sliding a lace skirt above his new wife's knee, preparing to hook his finger into her garter. A lascivious action made tender by the gentleness.

That was the first time I imagined Lorenzo's hand on my bare skin, an ordinary Monday in his book-cluttered office with the music box tinkling out "Torna a Surriento" and the espresso maker bubbling its thick, sweet coffee.

Lorenzo isn't a believer or a hater or a coward. He's in his own category, tucked inside a dark and pleasant corner of my mind.

SEVENTEEN

Steven is the first to wake up and is out of the house before either Patrick or I start our morning routines. The twins, in a rare feat of self-sufficiency—if not color coordination—have dressed themselves and now pour the last of the milk into bowls laden with multicolored, teeth-rotting puffs of sugar. Leo has his sweater on inside out, and Sam fixes it. Neither of them says much over his cereal.

"What happened last night was only an argument," I say.

"It's strange when you talk, Mom," Leo says.

I suppose it would be, after a year.

By the time Patrick comes in, looking as if he's had less sleep than he has, the twins are on their way to the bus stop, and I'm dressing Sonia, sliding one thin arm at a time into her Windbreaker. My hand lingers on her red bracelet, and she tugs her wrist away, her small hand slipping from my grasp.

"I'm sorry you had to see that yesterday. With Steven."

She nods, as if she's sorry she had to see it too.

We walk to the bus together, as quiet as we've been on all the other days of the school year. I have words now, but no idea how to use them, no clue how to make my daughter's life better, if only for a while.

"No more scary dreams, right?"

Sonia nods again. Of course, she wouldn't have had any nightmares last night, not with the small dose of Sominex I stirred into her cocoa. Patrick still doesn't know about that, and I'm not sure I'll tell him.

"Be good in school," I say, and help her clamber up on the bus.

Be good in school. What a crock of shit.

I imagine my daughter sitting behind a desk, one of that kind that has the cubby under the seat where books and bright Hello Kitty pencil cases and, later, secret notes spelling *Do you like Tommy? I think Tommy likes you!* would hide. Formica-laminated writing surfaces where you scratched hearts and initials, or where you traced the carvings of some other boy or girl in some other year, wondering if BL ever married KT or if Mr. Pondergrass the algebra teacher really was a pig-monster with eye boogers. Black-and-white composition books, later thinner and bluer when the writing assignments shifted from "What I Did During Summer Vacation" to "Compare and Contrast Shakespeare's Hamlet and Macbeth." All those things, simple and ordinary, that we assumed we would never lose.

What do they study now, our girls? A bit of addition and subtraction, telling time, making change. Counting, of course. They would learn counting first. All the way up to one hundred.

When Sonia entered first grade this past fall, the school held an open house. Patrick and I went, along with the rest of the parents. I never saw the announcement that was sent to the fathers—or grandfathers, in the event one of the girls was a Heather with two mommies. Of course, there aren't any two-mommy or two-daddy families anymore; the children of same-sex partnerships have all been moved to live with their closest male relative—an uncle, a grandfather, an older brother—until the biological parent remarries in the proper way. Funny, with all the talk before of conversion therapy and curing homosexuality, no one ever thought of the foolproof way of getting gays in line: take away their kids.

I suspect attendance at the open house that night was mandatory, although Patrick didn't say so, only urged me to go check out the facilities, which were supposed to be state-of-the-art.

"State-of-the-art what?" I said, checking my counter before speaking. An hour later, we found out.

There were still classrooms, complete with desks and projection screens. The bulletin boards were wallpapered with drawings: a family picnicking here, a man in a suit holding a briefcase there, a woman wearing a straw hat and planting a bed of purple flowers in another corner. Children on a school bus, girls playing with dolls, boys arranged in a baseball triangle. I didn't see any books, but, of course, I hadn't expected to.

We didn't spend much time in the classrooms before teachers, each one wearing a small blue *P* pin on his collar, marched us along the corridors for the tour.

"Here's the sewing room," our group leader said, opening a set of double doors and motioning us inside. "Each girl—once she's old enough to work the machines without pulling a Sleeping Beauty"—he laughed at his own joke—"will have her own digital Singer. Really amazing equipment, these." He stroked one of the sewing machines as if it were a pet. "Now, if you'll follow me, we'll have a peek at the kitchens before heading outside to the gardening area."

It was home ec on drugs, and not much more.

I wave to Sonia as the bus pulls away from the curb. Today, she'll be in a room with twenty-five other first graders, all girls. She'll listen to stories, practice her numbers, help the older students in the kitchen as they cut cookies and knead dough and crimp pies. This is what school is now, and what school will be for some time. Maybe forever.

Memory is a damnable faculty.

I envy my only daughter; she has no recall of life before quotas or school days before the Pure Movement took off. It's a struggle to remember the last time I saw a number greater than forty on her fragile wrist, except, of course, for two nights ago when I watched that number creep upward to one hundred. For the rest of us, for my former colleagues and students, for Lin, for the book club ladies and the woman who used to be my gynecologist and Mrs. Ray, who will never landscape another garden, memory is all we have.

There's no way I can win, but there's a way I can feel like a winner.

In the minute it takes to walk back across the street and climb the steps to our porch, I decide.

Patrick has the television on, and Reverend Carl is holding a press conference. The White House room looks much the same as it always did, except there are no women, only a sea of dark suits and power ties. All of the reporters nod as they listen to Reverend Carl's updates on Bobby Myers' condition.

"We have someone who can help," Carl says.

A chorus of "Who?" and "Where did you find him?" and "Wonderful news!" rips through the press hall. Patrick interrupts his watching and turns to me. "That's you, babe. Back in business."

But I don't want to be back in business, not for Bobby Myers' sake or the president's sake or the sake of any of the other men in that room.

Reverend Carl does his usual double-handed press of the air in front of him, as if he's deflating an air mattress. Or squashing some weaker object. "Now, everyone listen up. What we're doing is a little unconventional, a little radical even, but I'm sure Dr. Jean McClellan is the right person for the job. As many of you know, her work on the reversal of"— he checks his notes to get the technical wording right—"fluent aphasia, also known as Wernicke's aphasia, was groundbreaking. Of course, that work has been on temporary hold until we get things sorted out, but I want to say—"

I switch the TV off. I don't give a shit what Reverend Carl wants to say. I never will. "I won't do it," I tell Patrick. "So call Reverend Carl before you leave for work."

"What am I supposed to say?"

I look at my wrist, clear of its electrical burn, clear of its silver-toned collar. "Tell him I said no."

"Jean. Please. You know what will happen if you don't agree."

Maybe it's the way he says this. Maybe it's the look in his eyes, that tired, beaten-down-like-a-disobedient-puppy look. Maybe it's the sour smell of milk and coffee on his breath when he speaks. It might be a combination of all three, but at this moment, in the house where we conceived four children, I realize I don't love him anymore.

I wonder if I ever did.

EIGHTEEN

This time, Reverend Carl comes to the house alone. His suit is the same expensive coal gray wool of yesterday, but double-breasted instead of single. I count the buttons on it: three on the right, three on the left, four on each sleeve. The sleeve buttons are the kind that overlap by a few millimeters, kissing buttons as my father called them when he had his haberdashery, the sign of a bespoke suit. Also, they're real, working buttons, and Reverend Carl leaves each of the bottom ones undone. He wants the world to see what exquisite taste he has, I suppose.

Lorenzo never showed off like this.

Over coffee one afternoon—I think it was two winters ago while we were plowing through another roadblock on the Wernicke project—I accidentally brushed his jacket sleeve with my pen, leaving a small, but ugly, mark on the gray material.

"Leave it," he said.

"Be right back."

I kept a bottle of hair spray in my office in those days. By "those days,"

I mean the days after Lorenzo and I started working together. I hadn't bothered before, usually content to let the dark curls that I inherited from my mother have their own unruly way. But that afternoon, I had a canister of Paul Mitchell Freeze and Shine lurking in a drawer along with a nail file, a pick, and an emergency makeup kit. Just in case Lin called any surprise project meetings.

The things we girls do.

After I sprayed and dabbed at the ink mark, I ran a fingernail down the waterfall of four buttons. They clicked as I touched them. "Kissing buttons," I said. "Haven't seen those in a while." My father had told me they work sleeve buttons that way only in Italy.

And so, that's how it happened. A stupid, offhand comment about a childhood memory, and Lorenzo's foot kicked the door shut as his mouth found mine.

That was a nice place to be, but now I'm back in my living room with Patrick and Reverend Carl and Carl's sleeve buttons, the bottom one on each wrist undone.

"We were hoping, Dr. McClellan, that you would—," Reverend Carl starts. He's staring longingly at my coffee mug.

I don't offer him a drink of his own, and I don't let him finish. "Well, I won't."

"We could up the pay."

Patrick's eyes flash, first at Reverend Carl, then at me.

"We'll make do," I say, and take another sip of coffee. I've grown used to defiance in small forms, like when I picked that bloodred counter for Sonia.

There's no desperation in his voice, no pleading, only a slight turning up at the corners of his mouth when he says, "What if I told you we had other incentives?"

Now I imagine myself in a room somewhere, a dirty and barren place with sound-attenuated walls and no windows and with sweat-streaked, beady-eyed men who follow commands like "Take it up a notch" and "Give her a moment to think it over" and "Let's start again." It's all I can do not to flinch, to hold a steady gaze. "Such as?"

His smile broadens. "We could, for instance, increase your daughter's quota. Let's say to one hundred fifty? No. Two hundred."

"You can increase it to ten thousand, Reverend. She's not talking as it is."

"I'm sorry about that," he says, but nothing in his tone indicates sorrow. This is what he wanted: docile women and girls. The older generations need to be controlled, but eventually, by the time Sonia has children of her own, Reverend Carl Corbin's dream of Pure Women and Pure Men will be the way of the world. I hate him for this.

"Anything else?" I say.

Patrick shoots me a look but doesn't speak.

Reverend Carl only takes a slim metal box from his pocket. "Then I'll have to put this back on." The "this" he's referring to is the narrow black band inside the box.

"That's not mine," I say. "Mine is silver."

Another smile, but now Reverend Carl's eyes join in. "A new model," he says. "You'll find it functions exactly as your former bracelet did, but this one has two additional features."

"What? A built-in miniature bullwhip?"

"Jean!" Patrick says. I ignore him.

"Nothing like that, Dr. McClellan. The first feature is a courtesy tracker."

"A what?"

"We like to think of it as a gentle nudge, nothing more. Just keep things clean, and everything will function normally. No four-letter words, no blasphemy. If you slip up, that's okay, but your quota reduces by ten for each infraction. You'll get used to it."

I feel like Cartman in that *South Park* movie, the one where he gets a chip implanted in his head that shocks him every time he says "fuck," which, because it's *South Park*, is effectively all the time.

"The second requires a bit more action on your part." He taps the red button at the side of the band. "Once a day, at a time of your choosing, you will press this button and speak into the bracelet. There's a microphone here." He points to the other side, opposite the red button. "We're hoping this practice will help get people—"

"Women," I interrupt.

"Yes. Women. We're hoping it will help put you in the mood, understand the fundamentals."

"How?"

From his breast pocket he removes a folded sheet of paper and smooths it out. It's a typed list. "You'll read this, once a day, into the microphone. Press the red button twice before you start, and twice when you've finished. It won't count against your quota."

"What won't count?" My mouth has gone dry. I take another swallow of coffee, now cold.

He hands me the sheet. "Why don't you read it now while I train the device to your voice? We'll kill two birds with one stone that way."

The first words I read are in bold blue type at the top of the page:

I BELIEVE that man was created in the image and glory of God, and that woman is the glory of the man, for man was not made of woman, but woman was made from man.

"I can't read this," I say.

Reverend Carl checks his watch. "Dr. McClellan, I have a meeting downtown in an hour. If we can't finish this, I'll have to call someone who can."

I'm picturing Thomas of the dark suit and dark complexion and even darker eyes, the one who took my counter off yesterday morning. The man I saw once before, a year ago, when men first came for us.

On the day I announced our team's progress to a packed seminar room, two dozen uniformed men, their left arms banded with the presidential seal, midnight black weapons in their right hands, pushed through the crowd. My projector dimmed in the time it took me to catch a breath. Behind me, only ghosts of my formulas remained on the white scrim.

It had begun, the terrible, unthinkable thing Patrick had warned me about only days earlier.

They separated our crowd, sending the men away, lining the rest of us up and leading fifty students and faculty women, some tenured, some new, through empty hallways. Lin was the first to voice her resistance.

Thomas was on her like a cougar after prey, that midnight black torture stick of his now pointing menacingly at Lin Kwan's petite frame.

I watched her fold and bend and collapse on herself, wordlessly, only the thread of a pained sigh, high-pitched and taut, coming from her lips. Five of us ran to the crumpled mass of woman on the tile floor, only to be beaten off. Those who lingered were also tased or stunned. Like misbehaving animals. Cows. Pets.

None of this happened without a fight, is what I'm saying.

"Dr. McClellan?" Reverend Carl has his phone out now, one long finger poised over the green Send button, ready to tap and summon a man who is short on charm and long on persuasive techniques.

"Fine. I'll read it," I say, thinking I can speak these horrible words without letting them invade me.

So I begin.

By the time I'm halfway down the page, Patrick's skin has blanched to a paste color. Reverend Carl nods each time I speak one of the beliefs or affirmations or declarations of intent into the black bracelet.

"We are called as women to keep silence and to be under obedience. If we must learn, let us ask our husbands in the closeness of the home, for it is shameful that a woman question God-ordained male leadership."

Nod.

"When we obey male leadership with humility and submission, we acknowledge that the head of every man is Christ, and that the head of every woman is the man."

Nod.

"God's plan for woman, whether married or single, is that she adorn herself with shamefacedness and sobriety, and that she exhibit modesty and femininity without fanciful or proud displays."

Nod.

"I will seek to adorn myself inwardly, and to be pure, modest, and submissive. In this way, I will glorify man, thereby glorifying God."

Nod.

"I will honor the sanctity of marriage, both mine and that of others, for God will judge adulterers with vengeance."

Nod.

I hope Patrick interprets the break in my voice at this as a sign of discomfort.

Reverend Carl nods once more, when I'm finished with the page, and taps the red button twice. "Well done, Mrs. McClellan." There's an emphasis on "Mrs." "Patrick, will you do the honors?"

Patrick shifts and sets his still-full coffee cup on the end table, spilling it. Then he takes the black thing from Reverend Carl's hand, encircles my left wrist with it, and snaps it closed.

So this is how I lose my voice for the second time. With a click that sounds like a bomb.

think I've developed superhuman hearing.

This afternoon, as I wait for Sonia's bus to snake along the lane toward our bungalow, I hear every sound. Not the sounds I used to hear: not the CNN reporters droning politics from the mini-television in the kitchen; not John, Paul, George, and Ringo telling me through the stereo speakers they want to hold my hand; not my own voice singing—badly, I'll admit—along. I hear the wet slap of the dough as I knead it into submission, the deafening hum of the refrigerator, the high-frequency whine of Patrick's computer through the locked door of his study. I hear my own heartbeat, steady, incessant.

There's the motor now, the Doppler effect amping up the frequency as the bus approaches. Already I have my three words planned for when Sonia arrives: *Mommy loves you.* More may be said later, but this is enough for now.

I place the dough in a large glass bowl for its second rise and towel off the flour that's stuck between my fingers. Should have taken off my ring, but I forgot. Then I force on a smile—not too wide, not too clownish; I don't want it to look like a bad makeup job—and head for the door.

Sonia leaps from the bus's steps, waves to Mr. Benjamin before he drives off toward his next drop-off point, and covers the hundred feet between bus stop and porch like an adrenaline-charged feline. Normally steady and deliberate, she's got a bounce in her this afternoon, a jitterbug type of anxiety. My girl is shiny with excitement as she leaps into my arms, the paper she's holding grazing my left ear, her downy cheek sticky and sweet with a glaze of chocolate.

"Mommy loves you," I say. *Pulse, pulse, pulse.* I've hardly registered my own words when she breaks the hug.

"Won prize!" Sonia squeals, thrusting the paper into my hands, pointing to her mouth, licking at it with a pink tongue. When I wrinkle my eyes at her, she makes three stabbing motions with her index finger at the smear of dried ice cream lingering at the corner of her mouth. I take her hand and move it away from her mouth, shaking my head. She forgets, sometimes, about the cameras.

And Steven.

Sonia points to her mouth again, desperate to make me see the chocolate smear, and again, I press her hand down, holding her fingers in my fist. A few seconds of pointing or gesturing at home might not matter—unless it becomes a habit. A single, painful image of Sonia doing this in public flashes in front of me—or worse, in front of Steven the goddamned Spy Kid. I squeeze her fingers a little more tightly while my other hand turns over the envelope she's brought home.

On the front there's a label, addressed to Dr. Patrick McClellan. And, of course, the envelope is sealed.

So there we are. My three words of the day, unless you count the ingredients list on the bag of flour, and the green LED message *Your beverage is ready* glowing from the microwave when I reheated my coffee.

"Why?" I say, leading Sonia inside, trying to ignore the next pulse on my wrist. "Careful with your words." This is more conversation than we usually have, but I'm desperate to know what news my girl's brought home. I'm also desperate to keep her from blurting out more than she should—I haven't yet checked the total on her counter.

In the kitchen, while I fix a mug of cocoa for us—our silent afternoon ritual—Sonia hops onto a barstool, thrusts out her left hand, and speaks one ear-splitting word. "Lowest!"

What the hell?

Then I read the counter on her red bracelet. They call them bracelets in school, at the doctor's office, in the advertisements they show before movies. I consider this as I wet a paper towel and wipe the smudge of chocolate—what I suspect is Sonia's prize—from her mouth and watch her create a new mocha-colored mustache as she spoons hot cocoa from the mug. Advertisements for electric-shock-inducing silencers: pick your own color, add some sparkles or stripes. They've got a mood-ring type that will match your clothing if you're obsessive about being coordinated, a variety of ringtones, cartoon character designs for the younger set.

It's everything I can do to keep from cursing the men who made these, or the marketers and their sinister efforts to persuade us we have any kind of choice. I suppose, if things ever return to normal, they'll use that old chestnut of a line: *I was only following orders.*

Where have we heard that before?

I can't be in this kitchen now, can't watch my girl sip cocoa and study the white envelope on the counter as if it contained a fucking Congressional Medal of Honor. So I go somewhere else. I try to imagine her on the playground, skipping rope and playing alphabet games, singing "Miss Lucy Had a Steamboat" and giggling at the thinly veiled curse words. I see her lining up, whispering about the new boy in class, writing love notes and fortunes on paper she'll fold into cootie catchers. I hear her speak thousands of useless, but precious, words before the first bell rings.

Another motor purrs, then growls, through the screen door of the back porch, and I'm out of my daydream. At least Patrick is home before the boys return from school. I don't have anything to say to him, but I need him alone; I need to see what secrets Sonia's mystery letter holds.

But I don't, not really. Across the kitchen island, my daughter's counter glows its horrid and up-to-the-second report.

Won prize! she said. *Lowest!*

I know what her school is up to. I know, because the counter on her thin wrist says the number 3.

My daughter has been silent all day.

was right; it is a contest.

The letter Patrick opens and reads to me announces with great pleasure the launch of a monthly competition for all students enrolled at PGS 523—the PGS stands for Pure Girls' School. Obviously, the boys attend PBS, Steven at the high school, Sam and Leo in another for grades five through eight. They don't divide the girls this way, possibly as a method of fulfilling yet another pledge from the manifesto—that older women provide teaching and training to younger women—possibly because they don't want to double up on the number of digital sewing machines and garden equipment.

"They're doing daily contests first," Patrick says, settling onto the barstool across from me after grabbing a beer from the fridge. It's early for him, but I don't say anything. "Ice cream for the girl in each grade with the lowest"—he takes a rather large swig from the bottle—"with the lowest number on her counter."

So it was exactly as I expected.

He continues. "At the end of the month, they'll tally all the counts, and—"

"Words," I interrupt. The black band on my left wrist pulses once.

"Right. Words. There's a grade prize of what they're calling an age-appropriate gift. A doll for the younger girls, games for the middle graders, makeup for the over-sixteens."

Super. Trading voices for crap.

The worst part is that Patrick is smiling.

"Enough of this," he says. "It doesn't matter."

"Like hell it doesn't." The contraption circling my wrist pings four times and I watch the number tick up from 46 to 50. Then it emits a sound like a diseased frog, and the 50 becomes 60. Okay. "Hell" is now out of my vocabulary. So much for George Carlin's list of seven dirty words. I wish I knew why Patrick was beaming at me.

As if he's read my mind, he leaves the kitchen, retrieves his briefcase from the front hall, and sets it on the counter dividing us. "Present from the president, babe," he says as he removes an envelope from the leather case. In the upper-right-hand corner is the presidential seal. In the left, where the return address would normally go, is a silver embossed capital *P*, the model for Steven's new pin.

And speak of the devil: the boys are home.

Leo and Sam bound into the kitchen first, kiss me hello, and make a beeline for the snack drawer. Steven, more composed than even he usually is, goes for the fridge after a curt "Hi, Dad. Hi, Mom."

He'll be looking for milk, which of course I forgot to buy.

"Nice," Steven says, shaking the last teaspoon of milk in the carton. He seems surprised when I don't come back with a response, then sees the latest addition to my wardrobe. "You got the new model! Awesome. Julia has one too, except hers is purple with silver stars. Just got it today. She showed me when I was walking home from the bus."

I don't hate my son. I don't hate my son. I don't hate my son.

Except right now I do, a little bit.

"Read the letter, Jean," Patrick says.

President Myers was on television again today. He's always on television, it seems, always trumpeting a new plan to turn the country around, constantly telling us how much better off we are. The economy's up—but not in our household, as the broken air-conditioning reminds me; unemployment is down—as long as you don't count the seventy million women who lost their jobs. Everything's great and everything's fine.

Everything wasn't so fine today as he fielded questions from the press.

"We'll find someone," he said. "Whatever it takes, we'll find someone to cure my only brother."

Like hell you will, I thought. The same slight smile on Anna Myers' lips told me she thought it, too. Good for you, sister.

Even if I agreed, there were no guarantees of success. Wernicke's aphasia is a tricky devil. Maybe I'd have a chance if I could make sure Lin Kwan was actually on the team, and not just the backup Reverend Carl mentioned. Even better, Lin and Lorenzo.

But I don't want to think about Lorenzo just now. I don't like to think about him when Patrick is around.

"You going to open it?" Patrick says.

I slide a nail under the flap of the envelope. Inside is a single trifold sheet of bond paper, off-white letterhead. It's addressed to me, Dr. Jean McClellan. So I'm back to "Dr." for the time being.

The body of the letter is one sentence long.

"Well?" Patrick asks the question, but his eyes tell me he already knows what the president has to say.

"Hang on."

He gets another beer from the fridge but doesn't drink it with the same celebratory mood as he did the first bottle. This one is medicinal, liquid anesthesia to get him through the wait while I remove myself from the kitchen with my yet-unvoiced decision. Maybe he expected me to do backflips on the tile. I don't know.

Anyway, it's too hot in here to think. The back garden, under Mrs. Ray's magnolia, is better.

Please call me with your price, the president says. It's rather pleasant to see that the bastard is begging.

My price. My price is to turn back the clock, but that's not feasible. My price is to eradicate the Pure Movement from the ground up, like pulling weeds from what was once a lively garden. My price is to see Reverend Carl Corbin and his flock hanged or torn to shreds by wild dogs or burnt to cinders in hell.

The back door creaks open and slams shut, and I expect to see Patrick coming toward me, but it isn't him. It's Sonia. She's holding a sheet of pink construction paper, the same color as her lips. When she reaches me, she holds it out.

For a six-year-old, she's got some talent, and this drawing is among her better ones, in a way. The six figures actually resemble us—Patrick, Steven, the twins, me, and Sonia. We're all standing in our garden, holding hands under a tree that's blooming with white stars. She's got the twins in matching outfits and she's drawn something that looks more like a suitcase than a briefcase in Patrick's free hand. Steven wears his new pin; my hair is pulled back into a ponytail. Around my wrist and Sonia's are bracelets: red for her and black for me. We're all smiling under a sun she's decorated with orange hearts.

"Beautiful," I say, taking the drawing. But I don't think it's beautiful. I think it's the ugliest fucking thing I've ever seen.

Instead of standing next to Patrick, or even at the far end of the family line, bookending our kids, I'm fifth. After my husband, after Steven, after the eleven-year-old twins. And Sonia has made me smaller than everyone except for her. I manage a forced smile and take her into my lap, pressing her head against me so she can't see the tears that are welling up, that I won't be able to contain.

I think of Jackie, and those last words she spoke in our crappy

Georgetown apartment, the accusations and admonitions. Jackie was right: I was living in a bubble. I inflated it myself, one breath at a time.

And so here we are. Me, my daughter, and the wrist counters that keep us in line. I wonder what Jackie would have to say about it. Probably something like *Good work, Jean. You gassed up the car and drove it straight into hell. Enjoy the burn.*

Yeah. That's what she'd say. And she'd be right.

I blot tears with my sleeve and set my face into a less crooked state before turning Sonia's tiny head toward me and planting a kiss on her cheek. Then I check my word counter.

Sixty-three words so far today. Plenty left for what I have to say to President Myers.

TWENTY-ONE

I can do this, I think.

I can do it in fewer than the thirty-seven words I've got left. In my head, I rehearse my half of the telephone conversation:

I want three things, Mr. President. I want my daughter's counter removed. I want her excused from school; I'll teach her at home Friday through Monday. I want Lin on the project full-time, not just backup.

No need to mention any other names. Lorenzo will be back in Italy now, anyway.

Sonia and the boys are in the add-on rec room watching cartoons whose sound effects trickle all the way into the kitchen. It's cooler in there, because of the window unit, and that leaves Patrick and me alone.

"Go on, babe," he says after yelling to Steven to turn the volume down. "Make the call."

I've never dialed the White House before. Patrick's job there started after the wrist counters went on, and I have little reason to phone him at work, unless all I want to do is engage in some telephonic heavy breathing. I don't. Not with Patrick.

My fingers find the numbers and press each one, hovering over the last. I almost miss it and dial a five instead of a four; that's how badly my hands are shaking. A voice answers, not of a secretary or any other gatekeeper, but his, and I speak my thirty-six words.

"I'm sorry, Dr. McClellan, but I can't do that."

Except these aren't the words he says in his gruff voice, a voice I sometimes think is unnatural in its harshness because I suspect the president is, at heart, a weak and insecure excuse for a man. I suspect they all are.

What he says, after a slight pause, is, "Very well, Dr. McClellan." And he ends the call.

"Wow," Patrick says. He's been close to me, breathing beer-scented air into my nostrils as he listened in. He seems shocked.

A moment later, the phone rings. Patrick answers it with a cheery "Hello!" and says single words: "Yes." "Fine." "Okay." I have no idea what he's agreeing to.

"Thomas will be here in a half hour," he says. "To take off the—um—"

Don't you dare call them bracelets.

"Counters," he says.

I nod and take out two boxes of pasta for dinner. Tomorrow, I've already decided, it's going to be steak. A mountain of steak. We haven't been eating much of it lately.

While I'm squeezing peeled tomatoes into a pot for sauce, I think about Sonia, how in less than thirty minutes she'll be free of that metaphorical collar, free to sing and chatter and answer questions that involve more than a nod or a shake of her head. What I don't know is how she'll greet this freedom.

In college, before I switched gears and plunged headlong into the black hole of neuroscience and linguistic processing, I'd studied psychology. Behavioral, child, abnormal, and all of that. Now, staring into this pot of tomato mush and garlic, I'm thinking I did a crackerjack job on the behavioral part, conditioning Sonia with bribes of cookies and marshmallows to keep her words unspoken. Someone should take away my mothering license.

I keep reminding myself it isn't my fault. I didn't vote for Myers.

I didn't vote at all, actually.

And here's Jackie's voice again, telling me what an acquiescent shit I am.

"You have to vote, Jean," she said, throwing down the stack of campaign leaflets she'd been running around campus with while I was prepping for what I knew would be a monster of an oral exam. "You have to."

"The only things I have to do are pay taxes and die," I said, not holding back the sneer in my voice. That semester was the beginning of the end for Jackie and me. I'd started dating Patrick and preferred our nightly discussions about cognitive processes to Jackie's rants about whatever new thing she had found to protest. Patrick was safe and quiet, and he let me bury myself in my work while he crammed for one medical school exam after another.

Naturally, Jackie hated him.

"He's a pussy, Jean. A cerebral pussy."

"He's nice," I said.

"I bet he quotes from *Gray's Anatomy* while he's eating you out."

I put my notes to the side. "The book or the television show?"

This time, Jackie sneered.

"He doesn't talk politics, Jacko." It was my pet name for her, or had been. "That's all I hear in this fucking city."

"One day, hon, you're going to change your mind." She tossed a paperback onto our thrift shop sofa, which I'd spread out on. "Read this. Everyone's talking about it. Everyone."

I picked up the book. "It's a novel. You know I don't read novels." It was true; with five hundred pages of journal articles a week, I had no time for fiction.

"Just read the back cover."

I did. "This would never happen. Ever. Women wouldn't put up with it."

"Easy to say now," Jackie said. She was in her usual outfit: low-rise jeans; a cropped T-shirt that didn't cover her belly, which Jackie didn't care to hide, even with its slight paunch; ugly-but-comfortable sandals; and three hoops in her right ear. Today, her cropped and spiked hair had a few green streaks in it. Tomorrow, it might be blue. Or black. Or cherry-cola red. You really never knew with Jackie.

She wasn't unattractive, but that square jaw and sharp nose and oil-drop eyes of hers didn't have guys banging down our door for her company. Jackie didn't seem to mind, and I found out why one night in September after she'd dragged me to a party. It was less of a party than a Planned Parenthood commercial with snacks and booze, both of which Jackie sucked down as if Armageddon were set for tomorrow morning. We didn't have a lot of spare change for liquor and junk food, although Jackie always managed to find a few bucks to keep her in cigarettes.

Christ, she was drunk. I ended up having to half carry her back through cobblestone streets to the apartment, no small trick when the person you're carrying is trying to chain smoke.

"Love you, Jeanie," she said when I finally got her through the door.

"Love you too, Jacko," I said automatically. "Want a cup of tea or something?" We didn't have any tea, so I popped open a can of Coke and tried to feed her a few aspirin.

"I want a kiss," she said after she'd fallen onto her bed, taking me with her. She smelled of patchouli and red wine. "Come here, Jeanie. Kiss me."

What Jackie wanted wasn't a kiss; it was full-on spit swapping.

The next day over coffee, she laughed it off. "Sorry if I got a little crazy last night, hon."

I never told Patrick about that.

"Whatcha thinking about, babe?" Patrick says, startling me and sending a peeled Roma tomato squirting against the backsplash.

What am I thinking about? Maybe where Jackie Juarez ended up, whether she decided to convert, or whether she ended up in one of the camps along with the rest of the LGBTQIA crowd. My money's on the camp.

Reverend Carl dreamt up the idea, which was a hit with the Pure Majority until they balked at the idea of putting gay men and lesbians in cells with each other. It would be counterproductive, they argued; think what they'd get up to. So Reverend Carl modified his plan and decided to pair one woman and one man in each cell. "They'll get the idea soon enough," he said.

Of course, the camps are only a temporary thing, "until we get on track," in Reverend Carl's words.

The camps aren't camps at all; they're prisons. Or they were prisons before the new executive orders on crime were signed. There isn't much need for prisons anymore, which isn't to say there's no crime. There is, but the criminals don't need to be put anywhere, not for long.

I answer Patrick after cleaning up the red mess of tomato on the tile. "Nothing." *Pulse. Ding. You're out, kiddo.* The clock's hands have decided to move at a snail's pace since our telephone rang.

He gives me a kiss on the cheek. "Another few minutes, and everything's going to be back to normal around here."

I nod. Sure, it is. Until I find a cure.

TWENTY-TWO

Dinner, despite my best efforts at my mother's sauce, is a disaster. Sonia isn't here, but in her room. I stayed with her for an hour after Thomas of the dark suit and dark attitude came and re-moved the counters. He did have a time with Sonia's because she wouldn't stop wriggling away. She even bit his hand on the second try. No blood, but Thomas yelped like a surprised puppy and cursed under his breath on the way to his car.

"It's all right, baby. You can talk now," I said, soothing her when we were alone in her room.

She said one word: "No."

"You don't have to go to school anymore," I said. "We'll have our own classes here at home. We'll read stories. And when I'm at work, you can watch cartoons over at Mrs. King's house." I hated the idea of Sonia spending even a minute in the company of Evan and Olivia King, but I hated it less than sending her back to PGS.

Everything lately seems to be a choice between degrees of hate.

At the mention of school, she started bawling again.

"You don't really like it there, do you?" I said.

She nodded.

"Use your words, Sonia."

She sat up and pressed her lips together. At first, I thought she was playing the tough girl—as tough as a six-year-old can be when she's swathed in pink sheets and surrounded by stuffed bunnies and unicorns. She was only getting ready.

"I was going to win tomorrow!" she said, and her mouth clamped shut again. I could almost hear the click of a steel key turning in its lock while she looked longingly at her naked wrist.

Finally, Leo poked his head in the doorway. "Sauce is bubbling, Mom. A lot."

"How about turning off the gas?" I said, wondering how I was going to work, teach Sonia, and deal with a household of incompetent males over the next several months. Then, turning back to Sonia, I said, "We'll work on a different kind of prize tomorrow, okay? Let's go eat."

She only shook her head and grabbed hold of Floppy the Bunny.

At the table, it's Steven who puts words to my worries. "How're you going to teach Sonia and work and take care of the house, Mom?" he says around a mouthful of pasta. "We still don't have any milk."

In my mind, I take hold of him by the collar and shake him until he's dizzy. In reality, I say, "You could ride your bike over to Rodman's and buy it yourself. Or you could walk to the 7-Eleven."

"Not my job, Mom."

Sam and Leo bury their noses in bowls of pasta.

Patrick goes red. "Steven, one more word like that and you can leave the table."

"You need to get with the program, Dad," Steven says. He takes another bite—a shovelful, really—and leans forward on his elbows. One finger pokes the air. "See, this is why we need the new rules. So everything can run like it's supposed to."

He doesn't seem to notice that I'm staring at him as if he's from outer space. "Take me and Julia—"

"Julia and me," I say.

"Whatevs. Me and Julia have it planned out. When we get married and have kids, she'll take care of that house stuff while I'm at work. She loves it. I'll make the decisions, and Julia will go along. Easy-peasy."

I put my fork down, and it clangs against the rim of the plate. "You're too young to get married. Patrick, talk to him."

"What your mother said," Patrick says. "Way too young."

"We've talked about it."

"You've talked about it," I say, still not eating. "How exactly do you do that on Julia's one hundred words a day? I'm curious."

Steven sits back, done with his second bowl. "I haven't talked about it with Julia," he drawls. "I've talked about it with Evan."

My blood is beginning to boil. "Does Julia get a say?"

There's no response from my son, only a bewildered look, as if I've suddenly begun speaking in tongues. We stare at each other across the table like strangers until Patrick interrupts.

"Let it go, Jean. No sense in fighting about it. He's too young, anyway." Then he looks over at Steven. "Way too young."

"Wrong again, Dad. A guy from the Department of Health and Welfare came to our school today. Major assembly. He talked about how next year they're rolling out a new program. Get this: ten thousand bucks, full college tuition, and a guaranteed government job for anyone who's married by eighteen. Boys, of course. And another ten thousand for each kid you have. Pretty sweet, huh?"

Sweet as snake venom, I think. "You're not getting married at eighteen, kiddo."

A smile works its way onto Steven's face, only a touch of a smile that isn't joined by his eyes. It's really not a smile at all. "You don't have anything to do with it, Mom. It's Dad's decision."

Maybe this is how it happened in Germany with the Nazis, in Bosnia with the Serbs, in Rwanda with the Hutus. I've often wondered about that, about how kids can turn into monsters, how they learn that killing is right and oppression is just, how in one single generation the world can change on its axis into a place that's unrecognizable.

Easily, I think, and push out my chair. "I'm going to call my parents," I say. I tried yesterday and got no answer. This morning, no answer. Before dinner, no answer. It will be late over there, nearly midnight, but I want to talk to my mother.

It's been way too long.

TWENTY-THREE

On Thursday morning, I put on a suit for the first time in more than a year. I had to climb up into the attic for it, forage through the boxes I'd stuffed with my better clothing in the days after Sonia and I were fitted with our counters. I hardly remember what I was doing, only that I had to keep my hands busy at trivial tasks. Otherwise, they would have found their way into walls or windows.

The outfit I choose is beige linen, for the heat. There's barely time to press out a year's worth of wrinkles and get my act together before the doorbell rings. Patrick lets the man in, and I recognize him instantly.

It's Morgan LeBron, from my old department, the all-too-young and completely incapable little shit who took over Lin's position. No wonder the president agreed so quickly to my conditions; Morgan is an idiot who doesn't know he's an idiot. The worst kind.

He steps in and holds out a manicured hand. "Dr. McClellan, I'm so happy to have you on my team. So happy."

Of course you are.

And it's his team. Not the team, not our team.

I take his hand. I've always had a firm grip for a woman, and shaking hands with Morgan is a bit like shaking with a newborn kitten. "I'm happy, too," I say. *Pussy.*

"So," he says. "Shall we get to business? I've got some paperwork for you to sign, and we'll need to set up a direct deposit to your husband's account. Whew. Hot in here."

"The AC's on the fritz," I say. "We can go into the back room. There's a window unit in there." No sense in asking why my paychecks will go to Patrick's account; all my money has been sitting there since last year. Words, passports, money—even criminals get two out of three. At least they used to.

I lead him through the house, stopping at the kitchen to refill Patrick's and my coffee and pour Morgan one of his own. He takes it with three spoons of sugar and a fat inch of milk, which I remembered to run out for last night after the disaster of a dinner with Steven and Sonia's meltdown. She seemed to brighten a little when Olivia King came to pick her up, possibly because I told her Mrs. King had a cartoon cable channel and would bake some cookies today. Possibly, the smile on my daughter's face had to do with the lavender counter on our neighbor's wrist. Something normal.

The first set of papers Morgan takes out of his briefcase is a contract, a noncompete agreement (as if I had any other job prospects), a nondisclosure agreement, and a work-for-hire acknowledgment. This last is a five-page-long reminder in legalese that all of the work I create belongs not to me but to the government. I take the pen Morgan offers and sign everything without reading, wondering why they even need a signature, since they'll do what they want in any case. Patrick signs the direct deposit forms and hands them over.

I do, however, note the compensation terms: five thousand dollars a week and a bonus of one hundred thousand if I complete the cure by August 31. The bonus is reduced by ten percent for every month after this date. So there's incentive to work fast, in a way, but the sooner I'm done, the sooner the metal counters go back on Sonia's and my wrists. I know they will eventually; it's only a matter of time.

"Perfect," Morgan says, removing a machine from his briefcase. The slim black object is like an iPhone, only larger. He sets it on the coffee table between us. "Security check." He presses a button, swipes, and enters my name. "Thumb is one, index finger two, and so on. Just follow the instructions and hold your finger to the screen until you hear a beep."

Naturally, they'd want a fingerprint check. I do as I'm told, and after the machine scans my left pinkie, Morgan picks it back up and waits. "This will only take a few seconds. If you're cleared, we can unlock your files and head over to my lab."

Again with the "my." I wonder how much of my work—my and Lin's work, that is—will wind up with Morgan's signature on it.

"Okeydokey," Morgan says when the machine pings. "You're clear." He turns to Patrick, who has been holding a set of keys in his hand throughout the signing-and-fingerprinting party. "Sir?"

Patrick leaves, and doors start to open. First his study. Then the metal file cabinet next to the window. Then the closet where I suppose my laptop and files have been living for the past year. While he's gone, Morgan shuffles through another set of papers. "Here's the team," he says, handing me a copy. At least he hasn't said "my" again. If he did, I might have to slap him.

The team leader, of course, is Morgan LeBron himself. There's a short bio after his name, including a reference to his latest position: Chair, Department of Linguistics, Georgetown University. Underneath, the rest of us are in alphabetical order: first Lin Kwan, and her credentials, which include the word "former"; then me, also "former." Each instance of that word is a poke in the eye.

But I'm not ready for the gut punch that follows.

The third surname on the list is Rossi. First name, Lorenzo.

TWENTY-FOUR

It's been so long since I've used my laptop, I'm worried it might not power up, that a year of nonuse will have sent it into the same dormant silence I fell into. But it's obedient, like an old friend waiting for a phone call, or a pet sitting patiently at the door until its owner comes home. I trace a finger over its smooth keys, wipe a smudge from the screen, and collect myself.

A year is a long time. Hell, when the FIOS in our house went down for two hours, it seemed like the end of the world.

Eight thousand seven hundred and sixty hours is a lifetime longer than two, which is why I need a moment before I walk out of this house, start the Honda, and follow Morgan to the lab where I'll be spending three days a week from now until I finish fixing the president's brother.

Also, I need a moment to sift through my files, the ones I copied and kept at home so I didn't have to lug the same shit back and forth to my campus office. There are reports I don't want Morgan to see, not until I can speak to Lin.

The bottom folder is the one I want, the folder with the red *X* on its front flap. Patrick has already gone to work, and Morgan is out in his Mercedes making phone calls, likely gloating to Reverend Carl about what a fantastic team he's put together, which leaves me here in the paneled room with its humming window air-conditioning unit and—I don't know—about five million pounds of books. They don't weigh that much, but the teetering piles of texts and journals are like academic mesas littering the rec room.

We haven't used the sleeper sofa in a year and a half, not since the last houseguest came to visit. No one really visits anymore. There's no point. We tried it once, a dinner party for some old friends I'd met when Steven was still in diapers, but after an hour of the men talking and the women staring into their plates of salmon, everyone decided to go home.

I pry up the corduroy-covered cushion next to me and slip my red-*X* folder in among a few cracker crumbs, a stray piece of popcorn, and some spare change.

This "it," encased in a dull manila folder rubbed shiny by my own hands, is the work that will, when I'm ready, reverse Wernicke's aphasia. I've thought about finding a more permanent hiding place for it, but given the year's worth of crap I find beneath the sofa cushions, I don't see the need.

No one, not even Patrick, knows we had passed the brink from "close" to "finished," although I believe Lin and Lorenzo suspected.

The day before Thomas and his Taser-carrying men came for me the first time, I had been winding down a lecture on linguistic processing in the posterior left hemisphere—the area of the brain where temporal and parietal lobes meet. Wernicke's area, and the language loss that accompanies damage to this complex cluster of gray matter, was the reason most of my students signed on for this seminar, and on that day the room was packed with colleagues of colleagues, the dean, and a few out-of-town researchers intrigued by our group's latest breakthrough. Lin and Lorenzo sat in the back row as I talked.

They must have seen the gleam in my eyes when I moved through the slides of brain imagery on the projector, zooming closer to the target area. The serum we would use wasn't mine. Repairs would happen naturally with the aid of an interleukin-1 receptor antagonist, a drug already widely in use to counter the effects of rheumatoid arthritis, and infant stem cells, which would increase the plasticity of the subject's brain, encouraging rapid repair and rebuilding. One of my contributions—*our* contributions—involved pinpointing the exact locus of application without affecting the surrounding areas of cortical tissue and causing further damage.

We had another ace up our sleeves. One Wednesday morning last spring, when the cherry blossoms had exploded into photogenic candy and Washington had begun to flood with its annual onslaught of tourists, Lorenzo pulled me into his office.

Of course, he kissed me. I can still taste the bitter espresso on his lips. Strange how a kiss can turn bitter into sweet.

He kissed deep and hard, as lovers do when kisses are stolen or come with a price, but then he broke away and smiled.

"I'm not done yet," I said.

His eyes swept up and down, from the widow's peak on my forehead all the way to my black pumps, the ones I had started wearing to work instead of my more comfy loafers. "Neither am I," he said. "But first I've got a surprise for you."

I did like Lorenzo's surprises. I still do.

While I floated down from my kissing high, he pushed files and journal articles aside on the desk until he landed on whatever he was looking for. "Here. Check the numbers for me."

The stats looked good. Fine p values showed significance; solid chi-squares and experimental design told me he knew his statistics shit. I took in the data as if they were water and manna sent to a deserted Robinson Crusoe.

"You're sure?" I said, checking over the data.

"Positive." He stood behind me, his arms circled around my waist, creeping up like five-legged spiders to my breasts. "Of a few things."

We hadn't done it on campus, not the big *It*, not the holy grail of physical intimacy, only kissed and run our hands over each other's bodies behind the locked door of Lorenzo's office. Or mine. Once, he followed me into the faculty washroom and—I'm ashamed to say it—made me orgasm with nothing but a finger. After seventeen years of marriage and four kids, it didn't take long.

He must have felt the heat growing in me, because he let go, let me read through the reports.

"Holy shit," I said. "You isolated the protein?"

We had been searching for that one last piece, the biochemical substance we knew was present in some people and absent in others. Lorenzo had run the numbers on more than two thousand subjects, searching for an indicator that might predict lexical proficiency. He called it the Kissinger Project, and his background in both biochem and semantics made him exactly the right person to find the link between meta-eloquence and brain chemistry.

"You've got the map, and I've got the key, love," he said while his hand snaked into the waistband of my skirt.

"How about we do a little practice unlocking?" I said. Lorenzo brought out my inner coquette. "Later?"

"Later. Same place."

We had a small cottage—the Crab Shack, as we called it—over in Anne Arundel County by the Chesapeake Bay, far enough from the suburban Maryland bungalow I share with Patrick and the kids to be discreet. The lease was still in Lorenzo's name two months ago.

Better not to go there right now. Besides, he'll have already given the place up.

I pack my laptop and files, all but one, into the briefcase I've carried since my days in graduate school with Jackie, and head out the door, a pleasant smile on my face that I hope hides my trickery from Morgan. I want to buy as much time as I can this summer, stretch out the work long enough to get Sonia on track.

In my car, driving from rural Maryland into the congestion of Washington, DC, I think about how I found the physical locus and how Lorenzo's work on verbal and semantic fluency identified the protein. I knew it; Lin and Lorenzo knew it. But Morgan doesn't need to know it. Not yet.

TWENTY-FIVE

My office is something between a cave and a monk's cell, but less luxurious given the pair of desks and chairs crammed inside. Also, it lacks a window, unless you count the glass pane in the door that gives the work space all the privacy of a fishbowl. A scarf and purse, both on the tattered side of wear, sit on one of the desks. I recognize both as Lin's.

Morgan shows me inside and leaves me to get settled. He says he'll come back in a few minutes to take me around the lab, get me set up with an ID tag, and show me where the copier room and the printer area are. I now know nothing I do here will be unseen by other eyes.

Oddly, I don't care. The idea of seeing Lin again, of talking to her and working with her, has me as high as a schoolgirl at her first dance.

"Oh my god," a wisp of a voice says from the doorway.

Lin Kwan is a small woman. I often told Patrick she could fit in one of my pants legs—and I'm only five and a half feet and 120 soaking wet, thanks to the stress diet I've been on for the past several months. Everything about her is small: her voice, her almond eyes, the sleek bob that barely reaches below her ears. Lin's breasts and ass make me look like a Peter Paul Rubens model. But her brain—her brain is a leviathan of gray matter. It would have to be; MIT doesn't hand out dual PhDs for nothing.

Like me, Lin is a neurolinguist. Unlike me, she's a medical doctor, a surgeon, to be specific. She left her practice fixing brains fifteen years ago, when she was in her late forties, and moved to Boston. Five years later, she left with a doctorate in each hand, one in cognitive science, one in linguistics. If anyone can make me feel like the class dunce, it's Lin.

And I love her for it. She sets the bar as high as Everest.

Lin steps in and glances down at my left wrist. "You too, huh?" Then she bear-hugs me, which is interesting since she's shorter and narrower than I am. It's a little like being bear-hugged by a Barbie doll.

"Me too," I say, laughing and crying at the same time.

After what seems like an hour, she releases me from her clutch and steps back. "You're exactly the same. Maybe even younger-looking."

"Well, it's amazing what a year off of working for you has done," I say.

The humor doesn't work. She shakes her head and raises a hand, thumb and forefinger a fraction of an inch apart. "I was this close to going to Malaysia to visit my family. This close." Her fingers fly apart into a starfish as she blows out air. "Gone. Gone in a bloody day."

"You sound like the queen," I say. "Except for that bloody part."

"Don't kid yourself. Even QE2 knows how to curse. Speaking of which, did anyone tell you about the latest model of wrist monster?" When she says this, it comes out like "mon-stuh," *r*-less and elegant.

"They didn't just tell me about it." I explained my eight-hour experience with the upgrade. "If I'd had to read that manifesto shit once more, I would have cut out my own tongue."

She perches on the desk, one bare leg swinging in the air, and lowers her voice after checking the door. "You know they'll put them back on, Jean, don't you? As soon as we finish."

"We don't have to finish right away," I say, my back to the door. "Even if we can, we don't have to." I pick up the silk scarf. "Tell me you haven't started wearing this on your head."

"What do you think?"

I think that's—in Lin's terms—about as bloody likely as a pig with wings, and I tell her so, which gets a laugh.

Then she's serious again. "We need to do something, Jean. Something besides working on the Wernicke project."

"I know. How about we reverse the serum and spike the White House's water supply?" I say this knowing it's even less likely than Lin walking around with a head scarf and a Pure pin on her collar.

"Now, there's an idea," she says. I can't tell whether her voice carries a hint of sarcasm or approbation.

She hops up and takes my arm. "Let's go get an espresso before Morgan the Moron comes back."

"They have an espresso machine here?" I say, letting her lead me out of the office and down the gray corridor. All the workstations and offices we pass are empty.

"No. But Lorenzo has his little coffee maker."

Oh boy.

TWENTY-SIX

Lorenzo's office is an exact copy of the one Lin and I are sharing, except that it's twice as big, the desk is wood instead of metal, the chair looks as if it came off a *Star Trek* set, and there's a window that overlooks a park strewn with blooming cherry trees. I growl on the inside.

Lin pushes me through the doorway and escapes back down the hall before I can protest.

"Ciao," Lorenzo says. His voice is the same, and different. Still low and musical, with the same softened consonants that bring me back to southern Italy, to a slower life. But there's a weariness in that single syllable that matches the lines in his face, deeper now after only two months. I can't help but stare into his dark eyes, and when I do, I see every word trapped inside him.

All of a sudden, there's a lump in my throat the size of a beach ball. I try to say "Ciao" around it, and what comes out has all the force of a mouse fart. My knees give way as the room spins around me, multiple

Lorenzos and coffee makers and bookshelves, all swirling in a whirlpool of color and texture.

He catches me on the way down and props me in the large leather chair behind his desk, taking the smaller visitor's chair for himself. "Nice to know I still make you weak in the knees, Gianna."

In one reality, I recover completely from what women used to call *la petite mort*, stretch my neck to meet Lorenzo's face, and wrap both arms around him. We kiss, slowly at first, then furiously. Then all hell breaks loose and I've got him on the desk or he's got me on the desk or we've got each other under the desk. It's fantastic and loud and wet and sweaty and perfect.

Then there's the other reality, the one that's actually happening, the one where I have precisely enough time to drag the plastic-lined waste-basket from its corner, line it up under me, and lose my breakfast into it with a very unsexy slosh.

All Lorenzo says is, "Wow."

"I've gotta go," I say, pulling myself up, using the desk for leverage. "Ladies' room."

I think the true test of a man is how he acts when a woman pukes in front of him, in his office, into his wastebasket. What Lorenzo did, right before he walked me to the door of the women's restroom at the opposite end of the hall from my office, was smile. A "wow" and a smile, nothing more.

I love him for that.

"I'll be fine. Just need a minute," I say, pushing the door open and heading for the closest stall. The rest of my bagel and coffee comes up, and I flush it away before sitting on the toilet seat with my head between my legs and the bitter bile and stomach acid in my throat.

I never get sick, and I don't have a sensitive gut, and I can't remember the last time I puked.

Yes, I can.

The stainless steel box with its hinged lid and plastic liner is to my right, opposite the industrial toilet paper dispenser that could wipe the bottoms of a small country before it runs out. I don't have anything to put in it, no carefully wrapped tampon, no rolled and taped napkin, not even a mini pad.

Oh, holy shit.

I'm forty-three years old. I have four kids, thanks to Patrick and his Irish virility. I had twins eleven years ago. And I know enough about reproductive biology to realize that my chances of having multiples are higher now than they were then.

I also know I've got a one-in-two chance of having another girl. Will they snap a word counter on her wrist the second she pops out? Or will they wait a few days? In any case, it will happen quickly, and I won't have any more bargaining chips.

So I do what any woman in my position would do: I throw up all over again.

TWENTY-SEVEN

L in is waiting for me outside the restroom door, her face painted with concern.

"You okay, honey?" she says.

"Fine. Except half of my breakfast is in his office."

She puts an arm around my waist and leads me back to our hobbit hole, cleans a smudge of mascara with a wet wipe from the bottomless pit of her purse, and gets right to the point. "You put a rather literal definition on lovesick, Jean. And don't pretend you have no idea what I'm talking about. Still got a thing for our Italian colleague?"

I sink into the task chair behind my desk. "It's that obvious?" Now I'm wondering whether the entire department, including Morgan, was onto my regular meetings with Lorenzo in his office. "Who else knows?"

Lin leans in toward me, elbows on the desk between us. "If you're worried about Morgan, don't be. He's an idiot, he's self-absorbed, and he's a guy. He wouldn't recognize afterglow if someone poured a bottle of it on his head. I doubt he noticed your wardrobe change, either." Her smile fades into a line, and the line becomes a frown. "But be careful. You don't want Carl Corbin's adultery wagon coming for you."

"No," I say, and feel sick all over again.

In our new, abnormal world, a surprising number of things are exactly as they used to be. We eat, we shop, we sleep, we send our kids to school, and we fuck. Only there are rules about fucking.

"How long has it been going on?" Lin asks.

"About two years, I guess." There's no sense in telling her I can point to the exact date when I first noticed Lorenzo's hand on the satin wood of the music box, when I felt a pleasant electrical current run up and down my spine at the thought of that hand on my skin.

"Only before? Or after?"

I float away from her now, from the sterile functionality of our office to the cluttered crab shack in Maryland, its walls covered from floor to ceiling with marine-themed kitsch. A fishing net there, a bottled boat on the windowsill, a rusted anchor leaning against a wall in the corner. And a bed. It's the bed I remember best because it was lumpy and squeaky and too narrow for both of us to lie on comfortably without overlapping limbs. I loved that bed.

We shared it only once after the Pure Movement went national, which is what Lin meant by *Only before? Or after?* I'd taken the Metro down to Eastern Market in early March to the cheese shop that used to be run by an elderly couple and now was the sole concern of the husband. I can't remember what I was looking for, maybe smoked *scamorza*, maybe fresh ricotta. Or, maybe, I wasn't looking for cheese at all.

He stood there at the baker's stall with an armful of produce and flowers and with a distant look in his eyes. We'd spent ten months without seeing each other, not once, and we would have gone on not seeing each other if I hadn't left the cheese shop and walked straight across the market hall.

I risked two words. "Still here?"

"Still here. I have a ticket home in August," he said. "After the summer term finishes. I can't stay in your country any longer." As he spoke, he avoided my eyes and fixed on the silver bracelet. "I wouldn't have stayed out the summer, but they made a generous offer."

August was five months away. When he left, I knew he would never come back to the States. Who would?

Lorenzo paid for his bread. "Don't go anywhere. I'll be right back."

He disappeared through the crowded market to the far end where the café and the wineshop were. This was a Tuesday morning, unusually warm for March, which had a habit of hitting Washington with a fresh blast of winter, as if to remind us that the season wasn't over yet, not without one last bang. My head told me to run out the side door, forgetting the cheese, and hop the next train back home. Or anywhere. My feet disobeyed and remained glued to the floor. And then he was back, another bag added to the collection of groceries he'd already purchased.

"Meet me in the Eighth Street alley in ten minutes," was all he said.

Officially, premarital and extramarital sex were illegal. They'd always been illegal in most states, a holdover from the days of pre–Middle Ages sodomy laws that forbade even a married couple from engaging in anything other than vaginal intercourse. "Immoral" and "unnatural" were the benchmarks. Rarely was anyone charged and criminalized for fellatio or anal play, though, and affairs outside the marital bed were regarded as normal, if not commendable, acts.

And birth control? That's a good one. The pharmacy shelf that used to hold Trojan and Durex and LifeStyles boxes is stocked with baby food and diapers. A logical replacement.

Reverend Carl had a few things to say about sexual morality when he rose to his current seat of power. No elections were held, no confirmation hearings—the president wanted votes, and he got them. All Sam Myers needed to do was listen to an unofficial right-hand man, a man with the attentive ears of millions who thought moving one hundred years in reverse was actually desirable.

Blessed be the loophole.

I don't know if there's really an adultery wagon, but I do know what happened to Annie Wilson down the street when her husband called in the infraction. It was on television, a handful of days after my world changed.

Annie Wilson was a tart in housewife clothing—at least she dressed down when her husband was home. I expect she made a beeline for her wardrobe on Wednesday mornings after he left for work, and reversed the dolling-up process in early afternoon after the man in the old blue pickup started his truck and left for another week. They had an arrangement.

I shouldn't call her a tart. I'm no better, and Annie's husband was no Prince Charming. She'd been wanting to leave him for two years, and once he canceled her credit cards and stopped payments on her car, Annie might as well have been living in a maximum-security prison. One Wednesday, I remember cheering her on, silently urging her to just walk out of the house and get in that blue pickup and never look back.

If she hadn't had the two boys, both under ten, maybe she would have done that. And if she'd run off that Wednesday afternoon, maybe I wouldn't have had to watch her on television that night as Reverend Carl Corbin handed her over to two blandly dressed women with gray faces that matched their long habits. Maybe I wouldn't have had to hear him tell us about the convent in North Dakota where Annie Wilson would live out her life with a wrist counter set to a daily maximum of zero.

What made up my mind to walk out of Eastern Market and head for Lorenzo's car in the alley across the street wasn't only lust, and it wasn't only the one-sided argument I'd had with Patrick that morning. Rage had been crackling inside me like a fire, first a slow burn, then an inferno. I knew all about the double standard, the private clubs that had cropped up in cities and towns where single men of certain means could go to unload their stress and sperm on professional ladies of the entertaining sort. Patrick had told me about the clubs after overhearing a conversation at work. They were the last places where you could get your hands on a box of rubbers.

Prostitution, they say, is the oldest profession. And you can't kill anything that old. Also, the gays had been taken care of in their prison camps; the adulteresses like Annie Wilson were working farms in North Dakota or the grain belt of the Midwest. The Pure had to do something about single women who had no families to take them in—they couldn't very well live on their own with no words and no income. They were given a choice: marry or move to a cathouse.

When I thought of Sonia—of what would happen to her if Patrick and I were out of the picture, of whether she would be forced into a loveless marriage or sent away to a commune of whores where she could do nothing with her mouth but suck and moan—my blood boiled. Even the whores were supposed to shut up and behave.

So I walked out of Eastern Market and across the street, dodging potholes and semifrozen puddles, and got into Lorenzo's car. It was the only method I had of saying "Fuck you" to the system.

Thanks to raging hormones and my own idiocy, the system said "Fuck you" right back. Lorenzo and I went at it three times. One with a condom. The others? Bareback all the way.

Christ, it was good.

Lin takes my hand, bringing me from that afternoon to this morning. "Be careful, honey. You've got a lot more to lose than your voice."

"I know," I say, and pull myself together just as Morgan knocks at our door.

TWENTY-EIGHT

Morgan leads us along the hall, collects Lorenzo from his office, and pauses with his nose wrinkled. "What's that smell?" he says.

"I don't smell anything," Lorenzo says flatly, but his eyes are smiling at me.

Lin plays along. "Neither do I."

"Hmph. Well, let's get to it, people. Lots of ground to cover if we're going to meet our deadline."

This is the first I've heard about a deadline, and any respect I might have had for Morgan drops down another several notches. He can't possibly know we've already found the Wernicke cure, and I wonder what he's promised the president. It's not as if we're baking a goddamned cake.

"What deadline?" I say.

Morgan hesitates, as if he's inventing a story to tell us. When he finally speaks, it sounds like a well-rehearsed line. "The president is due to travel to France at the end of June, for the G20 summit. He needs his brother."

"This is May," I tell him. "I thought we had more time. The contract didn't say anything—"

But he cuts me off. "You didn't really read your contract, Dr. McClellan. If you had, you would have seen a clear deadline of June twenty-fourth, one week before the president flies to Europe. Any more questions?"

"We're scientists," I say. "We don't do deadlines."

Lorenzo, who has been quiet up until now, shuts his office door. "I'll explain it to them later, Morgan. Let's get on with the admin shit so we can start working on your problem."

I flash him a look of disbelief, as does Lin, but Lorenzo shakes his head. "Later," he mouths.

Our first stop is the security office, a series of rooms and cubicles staffed by twenty men. It isn't in our section of the building, which is unpopulated except for Lorenzo, Lin, and myself, but one floor down. There are no windows here, not even on the main door, which Morgan unlocked by inserting a card from the lanyard around his neck into the reader.

"We're all about security," he says, leading us through the sea of computers and surveillance equipment toward one of the smaller cubicles.

Lin and I exchange a look.

"Security for what?" I ask.

Morgan doesn't answer, but I know he's heard me.

I repeat the question.

"Just general security, Dr. McClellan. Not something you need to worry about." He turns to the man in the cubicle. "We'll need card keys for my team, Jack." Again with the "my."

Jack grunts but doesn't smile. I put him at about fifty, maybe pushing sixty. His suit jacket hangs on the chair behind him, wrinkled and well-worn. The white shirt stretches taut against an ample beer belly, and yellowish patches bloom under his arms. His collar is pierced with a silver pin, a blue *P* in a circle. I wonder if he's married, if some poor woman has to lie underneath him while he grunts and sweats. Or, if he's single, is he high enough up in the hierarchy to merit right of access to one of the city's private men's clubs? For the second time today, I picture Sonia, twenty years old, playing courtesan, satisfying a monster's appetite.

"Sit here," Jack says, nodding to me and indicating the chair next to his desk. "Right hand here, palm down." He points to a flat screen on the desk, polished to a high shine.

I place my hand on the surface. It's cold, but not as cold as Jack. The machine whirs, and a band of light scans my handprint.

"Look straight ahead. Don't smile," he orders.

The camera in front of me snaps a picture.

"You're done. Now you." Jack nods to Lin, and she goes through the same procedure. When Jack grunts another order, she stands up.

"You're in the dark as much as I am, aren't you, Jean?" Lin says.

"Shut up," Jack tells her. He turns to Lorenzo. "Dr. Rossi, please take a seat. Right hand on the screen."

Asshole, I think.

There are no pictures on Jack's desk, no family portraits, no school photos of kids against a cloud or forest background, no decorations. His lunch, or what I think is his lunch, is in a crumpled paper bag that looks like it might not stand up to another emptying and refilling. I'm thinking Jack isn't married and I find the thought appealing. Better to suffer through a few minutes of prodding and poking and heavy breathing once a week than to live with him 24/7.

Lorenzo's finished, and the printer behind Jack spits out three plastic ID cards. Jack holds out a hand toward Morgan, and they shake. When he holds the same hand out to Lorenzo, nothing happens.

"I don't think so," Lorenzo says. "Something might rub off on me."

This is why I love Lorenzo, or one of about a hundred reasons. Patrick would have shaken hands with the fat creep. Patrick would have smiled and said, "Thanks," when Jack handed him the laminated key card. Patrick would be seething on the inside, but he'd play the game.

We leave Jack's cubicle, and Morgan ushers us into a small conference room in the security complex. It's set up not in conference style, but with the table pushed off to one side, two chairs behind it, and three chairs lined up like school desks, facing the table. Morgan takes a seat at the head of the class and holds out a hand, motioning for the three of us to sit in the chairs facing him.

I exchange a look with Lorenzo, but he shakes his head, almost imperceptibly.

And we wait.

After ten minutes of listening to the wall clock tick, a sullen man with a scar on his right cheek and with all the charm of a Special Forces veteran enters through the open door to the conference room. "Morning, Morgan," he says. "Morning, team," he says to the rest of us. He doesn't sit, but stands behind the table, looking down at his audience.

A man of his size should have made at least some noise in the hallway, but this one crept up on us. It takes me exactly five seconds to realize I don't like him. By the sour look on Lin's face, she's spent even less time contemplating his likability.

"I'll keep this short and to the point, because you all have work to do," he says. "I'm Mr. Poe, and I'm in charge of project security." His lips barely move as he speaks; his heavy chest doesn't seem to rise and fall. I don't think he's blinked once since he entered the room. "You have one job to do here. The operative words are 'one' and 'here.' That means you do your work, you leave, and you come back the next day. I don't want any discussion of the work with the rest of the lab, or any socializing among you outside office hours. Clear?"

"As crystal," Lorenzo says, examining one of his own fingernails.

Poe glares at him. "You don't talk about the project with anyone outside these walls. You don't bring work home. If you need to work more than eight hours a day, you do it here. Lunch is in the cafeteria on the third floor." He checks a printed schedule. "You three have the one p.m. slot to yourselves."

Lin shifts in her chair, uncrosses her legs, then crosses them again. Her foot brushes mine, and I push back on it. *Yes, that sounds weird.*

I speak first. "Excuse me, Mr. Poe, but what about the lab assistants? We need to set up experiments, and we—"

Poe cuts me off. "Any instructions to the lab staff go through Morgan. Also, you won't be taking your laptops home. One of my men will set up appointments with you for this afternoon to secure your electronics and set up the intranet for your part of the team."

"I thought we were the team," Lorenzo says, a bit drily.

"That's what Mr. Poe means," Morgan says. His eyes dart toward the big man standing next to him. "Right, Mr. Poe?"

"Exactly. Any other questions?" He doesn't wait. "You'll each go through a security checkpoint when you enter the building and when you leave. The building is staffed around the clock." Poe nods once to Morgan before turning his back on us and leaving the way he came in. Quietly.

"Okay." Morgan claps his hands together once, as if he's calling an unruly class to order. "Let's get to work. If you'll follow me, I'll show you around the lab."

We file out of the conference room, past fat Jack, who is slurping down a Coke, and back through the windowless main door. Morgan opens this with his key card, which, unlike mine and Lorenzo's and Lin's, is blue. Ours are white.

Lin pulls me back as we walk down the hall toward the elevator bank. "That Poe. Silent-but-deadly type," she says.

"Very," I say. "What's with the segregation and the deadline?"

"Don't know. But if we're on our own at lunch, we'll have a chance to talk. Lorenzo seems like he knows something."

"Come on, ladies," Morgan calls from the elevator he's holding open.

We pick up the pace and arrive at the open doors. Morgan walks in first, Lorenzo last. When we're inside, he reaches behind and squeezes my hand.

"Very exciting day," Morgan says.

Yes. It is.

TWENTY-NINE

The first thing I hear as we walk the ten feet from the elevator to the lab complex is the squeak of mice. The animals are a necessity, but I still get squeamish about injecting the tiny beasts with untested sera. They're so helpless, like babies. I can't stand holding them and looking into their oil-drop eyes and squeezing whatever my latest potion is into their innocent veins. Lin has no problem with it; maybe her medical background makes her immune. I've always let her administer the injections.

"They're mice, Jean," she would say, back in our Georgetown lab. "You'd set traps for them if they invaded your pantry, wouldn't you?"

Well. She had me there. But the traps were passive devices. I could deal with them better than I could deal with needles full of chemicals. I've always been a textbook kind of a girl when it comes to anything brain related. Let the MDs fiddle with the practical stuff.

Morgan is poised with his key card at the door, then reconsiders.

"Might as well try one of yours, to make sure it works. Dr. McClellan? How about you do the honors?"

Lorenzo chuckles. "Come on, Gianna. You won't know what's inside until you open it."

I slide my white key card into the reader, wondering if Lorenzo realizes how like Pandora I feel as the doors swing open and we're momentarily blinded by the fluorescent lights that come alive inside the lab. There can't be any evil here, I think, only the hope that also hid inside Pandora's ancient box.

Still, something about Poe's slip of the tongue about our part of the team—if it was a slip of the tongue—makes me uneasy. For that matter, Poe himself makes me uneasy. He's built like a refrigerator and silent as a grave. And he has the look of a man who's killed for God or country. Or money.

Morgan beams as if the lab were his own firstborn son and motions us to follow him inside. Once again, Lorenzo waits for Lin and me to enter before walking through the double doors.

The squeaks of a few hundred mice fly out of the cages lining the left wall. On the right, there are rabbits, sniffing silently, their pink noses twitching at the intrusion into their space. We've never had rabbits before, and I know Lin will have to take care of the injections when we get around to the larger animals. No way I could plug an Easter bunny with anything unless I was damned sure.

But I am sure, and that's the hell of it. If I want to draw out the project as long as possible, I'll need to kill a few mice and bunnies.

Lab tables, ten of them, each with its own workstation, fill the empty area between the rows of cages. Like the offices and cubicles in our department of three, they're unoccupied.

At the end of the room is another door, also with a key-card reader. This time, it's Lin's turn, and once again, Morgan walks past us, into the belly of the lab.

"Holy shit," Lin says.

Morgan twitches at this. Good.

Lorenzo utters a single Italian word, as ubiquitous and productive as English's "fuck." *"Cazzo."*

They're both right. This space is like nothing I've ever seen.

On my right are three doors, marked with the sign PATIENT PREP ROOM: PLEASE KNOCK BEFORE ENTERING. Beyond these is an open area with a bank of computers and cabinetry to hold smaller equipment. PORTABLE ULTRASOUND, TMS, and TDCS are printed on neat labels below each cabinet.

"Nice," Lorenzo says. "Transcranial magnetic stimulation and direct-current stimulation. How many units?"

"Five of each," Morgan says, opening the cabinets one at a time. "And three portable ultrasound kits, all with various transducers." He reads the labels. "Linear, sector, convex, neonatal, transvaginal." There's a pause before the last item, as if he's put off by the mention of female anatomy, even though Morgan should know we need the transvaginal probes for our smaller subjects. I've said before, he's a shitty scientist.

Lorenzo winks at me.

"There's more over here," Morgan says, and leads our tiny parade past the open area and toward the back of the lab. Here, two doors lead to the MRI rooms.

"You've got two magnetic resonance imaging setups?" I ask, nudging Lin, who is almost drooling. Back at Georgetown, we had to beg for the use of one MRI in the hospital—a twenty-minute walk away. And that was when we were allowed the time, which wasn't often.

Morgan beams. "Two Tesla MRIs. And here's the PET facility." He opens another door and lets us peek inside.

We had to wait months for access to the hospital's positron-emission tomography, or PET, equipment.

"What about EEGs?" Lorenzo asks. "And the biochem lab?"

"All here. The electrocephalography stuff is over in the small-equipment area."

"Electro*en*cephalography," I correct. "That's why they call it EEG and not ECG."

Morgan's eyes scrunch together. "Whatever. Anyway, I forgot to mention it, but you'll find the electrodes and the printer in the far right cabinet. The biochem lab is through these doors." He motions to Lorenzo's key card. "Go ahead. You'll probably be most interested in the protein expression module. It's just here, to your right."

Morgan points, but Lorenzo is still scanning the room, which could hold five high school chem labs.

There are only three of us. Four, if we count Morgan, but I don't think any of us is counting him. And only one biochemist.

"Okay, people." Morgan checks his watch. "Got a meeting with the big guys, so I'll leave you to it."

"You do that," Lorenzo says, and slides his key card into the biochem lab door. "We'll be fine."

"Internet?" I say, pointing to a bank of computers with monitors the size of flat-screen televisions in the main lab.

"No way, Jean." Morgan fires up one of the workstations. "Excel, Word, SPSS in case you need to run statistics. MatLab. Whatever you need."

All I need if I want to work in a vacuum, I think. "How about access to the world of periodicals, Morgan? I don't carry the past five years of the *Journal of Cognitive Neuroscience* around in my purse."

"Oh, that. Right." He moves toward a rack filled with tablets. "All plugged into the academic databases. If you can't find what you want, call up on the intercom. I'll make it happen." Morgan smiles, showing two neat rows of small teeth. They remind me of a hamster. Or a lab rat. "Gotta buzz now, people," he says, and disappears through the rodent room and out the main doors.

Finally, we're alone.

"Fifteen million for the two Tesla MRIs and the PET machine," Lin says when we hear the double click of the main doors to the lab. "Fifteen million. And then there's everything else."

We all know the numbers. The National Science Foundation did all but stick a laughing emoticon on our last grant proposal when we asked for a single MRI setup. I run some rough calculations in my head and come up with a figure.

Lorenzo nods. "Twenty-five million sounds about right. But that's not what bothers me."

"Me neither," I say.

We lock eyes, the three of us, alternately, and I know we're thinking the same thing. Every piece of equipment is new, shiny, recently installed. And all of it is exactly what we need to work on the Wernicke cure. You don't set up a lab with twenty-five million dollars' worth of apparatus in three days. Also, there was that animal smell in the first room. The mice and rabbits have been here a while.

They've been here longer than the president's brother has been in intensive care.

"It's almost as if they already knew," Lin says. "As if they'd planned for it."

I look around, moving from the biochem lab, past the MRI and PET scan rooms, toward the open area housing small equipment. In our world, small doesn't mean cheap.

"We need to talk," I say, addressing them both, but I know I'm looking at only Lorenzo.

THIRTY

L in leaves us in the small-equipment area, with an excuse about wanting to check out the Tesla MRI tubes. For a woman as petite as she is, she has eyes that can bore into me like the punch of a heavyweight boxer. *Be careful,* those eyes say.

"Come with me." Lorenzo crooks a long finger and stays quiet until we're back in the biochem lab at one of the sinks. He turns the water on full blast, then leans on the black epoxy resin counter. Then he taps his right ear and looks up at the ceiling. "Cameras," he mouths.

I get it. If there are cameras, there are bugs as well. I lean in toward him and pretend to read the report he's taken from his breast pocket. It's a utility bill, but I focus on the page as if it's Fermat's last theorem.

"You told them we'd be ready in a month? Why?" I say.

"Because Morgan wasn't going to ask for you. Or Lin. He didn't want any women on the project. I guaranteed him we'd have a successful trial before the president left for France, but only if you two were on the team." After a moment, he adds, "And we're already there."

I don't know whether to kiss him or slap him. "You know what happens to me when we're finished, right? And to Lin?"

Lorenzo looks down at my wrist, at the faded ring of an old burn encircling it. "I know."

His voice is sad but holds an undercurrent of fury. Once again, I'm reminded of the difference between Patrick and Lorenzo. Both are sympathetic, but only Lorenzo has fight in him.

"Also, I need the bonus money," he says.

"For what?"

"A personal matter."

"What kind of personal matter costs a hundred thousand dollars?"

His eyes meet mine over the running tap. "A very personal matter," he says before turning off the water. "Okay, you feeling better now?"

"Sure," I say, not understanding whether he's talking about my pukefest this morning or our conversation. "Right as rain."

"Good. Because we've got work to do."

"Wait." I twist the cold water back on. "When did they contact you about the project?"

"Just after Bobby Myers broke his head."

I nod. "No one gets two Tesla MRI tubes ordered, delivered, and installed in three days, Enzo. Not even the government."

He cracks a smile at the old nickname. "Yeah. I know. Come on. Let's dig Lin out from her techno-orgasm and grab some lunch." The tap goes off for a second time, and we walk back to the neuro section of the lab as the clock pings one.

"Who do you have in mind for the first subject?" Lorenzo asks.

"Definitely Delilah Ray. I saw her son the other day, you know. He's our mailman."

He's also the man who blinked three times at me and said he had a wife and three daughters. I jot a mental note to be at the door the next time he makes his rounds. Right now, the only other thing on my mind is food.

THIRTY-ONE

This afternoon, as I wind along with the snake of cars on Rock Creek Parkway, hunched down behind the steering wheel to avoid the stares of the male drivers who populate rush hour, I think of Jackie Juarez again.

She called Patrick a cerebral pussy; she'd never hang that epithet around Lorenzo's neck.

"Men come in two flavors," she said once. "Real men and sheep. That guy you're dating—"

"—is a sheep," I finished. "I suppose you'd think that."

"I don't think it, Jeanie. I know it." Jackie lit a cigarette—she was in her Virginia Slims stage, and *You've Come a Long Way, Baby* kitsch decorated our flat that year—and blew out a cloud of menthol smoke. "I mean, if I were to switch over to your team, I'd want a man who—I don't know—stood up for me."

"Look at you, the romantic," I said.

She shrugged it off. "Maybe. I'd just want someone who was tough when he needed to be."

"Patrick's kind," I said. "Isn't that worth something?"

"Not in my book."

When I'd defended my thesis and Patrick started his residency, we got married. I invited Jackie, hoping she would come.

She didn't.

Maybe I wouldn't have, either.

I pull off the parkway and stop at the light beside a middle-aged man in a matte black Corvette. *Sports-car menopause,* I think. The back window is plastered with stickers: MYERS FOR PRESIDENT!; I'M SURE PURE, ARE YOU?; and MAKE AMERICA MORAL AGAIN! He honks, waits for me to turn my head, and rolls down his window. I do the same, thinking he wants directions around the labyrinthine Washington streets with their devilish diagonal avenues.

He spits into my car as the light turns from red to green, then roars off.

I realize I've still got the other candidate's sticker on my back bumper.

What would Jackie do? Speed on after him? Probably. Spit back? Likely. What's on my mind, though, is what Patrick would do: absolutely nothing.

He'd sigh and shake his head at the barbarism, and then he'd clean up the mess of phlegm and forget about Mr. Midlife Crisis. And Lorenzo? Lorenzo would beat the living shit out of the bastard.

For some reason, I find that appealing. I didn't use to. It hits me that I've turned into more of a Jackie than I expected, and suddenly I want to see her again more than anything.

I doubt she wants to see me, and even if she does, Jackie's in a place where the word "visitor" doesn't exist.

Jackie is in a camp (*Say it, Jean: prison*) somewhere in the middle of the country, where she works on a farm or ranch or fish hatchery from morning to night. Her hair—whatever color it last was—shows graying roots and split ends, and her arms are red with the sunburn of a farmer's tan. A redneck tan, we used to call it, the kind that leaves your shoulders pale. She wears a wide metal bracelet that does not display any numbers because, in Jackie's new world, there are no words to count. Like the women in the supermarket, the ones with those small babies, who did nothing more than try to finger spell a bit of gossip, a message of comfort, a mundane little *I miss talking to you, too.*

Jackie Juarez, feminist turned prisoner, now sleeps at night in a cell with a man she doesn't know.

I saw a documentary about these conversion camps on television last fall. Steven had turned it on.

"Freaks," he said. "Serves them right."

The last of my words flew out, little daggers aimed at my oldest son, who had begun acting less like my son and more like Reverend Carl Corbin. "You don't really believe that, kiddo."

He muted the television as an endless line of men and women marched from a hole in a concrete wall toward the working farm. Jeeps with armed soldiers flanked the parade of prisoners.

"It's a life choice, Mom," Steven said. "If you can choose one sexuality, you can just as easily choose another. That's all they're trying to do."

I sat speechless as I watched the faces of gray-clad people, once mothers and fathers and accountants and lawyers, make their way from wall to fields. Jackie might have been among them, tired and blistered from day after day in the sun.

Steven upped the volume and pointed at a screen of statistics. "See? It's working. Ten percent after the first month, up to thirty-two percent as of the end of September. See?" He was referring to the conversion success rate.

I didn't see at all. But I saw, and still see, Jackie Juarez in work boots and a khaki uniform, weeding and harvesting until her hands are raw and bloody.

Or.

Jackie is married. Maybe to a fat fuck like Jack the security man, maybe to one of the gay guys she knew before. She wears a word counter and spends her days baking and hoping to get pregnant, so the authorities will know the marriage is bona fide, more than a convenient arrangement to dodge life at one of the camps.

No. Jackie would never fold, never work the system, never whore herself out to the president's men in exchange for money or a voice or a month of liberty. Patrick would, of course. Lorenzo wouldn't. That was the difference between my husband and my lover.

But Lorenzo did, the second he signed the contract and agreed to work on the aphasia project.

As I pull into my driveway, the reason dawns on me:

Lorenzo has another agenda, and I think it bears my name.

THIRTY-TWO

I put on my Mother and Wife face when I walk through our back door. Sonia and the twins are playing a game of cards on the den carpet; Patrick is chopping vegetables in the kitchen, an open bottle of beer next to his cutting board. I wonder if this is his first of the afternoon.

"Hey," I say, dropping my purse—thoroughly searched at the security checkpoint before I left the office—onto a side counter.

"Hey, babe." Patrick sets the knife down and gives me a squeeze. "Everything go okay?"

"Well enough."

"What was it like?"

"We're under the pain of torture not to talk about it outside the office," I say. It's probably truer than I think. "Where's Steven? He's about to miss his six o'clock predinner feeding."

Patrick knocks his chin toward the left side of our house. "Next door."

"He and Julia must be talking again," I say. "You really need to speak to him about this marriage thing. He's too young."

"I will. Oh, and your parents FaceTimed. I said you'd call tomorrow, but your mom wants to talk to you tonight."

"Can I use your laptop?"

"Where's yours?"

Mine is currently in quarantine with one of Poe's computer geeks. "Locked up tight in a building with no name somewhere in Washington," I say. "Sure I can't help in here?"

He flicks a dish towel at me. "Go on. Git. I don't need no jive sous chefs in my kitchen." We both laugh at his attempt at Southern fry-cook slang.

Well. That's different.

After a lightning-quick round of old maid with the kids—Sonia manages a few careful words—I go to Patrick's study, which he's left unlocked, and call my parents. The Italian comes back slowly at first, then eases into a steady cadence, all vowels and rhyming syllables. Papà has nothing positive to say about the president, or the president's brother, or pretty much any part of this country; Mamma is more subdued, quieter than usual.

"Tutto bene, Mammi?" I say.

She assures me everything's fine, just a few headaches recently.

"You need to stop smoking," I tell her.

"It's Italy, Gianna. Everyone smokes."

This much is true. Second to soccer matches, smoking is the national pastime, especially in our part of the South. I let it go for now and focus on happier talk. For a while, I listen as they tell me about the lemon and orange trees in the yard, the vegetable garden, the gossip about Signore Marco, the fishmonger, who is finally going to marry Signora Matilda, the baker. It's about time—put together, Marco and Matilda must be 170 years old.

The axe falls when Mamma asks if I'm coming for a visit this summer. "You don't want me to die all alone," she says.

"Nobody's dying, Mammi," I say. Still, a cold current jitters up and down my spine. "Promise you'll go see Dr. Michele, okay?"

Between the "Ciaos" and the kisses and the promises to talk again tomorrow, it takes a full ten minutes to end the call. If the Italian women had quotas like we do, they'd spend every last word on the goodbye part of a phone conversation.

Only after I've shut down FaceTime do I notice the manila envelope with its TOP SECRET stenciling on Patrick's desk. Whoever came up with the idea of labeling classified documents with larger-than-life red stenciling that advertises—or at least hints at—the contents was a schmuck, I think. You might as well put a tag that says OPEN ME! on it. If it were up to me, I'd hide all secrets in back copies of *Reader's Digest*.

Patrick whistles in the kitchen, and the kids are now arguing over whether Sam cheated at cards by swiping one queen of spades from another deck and hiding it in his shirtsleeve.

It would be so easy to take a peek at the contents of this envelope. I can practically feel the weight of that little red devil on my left shoulder, urging me on. *Go ahead, Jean. Have a look. No one ever has to know.*

So that's what I do.

The contents don't surprise me. As the president's science adviser, Patrick would of course be in the loop on the Wernicke project. What I don't understand is why the first page inside my husband's top secret envelope refers to three separate teams: Gold, Red, and White. Lorenzo, Lin, and I are on the White team. Other names, all unfamiliar to me, are listed under "Gold" and "Red." A few of them have military ranks attached.

"Mommy!" Sonia's voice in the doorway startles me. "I won old maid!"

Now the sequestered queen of spades that Sam had makes sense. Quickly, I slide the project memo back into its envelope, hoping I've left things as they were on Patrick's desk, which always seems to be organized with the help of a T square.

"That's super, baby girl," I say. "How about we go check on Daddy in the kitchen?"

"I love you, Mommy. I love you so much."

Nine words are all it takes to make my heart skip a beat.

THIRTY-THREE

"Anything interesting?" Patrick says when I'm back in the kitchen. I've always been lousy at secrets. The merest hint of a lie forces my lips into a curl; then my eyes join in the game. Only once did I try to throw together a surprise party for Patrick—his thirtieth birthday, I think—going through his then secretary and a couple of guys from work. When the day finally arrived, Patrick acted as stunned as if a bomb had fallen from the sky.

Success! I thought. Right up until the next morning when Evan King blabbed about what a terrific show my husband had put on.

"Saw it in your eyes, babe," Patrick said. "Good thing you're not the one with the security clearance."

So. No more surprise parties.

He looks up from the stove. "Good news?"

"What?"

"Was it good news? From your parents?"

I feel the weight of terror slide off me and melt into a puddle on the kitchen tile. "Um, I guess. Papà's sold a store to some chain. So I guess that's good news."

"Time for the old man to retire," Patrick says. "Here. Taste this and tell me what it needs." He spoons up a bit of the veg he's been sautéing.

"Perfect," I say, even though it tastes off. Nothing smells good right now. The red wine Patrick pours stinks like rancid oil; the meat, which I think is chicken, but could be goat liver for all I know, fills the kitchen and dining room with a hellish stench. I should be starving, but I'm not. "Steven's not back yet? Oh. Speak of the devil."

My son walks in, slamming the back door behind him. Sonia brightens, as do the twins. Patrick and I are about to say a "Hello," but Steven walks past us, past the fridge, and straight down the hall toward his room. His face is flushed, a bloom of mottled red on his cheeks and neck. Somehow, he looks thirty-seven instead of seventeen, the entire world on his shoulders.

And here's the shittiness of parenthood, wrapped up in one sullen teenager.

"I'll go," I say. I need a break from food odors before my olfactory nerves decide to rebel. "Ask Sonia to tell you about her card game."

Steven's music shakes my bones as I walk down the hall to his bedroom door. I knock once; there's no answer. On the second knock, Steven grunts a bored "Enter."

"You okay, kiddo?" I say, sticking my nose in the doorway.

Whatever he's listening to fades to dull background noise. "Yeah," Steven says.

"School go okay?"

"Yeah."

"How's Julia?"

"Fine."

"Coming out for dinner? It's almost ready."

"Soon."

I turn to go, and he breaks the chain of monosyllables. "Mom? If someone you knew—maybe even someone you really love—did a shitty thing, would you rat them out?"

It's necessary for me to think about this.

Once, I'd have said yes. See someone go sixty in a school zone, take down their license plate. Watch a parent hit his kid in the Walmart, call the cops. Witness a robbery next door, report it. For every action, there's an opposing and appropriate reaction. Except there isn't, not anymore. The reactions might be opposing, but they sure as shit aren't appropriate. I knew about Annie Wilson and her backdoor man in his blue pickup truck, although he didn't bother using the back door. I know Lin Kwan, who now lives with her brother, is the type of woman who prefers other women. I also know that if I—in Steven's words—had ratted Annie out, I'd have a hell of a time facing myself each morning. The idea of playing informant on Lin is anathema, whatever Reverend Carl and the rest of the Pure have to say about it.

"Depends," I say. "Why?"

"No reason," Steven says, and hoists himself off his bed. "Guess I should take a shower."

As he brushes past me, leaving me with the hum of electronic music— a tune from the time before, whose lyrics probably don't mesh with *Fundamentals of Modern Christian Philosophy* or Pure Manhood or Carl Corbin's twisted worldview—I feel the heat of trouble settle on me again. It presses, squeezing out the air from my lungs, forcing me into a breathless state.

There's no way Steven could know about Lorenzo, I tell myself. No way. We were careful that last time, meeting accidentally at Eastern Market, driving through traffic toward our Maryland crab shack with all of me scrunched down on the floor of the back seat. It was March, and Steven would have been in school.

Fatigue and worry hit me like bags of bricks, one on each side, and I head back down the hall to join Patrick in the kitchen.

He's still whistling.

THIRTY-FOUR

The sirens wake me up. They're like screaming animals in the quiet of the night, growing louder and louder until it seems they're at my bedroom window. Reds and blues flicker through the blinds, and I know I'm not dreaming.

"What the hell?" Patrick says, rolling over once, then twice, then pulling a pillow over his head. He doesn't last long in his cave; reality seeps in, drawing back the curtain of sleep, and he's up.

All I can think about is the conversation I had with Lin in our office this morning. *Still got a thing for our Italian colleague? . . . How long has it been going on? . . . Be careful, honey. You've got a lot more to lose than your voice.*

And then there's Steven, his cryptic question ringing in my ears now.

"Oh my god," I say, and go to the window.

As best I can see, there are two cars and one larger vehicle, boxy, like an ambulance, but not white. A third car pulls up behind the boxy van, blocking our driveway.

Blocking any cars from getting in. Or out.

The next words I say scratch the air, hardly more than a hoarse whisper. Nothing inside me is functioning, not my knees, which have gone to jelly, not my voice, not my stomach. Wave after wave of nausea ripples through me as I stare at the electric colors lining the street in front of our house.

I'm expecting the doorbell to ring, such an ordinary event, one I used to look forward to. Doorbells meant visitors on holidays; packages I was expecting; friendly pairs of young men from Utah who, despite my resistance to any sort of conversion, somehow always seemed pleasant and well scrubbed. Doorbells meant trick-or-treaters dressed as ghosts and goblins and the princesses or action heroes of the month.

"I'll go," Patrick says.

I wait for the ding of the bell and think about Poe with his scar and his ex–Special Forces mien and his eerie silence. They won't be silver or golden bells for me tonight, but iron ones.

Oh fuck.

Now I see them coming inside, uniformed and armed with black devices, walking over the polished hardwood of my house, leaving scuffs and tracks. I see Thomas and Reverend Carl and other men, one carrying a small box with a counter set to zero that will snap on my wrist like an iron shackle. I see the television cameras and the news reporters, all flashing and straining to catch a glimpse of the former Dr. Jean McClellan, now destined to a life of silence and labor in the fields of Iowa, the fisheries of Maine, the textile mills of Alabama. Subsequent to a public shaming, of course.

Steven, I think. *What have you done?*

They won't go after Lorenzo. I know this. The follies of men have always been tolerated.

Sonia comes running into my room, eyes glowing. The boys' footfalls move in the other direction, into the main part of the house, where Patrick has gone.

"It's okay, baby girl," I say, taking Sonia into my arms. "It's okay."

But it's not okay. Nothing is okay as I sit here with my back to the bed frame, rocking my daughter, waiting for the inevitable doomsday clang of the doorbell.

THIRTY-FIVE

Five horrible minutes pass before Patrick's footsteps come running back down the hallway.

"It looks bad," he says. "Whatever it is, it looks bad." His face is a map of worry, all lines on a parchment-pale landscape.

But the doorbell hasn't rung.

I pull myself up, scoop Sonia into my arms, and follow Patrick to the kitchen. The parade of vehicles is still in the street, still screaming their sirens and polluting the night with blue and red. Six men stand guard on the front porch of the Kings' house, two more at the back door.

It's not me, I think. *It's not me. It's not me. It's not me.*

A woman's scream pierces through, all the way into our kitchen, and I risk a look out the window.

Leo moves to turn on the light.

"No. Keep it off. Keep it dark," I say.

What could Olivia King have done?

If someone you knew—maybe even someone you really love—did a shitty thing, would you rat them out?

And then I realize these men are here not for Olivia but for Julia.

I turn away from the window. Here's Patrick, next to me, still a ghoulish pale. Sonia I've sat on one of the barstools by the island. Sam and Leo stare at the scene next door through rounded eyes the size of Frisbees.

Only Steven isn't here.

Outside, the screaming has gotten worse. Olivia—I think it must be Olivia of the pink head scarves and pink Bibles and empty measuring cup in her hand—has unleashed pure hell.

"You can't take her! Evan! Do something! For fuck's sake, do something instead of standing there with your fucking hands in your fucking pockets and watching. Kill them. Shoot the motherfucking bastards. Tell them it wasn't her fault! It wasn't—"

Her tirade is interrupted by a pained wail, but only for a moment, a slice of a second. Then she's back at it, half screaming, half wailing while two men haul Julia King out of the house, while Evan stands silently by with his hands in his pockets and the porch light casting a yellow glow on his face.

Before Patrick can stop me I'm out the back door of our house, ignoring the May rain that's started falling, sloshing with bare feet across our driveway and into the Kings' yard.

"Stop it! Take her counter off!" I scream.

Every head except Olivia's turns toward me.

Olivia continues on, begging and sobbing now. "Please don't take her. Please. Take me instead. Please." Each word is interrupted by the sickening zap of an electric charge and a wail.

"Take the fucking counter off her!" I scream again.

"Go back inside, ma'am," a voice says. I recognize it as that of Thomas of the dark suit and even darker soul. Then, to one of the others, he says, "Put her in the truck."

They mean Julia, who hasn't said a word. Not yet. When she turns under the wan glow of the porch light, her face is a complete blank. She's in shock. Around her left wrist is a wide metallic cuff. Julia is about to join the supermarket women, and Jackie, and god only knows how many others in their twisted version of solitary confinement. *Zero words per day, girlies. Let's see how long it takes you to fall into line.*

I've never much cared for Olivia, but my feet take me farther into her yard, over to the bent and convulsing body in its peach satin nightgown, now sticking to her like a film, as mine is to me. From sweat, it must be, since the Kings' porch is covered and the rain isn't driving. Thomas motions to one of the other men, and he steps toward me, hand poised like a starfish next to the weapon on his belt.

"Go home, ma'am. Nothing to see here."

"But I—"

The starfish hand moves an inch closer to his belt.

Now I'm witnessing the single most terrible event of my life as Julia King is led from the porch, away from her mother, and toward the dark van. The man escorting her, which is really to say holding her limp frame semi-upright, reads her rights.

Except they aren't rights. There's nothing that rhymes with "You have the right to," only the monotonous repetition of phrases that all begin with "You will."

My foot catches a piece of gravel as I walk back across our driveway to the rear door. There are so many pebbles, so many bits of stone, and I want to cram them by fistfuls into my eyes to blot out everything I've seen, and everything I'm going to see.

For instance, Patrick, standing in the kitchen, doing nothing. Steven, who has emerged from his room by the time I drip all over the doormat, and is now watching with expressionless eyes—doll's eyes—as the black van that is not an ambulance takes Julia King to her new, and permanent, home.

Sam and Leo have brought me towels. I take them and send the twins and Sonia to bed. Then I go for the kill.

"What the living hell did you do, Steven?"

He shirks away at the sound of my voice, no longer the cocky teen he was yesterday at dinner. "Nothing."

"What did you do?"

"Let go, Mom!"

Right. So I have my seventeen-year-old son by the shirt collar now, and I'm feeling like I could squeeze and squeeze the fabric around his neck until he's ruddy and sweating. But this isn't how I want to be. This isn't the image I want to see in the mirror tomorrow morning. I lower my voice. "What did you do, kiddo?"

Steven seems to shrink, folding himself into the corner of the kitchen next to the fridge and the shelf that used to hold my cookbooks, a thousand or a million years ago. My eyes slide to Patrick. *I need you now,* they say, these eyes of mine.

"I d-didn't—," Steven stammers. "It wasn't my fault!"

It. What is *it*? An old Eartha Kitt tune hammers through my head: *Let's do it.*

"Oh, Steven," I say.

And it—*It*—all spills out.

"She said she just wanted to make out, to try something. And—" Steven looks to Patrick for help. Finding nothing but a quiet shake of a head, he goes on. "It wasn't supposed to happen."

It.

I make a silent promise never to use this word again.

Outside, under the light of the Kings' porch, Evan is shouting something I can't understand while Olivia slumps against the brick wall.

"She'll never get over this," I say, but not to anyone in particular. Then, turning to Patrick: "Can you do something? Can you talk to Carl Corbin or Myers?"

Patrick's words are stale. "What would I say?"

"Christ. I don't know. You're smart. What if you told them it was Steven's fault? That he started it and Julia said no, and he went on anyway. That they were confused. Or that it didn't actually happen." There's that *It* again. "That they didn't actually have sex. Can you do that?"

"That would be a lie," Steven says before Patrick can answer.

"I don't care," I say. "Do you realize what's going to happen to Julia? Do you?"

She comes into my vision, as in an old family movie, skating or biking down the street with her halter top and her music, talking over the fence while I pruned Mrs. Ray's roses, holding Steven's hand. Now I see her on the television, dressed in a gray smock, flinching at the flash of a hundred cameras, standing silent while Reverend Carl reads out lines from his Pure manifesto. Fast-forward some years, and Julia is tired and bent, thin as a rail, pulling weeds or gutting fish.

And no one in this room can do anything about it.

Like I said: the follies of men.

THIRTY-SIX

Friday, according to my contract, is my day off, but too much adrenaline is coursing through me to sleep, so I get up, leaving Patrick to snooze, and go to the kitchen. It's where I do my best thinking.

I want to fight, and I don't know how.

If Jackie were here, she'd have a few words for me. Mostly, I think of one of her last lectures, that late April afternoon in our Georgetown apartment with its Ikea rugs and Ikea dishes and maybe a few pots and pans from a yard sale.

"You can start small, Jeanie," she said. "Attend some rallies, hand out flyers, talk to a few people about issues. You don't have to change the world all by yourself, you know."

And the usual catchphrases ensued: *grassroots, one step at a time, it's the little things, hope-change-yes-we-can!* All those words Patrick sneered at, and I sneered along with him.

At six, Steven drags himself into the kitchen and pours a glass of milk, which he takes back to his room.

Good. I can barely look at him.

I fix myself some dry toast and tea. My brain wants coffee, but the rest of my body rebelled as soon as I opened the bag of beans and poured them into the grinder. Even the toast smells off, as if the entire contents of my pantry went rotten overnight. Everything tastes like old fish.

Sonia's up next, full of questions about last night. "What happened at the Kings' house?" "Will I be going to play with Mrs. King today?" "Is Julia sick?" Her speech is like music, but the lyrics are all wrong.

"Everything's fine, baby," I lie. "But I think Mrs. King needs a break today." Which means, of course, I'll need to find another sitter for Sonia while I'm at work.

I rule out the other neighbors, one by one. Too old, too religious, too weird, too careless. The last thing any of us needs is Sonia falling off a swing set or—worse, I think—coming back home reciting passages from the Pure's manifesto. I rub sleep out of my eyes and search my brain for a solution.

It comes to me, all at once, that triple blink of my mailman's eyes. And he's got three girls.

While Sonia's crunching on cereal, I outline my day. Make a doctor's appointment, wait for the mailman, check on Olivia as soon as Evan leaves for work, get to the office and tell Lin what I found in Patrick's office yesterday. What I'm not planning on doing: watching Julia King's public shaming.

The program will air today, and tonight, and probably for most of the next month until there's a new victim to parade in front of the press. They always handle it this way, usually inserting the footage into some show they know people will be watching. It's sinister. No one is actually forced to watch, but the alternative is to keep your television off. And even then, reruns crop up when you least expect them—during cooking shows, *This Old House*, a documentary on zebras.

Steven pads back into the kitchen. "I don't feel so hot. Think I'll skip school today."

Of course he'll want to do that. Julia King will be the feature of the day at PBS.

"You're not sick, Steven," I say. "So go get your brothers up and put some clothes on." I check the clock. "Bus is coming in an hour."

"But, Mom—"

"Just don't, kiddo."

He needs to see this program, needs to be strapped down with his eyelids forced open like that son of a bitch in the Stanley Kubrick movie. Maybe, for good measure, they'll throw in a few clips of Julia's future life in the fields or fisheries.

The phone rings as I'm rinsing dishes. "Get that for me, please. Then wake Sam and Leo." I turn to Sonia. "How about you go check on your daddy? You can bring him this if you're careful." I hand her a half-filled coffee mug, wincing a little at the stench. Never before did it occur to me how much coffee smells like shit.

"Okay!" Sonia says, and goes off, holding the mug with both hands, walking at a snail's pace. With any luck, Patrick will get his coffee sometime in the next week.

"It's for you," Steven says. "It's Babbo."

It kills me, this pet name for his grandfather, a childish holdover from a time when my son was Sonia's age, when he was still running around in bright red corduroy pants and a sun yellow T-shirt with the words SUPER KID! blazoned across the front. I have a clear memory now, of us in this kitchen, before the remodeling job, when the appliances were still avocado, and gold-flecked white Formica covered the countertops. I was making a batch of brownies, and Steven, rather than asking for the spoon to lick, pulled the empty batter bowl toward him, using his tiny hand as a spatula.

Why do they have to grow up so goddamned quickly?

I take the receiver. It's my father. "Hi, Papà. How come you're calling on the phone instead of FaceTiming?"

Whatever answer he has for this, I don't hear it. My father is crying hoarsely, and the background noise of Italian hospital sounds filters through the phone line.

"Papà. What's happened?" I say.

A new voice replaces his. "Professoressa McClellan?" a woman asks. Only she pronounces Patrick's un-Italian surname as *macalella*, avoiding clusters and codas, turning it into something familiar to her.

"Yes." Tea and toast begin an obnoxious roiling in my stomach. "What is it?"

It again. Everything has become one looming *It*.

"Your mother," the doctor says after introducing herself. Her English is good, good enough that I don't have to worry about medical jargon in a language I haven't used for more than a year. "Your mother had an aneurysm. It burst early this morning."

My tea and toast climb up farther, into my chest. "Locus?" I say.

"In her brain," the doctor says.

"Yes. I know that. I mean, where in her brain? I have some background in neurology."

"In the posterior section of the superior temporal gyrus."

"Left or right?" I ask, already knowing the answer.

Papers rustle over the phone. "Left hemisphere."

I lean forward on the counter, my head pressed against the cool of the granite. "Wernicke's area," I whisper.

"Yes, near the area of Wernicke." Another blast of Italian comes over the phone, drowning out the doctor's words. "I'm sorry. I really am sorry. But I have another patient to attend to. If you can call back in a few hours, we might know more about your mother's situation."

She puts my father back on the line.

"Is she conscious?" I ask.

"No."

When we disconnect, I'm left with Jackie's words. *One step at a time, Jeanie. Start small.*

I don't know how to start, big or small, but I know whatever I do next needs to be huge.

I wish Jackie were here.

THIRTY-SEVEN

Everyone except Sonia is out of the house when the mailman's truck pulls up. He dodges puddles on the way to our mailbox, sifting through the stack of envelopes in his courier bag.

"Morning, Dr. McClellan," he says.

"Good morning," I say.

"Aw, don't waste your words on the likes of me, ma'am. I'll understand."

I hold up my wrists. "Temporary reprieve, courtesy of the president's brother."

"I don't get you."

"I'm back at work. And we'll be needing subjects for our clinical trials."

He processes this. "Well. That's some fine news. Can I tell Sharon? That's my wife."

"Sure."

"She'll be so happy. My ma always treated Sharon like one of her own." His face darkens. "I know she'll have to wear one of those counters, but still. A hundred words a day is better than nothing, right?"

"I guess it is," I say, unsure whether I agree. I'm trying to read the return addresses on the envelopes he's carrying, but he's holding them close. "Do you think your wife might want a babysitting job? I've got a little girl, and the people who were watching her—well—they're unavailable."

"I think we can work something out." He lifts the metal flap and peers inside the locked box. "Ah. Outgoing mail today. Just a sec." From the ring of keys on his belt loop, he takes a newish-looking silver one, with teeth in a pattern I haven't seen before except on the set of keys Patrick carries around. The box hinges open, and he takes out a single envelope, carefully covering with his palm the area where the address would be. He locks the mailbox again and, almost as an afterthought, lets the letters in his hand slide through the metal mouth.

"You Pure, Dr. McClellan?" he asks, blinking his eyes three times before raising them to the camera trained on our front door. A reminder.

I shake my head. It isn't much of a shake, only a slight move to the right and the left. Slow, but definite, enough to get the message across.

"Hmph," he says. "Well, lemme call the wife and see what we can do about taking care of your girl. What's her name?"

"Sonia."

"Pretty name." He speaks a few words into his watch, which beeps once when he's finished. "Sharon, darlin', I got that lady doctor here in AU Park who needs a little help with her baby girl. How 'bout I send her on over to the house in a while?" Another beep, and he ends the call. "Heh heh. Blink once for yes, twice for no, remember?"

I have zero idea what he's talking about.

"Okeydokey. I best get on with my route. When you see Sharon, you tell her I said I'll be home a little late today. Gotta take an extra shift, make a bit more jingle, keep the home fires burning and all that garbage. Know what I mean?"

"Sure," I say, although I'm beginning to think Mr. Mailman and I speak mutually incompatible languages. "And I'll make sure I leave my number for you so we can set up Mrs. Ray's appointment."

He scribbles on a scrap of glossy advertising flyer. "Hate these things. Everybody hates the Valpaks. Can't stop 'em, though. Anyway, here's the address. Sharon'll be expecting you."

I take the folded scrap from his hand. "Thanks. Be in touch soon."

And he's off, back down the gravel driveway, dodging puddles and whistling to himself. It's a curious whistle, not really a song, but tuneful all the same, and there's a touch of familiarity in it.

When I get inside, Sonia is still watching her cartoon.

"No, honey. Let's turn this off for a while."

"No!" she squeals.

There she is, Julia King, up on the screen in the time it takes me to locate the remote. She's in a drab gray smock, long-sleeved and down to her ankles, even in this heat, and her hair is cut, which I don't remember them doing to Annie of Mr. Blue Pickup Truck fame, but maybe they've changed something, introduced a new brand of humiliation into their ritual. Reverend Carl stands beside her, sober and sad, and begins reciting the relevant bits from the Pure's manifesto.

"Look you not on your own self, but on others, as Christ did in taking upon himself the form of a servant, obedient unto death, even the death of the cross."

And:

"If you suffer for righteousness' sake, happy are you. For it is better, if the will of God be so, that you suffer. For this affliction, which endures but for a moment, is your key to eternal light and glory in the kingdom of heaven."

Blah blah blah blah blah.

Sonia sits up, even more attentive than she was when the cartoons were on. "Julia?" she says.

I lie. "No. Just a girl who looks a little like her." And I click the television off as Reverend Carl begins another of his rants.

"Come on—let's get you ready. We're going to see some new friends today."

I do three things. First, get Sonia to brush her teeth for more than five seconds. Then I run to my own bathroom and spill toast and tea into the toilet. Then I unfold the scrap of advertising material my mailman gave me and read.

There's an address. Also, a note.

Don't be too surprised.

THIRTY-EIGHT

Sharon Ray's house is more barn than actual house, a weathered wood structure that looks as if someone has beaten it with a giant ugly stick.

I follow twin dirt ruts from the road, past a vegetable garden the size of a small farm, and kill the engine behind a Jeep with vanity plates. The Virginia tags read IMPURE.

Sonia unstraps herself from the car seat and vaults out in the direction of two goats.

"Whoa, little girl. Wait a minute," I say. In the forty-five-minute drive out here, I explained that the girls she's about to spend her day with might not talk very much. "Just like school," I said. "Remember that." But then, of course, the Ray girls would be at school on a Friday.

A screen door, tilted on its hinges, swings open, and Sharon steps out onto a porch that isn't quite parallel to the ground. She's in frayed overalls and a checked cotton shirt; a blue bandana tied on her head with the knot on top keeps her hair in check but doesn't cover it. Ropes of muscle line her forearms, where the shirt cuffs are rolled back, and in one hand she's holding a wrench. In the other, a plastic drywall bucket.

Sharon Ray could be a modern Rosie the Riveter, if Rosie had been forty-something, black, and wearing a silver-toned word counter on her wrist.

She smiles from the porch, sets the bucket and wrench down, and walks to where Sonia and I are standing. Then she tilts her head slightly to the right, toward an outbuilding that seems to be in better repair than the family's house. We walk in silence to the barn, Sonia wide-eyed at goats and chickens and three alpacas roaming freely around the property.

"What's that?" Sonia says, pointing toward one of the furry beasts.

"Shh," I say.

Sharon smiles again but says nothing until we've reached the barn. She slides a wooden beam as thick as a man's thigh aside and pushes the door open. Smells of sweet hay and not-so-sweet manure hit me like a slap.

"Nothin' like a little horseshit to wake you up, is there?" Sharon says. "Sorry. I mean poo. I forget myself sometimes."

"It's okay." I've never been one to mince words around my kids.

"So, you're Sonia?" She bends down and takes my daughter's left hand, running a thumb where Sonia's wrist counter should be. "I'm Ms. Sharon, and I think we're gonna be good friends, you and me. You like horses?"

Sonia nods.

"Use your words, girl. You got 'em, right?"

"I told her—," I start.

"You're probably wondering why I'm talking so much." Sharon un-snaps the silver band on her left wrist and slides it off. "Fake. Del made it for me last year, once he figured out how to get the real one off. Made three more for our girls." She turns back to Sonia, as if nothing she just said could possibly be more interesting than livestock. "So, that one in the back, he's Cato. Next to him is Mencken. And that bullheaded roan mare over on the side is Aristotle. How 'bout you go say hello to them while I talk to your mama?"

Sonia doesn't need to be asked twice, and runs off toward Aristotle's stall.

"She won't bite, will she?" I say, nodding to the mare.

"Not unless I tell her to," Sharon says. "You look surprised, Dr. McClellan."

"Jean. I guess I am."

"Del's an engineer in mailman's clothing. Got things all set up here so it looks like we're following along, nice and quiet like. Good man, my Del, even if he is a white boy from town. Come on over here, and I'll show you something." She leads me past Cato and Mencken—odd names for horses, I think; not as odd as naming a mare after a classical male philosopher—and opens a door at the back of the barn.

Del's workshop is both a science lab and the antithesis of any lab I've ever seen. Most of the machinery looks as if it were cobbled together from spare game console parts and kitchen equipment. On my right is an old slide projector that has been gutted; on my left, on a clean worktable, are five CPUs from the 1980s, their insides arrayed neatly in rows.

"What does he do in here?" I ask.

"He tinkers."

"Why?"

Sharon stares at me. "Why do you think? Take a good look at me, Jean. I'm a black woman."

"I noticed. So?"

"So how long do you think it's gonna be before Reverend Carl and his holy Pure Blue sheep get it in their heads that it ain't just women and men who were made differently under God's eyes, but blacks and whites? You think mixed marriages like mine are part of the plan? If you do, you're not as smart as I thought."

I feel myself going red. "I never thought about it."

"Course you never. Look, I don't mean to be unkind, but you white gals, all you're worried about is, well, all you're worried about is you white gals. Me, I got more to fret over than whether I have a hundred words a day. I got my girls, too. We still send 'em to that school and do what we can on the weekends, until we can figure out a way to get out of here and over the border, but Del and I know a tide's comin' in. I guess before the year's out, we'll start seein' more than just separate schools for boys and girls. And just like now, they ain't gonna be equal."

There's no emotion in her voice, no self-pity, only cold, clear observation, as if she were reciting a recipe or reporting the weather. I'm the one who's sweating.

"Anyway," Sharon says, opening up a cooler and taking out a handful of fat carrots. She feeds them to the horses, showing Sonia how to hold one hand out, palm up, so the beasts can take the carrot without taking the hand along with it. "Anyway, how about you go off to work and Sonia and I will do a little farming? Any idea when this magic potion of yours might be ready? I'd like to talk to my mother. Well, Del's mother, but she's the only one I've got now."

"Yeah. So would I." I explain about Mamma and her aneurysm.

"Looks like you and me are in the same barrel of pickles, Jean," Sharon says, and takes Sonia by the hand. "I don't envy your position, though. You get the cure done, that little bracelet goes back on. You don't, and your mama keeps babbling. One or the other, one choice to a customer, as my daddy used to say."

"I could set something up for early next week. Maybe Tuesday?"

"That'd be real nice."

We exchange numbers, and Sharon tells me Del will call over the weekend, if that's okay.

"Meanwhile," she says, "you don't say anything about our little talk here, all right? Del's got a lot to lose, with him being the errand boy for the resistance. I don't want him in trouble. Or anyone else."

"There's a resistance?" The word sounds sweet as I say it.

"Honey, there's always a resistance. Didn't you go to college?"

As we walk back to the house, the woman beside me seems more and more like Jackie. I imagine her carrying posters and organizing sit-ins while I stayed home with my nose in a book, or while Patrick and I went out for cheeseburgers and rolled our eyes at the latest campus protest. Sharon, even with her mud-caked boots and torn overalls, makes me feel dirty.

"I'll pick her up at six, if that's not too late," I say before kissing Sonia goodbye.

"That's fine. We'll be here."

On the way to my doctor's appointment, I think of Del, my mailman, running errands for some underground group of anti-Pure people, and I laugh.

They would use a mailman.

THIRTY-NINE

It's official. I'm pregnant.

The gynecologist who stepped into Dr. Claudia's place at the clinic tells me I'm about ten weeks along, give or take a few days. You never really know exactly when conception happens, he says before giving me a sealed envelope addressed to Patrick. It contains the date of my next appointment, some general literature, a schedule, and other information I might find useful. This is what he tells me.

My words tumble out like a geyser. "What if there are complications? Unexpected pain? What if I need to describe symptoms?" All I can think about is what will happen when the counter goes back on.

What I don't say is: *What if I don't want this baby?* I already know the answer.

Dr. Mendoza waits for me to finish, eyes calm, mouth drooping slightly at the edges. I can't tell whether this outburst of mine annoys him or invokes sympathy. "Mrs. McClellan," he begins.

Not "Dr.," not "Professor." "Mrs."

"Mrs. McClellan, you're a healthy woman and we've picked up a strong, regular heartbeat. We've marked you as advanced maternal age, yes, which would worry me if this was a first pregnancy. But it isn't. You have nothing to worry about. I'm confident you'll carry to term and, let's see"—he pauses, spins some dials on that little wheel doctors use, even though they have computers to do the work—"deliver a fine baby around December twentieth of this year. A nice Christmas present."

I don't want a fine baby around December 20 of this year. I don't want a baby at all. Especially if it's a girl.

"Dr. McClellan will have all the information." He taps the sealed envelope. "He'll be on the lookout for signs of trouble, loss of appetite, changes in skin tone or weight, and so forth. And we'll be monitoring your progress regularly. If you like, I can set up a chorionic villus sampling for you early next week. You'll find out the sex then." The doctor consults a schedule on his iPad. "How is Monday afternoon?"

I nod. Monday, Wednesday, next month, December 20. I might as well find out sooner.

Now he taps my knee. A fatherly tap. Or the kind of touch you'd use on a well-behaved dog. I wish the tap would send my foot shooting out and upward, smack into his groin. I could always say it was an involuntary reflex, a spasm. "Okay. All set. Congratulations, Mrs. McClellan."

He leaves, and I rush into my underwear, jeans, blouse. The smell of latex and hand sanitizer in this room has become unbearable. My sex is slippery with K-Y Jelly, or whatever they use for the ultrasound, because I didn't take the time to wipe it away. But I can't breathe here. I can't breathe at all.

I drive the long way back home, stopping at a 7-Eleven to pick up a pack of Camels. I could smoke it out of me, I think, poison the little palace, practice Teratology 101 in the privacy of my own home. Abortion the old-fashioned way.

An abortion is not an option.

It isn't just Reverend Carl and his pack of Pure fanatics. They have to put limits on choice for other reasons, for pragmatic reasons. The way things are, the way women are, no one would want a girl. No sane parent would want to choose a wrist-counter color for a three-month-old. I wouldn't.

In three days, I'll know if I'll have to.

FORTY

B y the time I arrive at work Lorenzo and Lin are in the lab, heads together, arguing over protein extractions and whether we need to add a primate to the menagerie of lab animals.

"We don't," I say. "What we need to do is check out the second MRI room."

There's no reason to check the MRI equipment; Lin has already done that. But I've been around the machines enough, and heard one subject after another complain about the banging, even with ear protection. Lying in an MRI tube is like snuggling up next to the amp while Eddie Van Halen wails out a guitar solo. In other words, almost painful.

When we're all in the room, I fire up the machine. The force of some sixty thousand times the earth's natural magnetic field shakes my bones. I tell them above 125 decibels of ear-splitting noise about my mother and about the envelope I found in Patrick's office last night.

"Three teams?" Lin shouts. "Are you sure?"

"Positive," I yell back. My voice is barely audible, but Lin gets it.

"Anyway, we're done. I have all the numbers at home and I want to set up the first trial on Mrs. Ray for Tuesday. Monday, if we can manage it. It means we'll have to work through the weekend, dose up a few mice. I mean, Lin can dose up the mice."

"I knew you were finished," Lorenzo says, and hugs me, which feels wonderful and awful at the same time. "I saw it in your eyes that day at Georgetown."

Right. I wonder what else he sees in my eyes. "Lin, I need a minute alone here."

She raises an eyebrow but says nothing. In a moment, Lorenzo and I have the MRI room to ourselves.

"I have some news. Not very good news," I say over the banging. I don't know when, or why, I decided to tell him.

Lorenzo's face goes as white as the walls. He punches the casing of the machine beside us, and the banging shudders, then steadies again. A flood of Italian cursing fills the room. "What is it, Gianna? What do you have?"

"No. I'm not sick. I'm fine. Well, I'm not fine, but—"

He checks all the corners of the room, examines the tile floor and the ventilation unit on the ceiling. For five full minutes, I'm standing in a sea of noise while Lorenzo combs the area around us. When he's satisfied, he comes to me, tangles his long fingers in my hair, and presses his mouth to mine. His hands roam down, stroking the nape of my neck, playing silent musical notes on my back. The skin under my blouse prickles and tingles and now I'm in the kiss, all of me is lips and tongue and saliva and mute love, and it's not a Patrick kiss, but a Lorenzo kiss.

I never want to leave this place.

When we break, we're both panting. His hardness presses into my belly, like he's probing to feel what's inside, what secrets I hold in that dark female place.

It's moments before either of us speaks.

"Is it mine?" he asks, moving slightly so there's room for his hand where that other part of him was. "Gianna, tell me."

I've already run these numbers, and I didn't need calculators or spreadsheets. Ten weeks ago was a cold day in March, when I went to Eastern Market for a hunk of cheese and returned home with Lorenzo in my body after an afternoon at our little Maryland shack. Love shack, crab shack, baby shack. Patrick and I hadn't been together for a while.

"Yes," I whisper.

He pulls me close. This time, it's all softness; no edges, no probing, only a warm cocoon of lips and arms and our mingled breath. I'm safe here, in this sterile room with its supermagnets and banging and no cameras to watch us or recorders to pick up our sounds. For a few moments, it's only us. I have no children, no husband, only Lorenzo and the baby inside me, and a desperate need to stay like this.

"I'm working on it, Gianna," he says into my ear. "I'm working on it."

I want to ask what he's working on. If it has something to do with the money and the personal problem he talked about yesterday. I want to ask if he has a way out for me, for Sonia, for our baby. It would mean leaving Patrick and the boys, maybe only temporarily, maybe until they're able to travel and find me. And what then? Would Patrick take me in his arms this way? Would we return to normal in some new place? Would Steven ever speak to me again?

But that's foolish talk. There's no way out for me.

Suddenly, every new bang of the machine is Jackie's voice, saying:
I told you so. I told you so. I told you so.

FORTY-ONE

The banging of the MRI stops.

"Okay, you two," Lin says. "Visitor. Good thing I looked up when I did. That Poe guy makes absolutely no sound. Zero. He's a fucking ghoul."

I uncoil myself from Lorenzo's arms with enough force to slam me backward, into the wall. My ears ring with the monotonous thunder of the machine and Jackie's words. Lin, cool as a cuke, takes me by the hand and leads me to the main area of the lab.

"What the hell was that?" Poe says. "It sounded like the goddamned building was falling apart."

"Magnetic resonance imaging," Lin says. "It's supposed to sound like that."

Poe grunts. "Why was it on? The other ones aren't on."

"We only have one other one," I say, looking toward the first MRI room.

Instead of responding, Poe starts a slow tour around the lab, opening drawers and cabinets. He makes no sound, as Lin said, and it occurs to me that, if Lin hadn't been here while Lorenzo and I were making out to the tune of a thrumming machine, I'd be joining Julia King on a podium, listening to Reverend Carl recite his morality tracts. We never would have heard Poe enter, not until it was too late.

By the look on his face, this possibility has occurred to Lorenzo as well.

"Morgan wants to see you in his office," Poe says, addressing me. "Now."

I leave Sharon Ray's number with Lorenzo and Lin, telling them to set something up for Monday morning. With any luck, we'll be ready over the weekend, and I want Mrs. Ray in here as soon as possible. If I can give her a voice again, Sharon and Del might be more receptive to the favor I plan on asking.

In the elevator, Poe sticks his key card into a slot and presses the button for the fifth floor. It's the first time I noticed the slot, and I assume only the floors with our offices and the lab are accessible without a key. The doors open, and Poe extends a hand.

"This way," he says.

The fifth-floor corridor is plush, more like a five-star hotel than a government science building. My shoes make no sound on the thick carpet—blue, naturally. As we walk, I read the names on the doors. General So-and-So, Admiral So-and-So, Dr. So-and-So. All men's names. A few of them stare out at me through semi-open doors. One scowls.

Morgan is at his desk when Poe knocks. He calls "Enter!" in a small voice he's trying to make big. I want to tell him it doesn't work.

"Where were you this morning?" he says without looking up from whatever he's reading.

"I had a family issue. A neighbor was supposed to look after my daughter, and—"

He cuts me off, closing the fat binder on his desk, moving a blank notepad on top of it so the label is obscured. Then he sits back with his hands behind his head, elbows pointing out. Maybe he thinks he looks bigger this way, more powerful.

"See," he says, "this is why the old way didn't work. There's always something. Always some sick kid or a school play or menstrual cramps or maternity leave. Always a problem."

I open my mouth, but not to speak. It just falls open in disbelief.

Morgan hasn't finished. He picks up a pen and jabs the air with it. "You need to get it in your head, Jean. You women aren't dependable. The system doesn't work the way it was. Take the fifties. Everything was fine. Everyone had a nice house and a car in the garage and food on the table. And things still ran smoothly! We didn't need women in the workforce. You'll see, once you get over all this anger. You'll see it's going to be better. Better for your kids." He stops stabbing. "Anyway, let's not argue about it. You be a good girl and get in here at nine from now on, and I won't report this."

"I have Fridays off," I say. "It's in my contract." I need every bit of concentration to keep my voice steady and my hands still.

"Well, I changed your contract," he says, tapping a folder on his desk. He still hasn't asked me to sit down. "Before you signed it. And we're moving up the deadline to the third week of June."

"Why?"

Now he's talking like a teacher to a small child. "Jean, Jean, Jean. You don't need to know."

"Fine, Morgan. Whatever. By the way, we'll be working over the weekend and running a trial on our first subject this Monday or Tuesday." I take a seat in the chair facing him.

He looks shocked.

"Surprised?"

"Well, yes. I didn't think—"

"You didn't think what, Morgan? That Lorenzo, Lin, and I could actually make this work? Come on. You were in the department with us. You know Lin's a rock star." I don't say, *You probably had to lower the chair in her office so your feet could touch the ground.* It wouldn't do to piss him off, not when I need something.

He studies me with those beady eyes, bright and alert, like a terrier's. No. That's not quite right. Terriers are clever little things. "That's just terrific, Jean. Really terrific." He stands up, an indication the visit is over. "I knew we could do it."

I don't correct him. Instead, I drop my purse. When I lean over to get it, I can read the label on the side of the binder Morgan covered up. It's upside down, but the two words are clear, blue block letters on a white field.

The side of the binder reads PROJECT WERNICKE.

FORTY-TWO

P oe, whose job seems to entail everything from site security officer to babysitter to office escort, is waiting outside Morgan's office to take me back down to the lab, and I follow him along the corridor of generals and admirals and doctors, along the blue carpet, to the elevator bank. Inside, he uses his key card again.

I didn't need the card to access the lab floor, so it must be the only way to leave floor five. Of course it is, I think. They would want to know who's leaving, and at what time.

Or they'd want to be able to block anyone from leaving.

On the way down, I think about the binder I saw in Morgan's office. Altogether, my files plus Lorenzo's and Lin's would fill several binders. We had reference materials, statistics, experimental designs, grant applications, progress reports—everything, the entire academic kitchen plus sink. The Institutional Review Board documents—all the paperwork and disclosures and subject consent forms we collected to assure the university we wouldn't be running another Tuskegee syphilis scandal on unsuspecting prisoners—would fill a file cabinet on their own.

There wouldn't be a single "Project Wernicke" binder; there would be a hundred, neatly housing years of our research.

But Morgan had only one, and it wasn't labeled with a number indicating its position in a sequence.

Also, the spine was broken. Morgan's binder was, evidently, well used.

I think about this as the elevator begins its descent, while Poe stands silently behind me, slightly to my left. He seems not to be breathing; he's that quiet.

First, there are three teams: White, Gold, and Red. That much I learned from spying in Patrick's study last night. Poe's slips about our team and the other MRI tubes make sense now—other teams mean other labs. Other labs mean other projects.

Second, our equipment wasn't installed three days ago. No way. This machine—however large it is, and whatever it encompasses—has been months in the making.

Third, Morgan's binder has a broken spine.

I catch my reflection in the polished steel elevator walls and realize I've been talking to myself. Poe is in the reflection too, dwarfing me. He has the slightest of smiles on his face, a sliver of a smile, and I think about what sharp teeth must be behind it. Sharp enough to tear me to shreds without making a sound.

"Here we are."

The voice shocks me. Its echo, cold and quiet, bounces off the interior walls of the elevator. I will the doors to open, and after a few interminable seconds, they do, onto the bone white hallway of the lab floor. My key card is still inside my purse, buried underneath lipstick and wallet and all the other crap my fingers find first.

Lorenzo, I think. *I need to find Lorenzo.*

My heel catches in the gap between floor and elevator; such stupid things, high heels are. Jackie always said they were as sinister as that old Chinese custom of foot-binding. *Fucking high heels. Made by some asshole of a man to hobble a woman, make her walk two paces behind him,* she said, twirling a sandaled foot while sitting on the sofa. But I'm not walking anywhere right now; I'm facedown, half of me inside the elevator, half of me on the tile of the corridor. More than hobbled.

Cheek to the ground, I can see the locked lab door only ten feet away, and I scramble to my feet. A cold hand, heavy as a meat hook, grips my arm and pulls.

"I'm fine," I croak. Or I think I do.

"Careful, Dr. McClellan," the voice belonging to the meat hook says.

I'm up now, key card clenched in my fist, running to the main door of the lab, footsteps behind me. Poe isn't as quiet as he was. I slide the card into the slot; nothing happens.

There's a laugh behind me, a soft laugh that makes me jump and drop the key card.

And that hand again, its long fingers digging into my shoulder, turning me around.

"You all right, Gianna?"

I turn and sink into Lorenzo's chest. Behind him, the corridor is empty. Poe is gone.

FORTY-THREE

We can't risk turning on the MRI machine again, so Lin and Lorenzo suggest a different plan when I tell them we need to talk.

"You're sick," Lin says as we approach the security checkpoint. "We're taking you out to your car."

She's to my right, pretending to support me, while Lorenzo has an arm around my waist. Our purses and briefcases are searched, and a uniformed man—army, I think, but he could be a marine—pats us down one at a time.

"They're clean," he barks to another man, and a light above the doors turns from red to green. "Have a nice weekend." The soldier says this as if he hasn't just spent five minutes groping us, as if this were any other office building in Washington.

The doors slide open, letting us out into the late May afternoon. Lorenzo doesn't let go of me, only holds me tighter, pressing his hip against mine. Someone is probably watching us from the windows five floors up, so I pause and bend over at the waist, hands on my knees, as if I'm catching my breath. It isn't that difficult an act.

"The projects are all color coded," I say, keeping my focus on the asphalt. "One red, one gold. The one we're on is the White team."

"Morgan told you that?" Lorenzo asks.

"Right," I say. "All Morgan wanted was to lecture me on how perfect the world was when women stayed home. No. Morgan didn't tell me anything, but he had a thick binder he tried to hide. Didn't work, of course. Morgan's twice as stupid as he looks."

"Can you ask Patrick about it?" Lin says. She's crouched beside me in the parking lot, her back to the building. "No, never mind. Can you get back into his study and have another look?"

"Maybe. Patrick's been drinking more lately, and it's Friday. I might be able to work something out tonight." I say this without really knowing where the words are coming from. They can't be mine, these spy-like thoughts. Jackie, maybe, would think up a scheme to get her husband drunk and pry his desk drawers open, but not Jean. In seventeen years of marriage, I've never snooped around Patrick's papers, either personal or business, never looked for clues of a mistress or a one-night tumble. Once, when I couldn't find my planner, I thought I might have left it in his car. Even then, as I clicked open the driver's-side door, I felt like an infiltrator.

"We don't keep secrets from one another, babe," Patrick said when I told him about the missing planner. "Never have, never will. I don't care if you go into my car. Snoop around all you want. You might find a dirty handkerchief in the glove compartment, though, so watch out. Cooties, you know." He played lightly with his fingers up and down my arms as he said this. "Beware the Irish cooties!"

Of course, I turned out to be the one with the secrets. Or with one six-foot-tall Italian secret.

Correction. Make that two secrets. One of them is about the size of a small orange.

"I'd better get going," I say. The drive out to Sharon Ray's farmette will take the better part of an hour in traffic, and I want to stop in to check on Olivia King before dinner, call the hospital where my mother is, and—*don't forget, Jean*—get my husband liquored up so I can steal classified government documents from his office. It's a tall order for a Friday evening.

Lorenzo helps me into my Honda—not that I need the help, but it keeps up the pretense. It also gives him the opportunity to talk to me without Lin hearing.

"Have you told him?" he says.

"No."

"Are you going to?"

"He's a medical doctor. He'll know the baby can't possibly be his." Lorenzo's face distorts into a question mark.

"We haven't—we weren't very active for a few months," I say.

He relaxes into a smile. "I see. So there's no doubt?"

"None at all." I already feel the slight bulge, sense where the waistband of my skirt cuts in more than it did two weeks ago. Sooner or later—sooner, I think—I'll have no choice but to tell Patrick.

He won't, in Steven's words, rat me out. I know that. Even if he wanted to, the news would run the kids over like a freight train. That train would keep coming, unexpectedly, in the form of an intruder while Sonia watched cartoons, during a soccer match, in between CNN news segments. School, for them, would become a daily trek into hell. Patrick would know this, and he would keep silent.

But the thing, that unspeakable *It*, will always hang over us like a storm cloud. No, that's not true. It won't hang. It will crawl and toddle and walk and laugh and be a living reminder of how I spent a cold March afternoon fucking Lorenzo. And fucking up everything else.

"That other matter I said I was working on—I may know something by Monday," Lorenzo says, snapping me back to the parking lot. "Hold on until then, okay?"

"What is it?"

Lorenzo straightens, pulling his hand away from mine.

"You two," a voice says. "What's going on?"

Poe is standing in front of the Honda, arms folded across his massive chest, aviator glasses masking his eyes. I hate Morgan, but the only person I'm scared to death of is this quiet giant named Poe.

I manage a smile, throw the car into reverse, and back away without meeting his stare.

ever let a child visit a farm, I think as I drive Sonia back home from the Rays' place. They'll want to stay forever.

Sonia, only two days free of her counter, has developed the gift of gab. Nonstop chatter about Aristotle the mare—who is really a girl horse with a boy's name, Sonia informs me—is interrupted only by a narrative about brown chickens laying brown eggs and white chickens laying the normal white ones. She can't wait to go back tomorrow, and I wonder if I should have left her at the Rays' overnight.

No, it's better to bring her home. If Delilah Ray's trial goes well on Monday, I may not have more than a week's talking time with my daughter.

I planned to ask Del if he would do us the same favor he'd done for his own family, remove our wrist counters and replace them with decoys, but I haven't. Not yet. A small voice keeps reminding me of Steven. He's drunk every flavor of Kool-Aid the Pure has handed him. Also, the twins might blurt something out, reveal the secret at school. I can't risk that.

As we drive, the landscape changes from rural to suburban. All those houses, I think, are little prisons, and inside them are cells in the shape of kitchens and laundry closets and bedrooms. Morgan's words come back to me, his matter-of-fact talk about how things were better before, long ago, when men worked and women stayed in their private sphere of cookery and cleaning and baby making.

I don't think I really believed it would happen. I don't think any of us did.

After the election, we started believing. Some of us became vocal for the first time. Women, for the most part, spearheaded the anti-Myers campaign—women like me, who hadn't ever tried on a pair of marching boots, piled into buses and Metro cars and froze in the Washington winter. There were men, too, I remember. Barry and Keith, who had three decades between them of fighting for gay rights, spent a Saturday painting signs at their house two doors down from ours; five of the graduate students from my department said they had our backs. And they did, for a while.

It's hard to pinpoint what—or whom—we were protesting. Sam Myers was a terrible choice for the chief executive. Young and inexperienced in big-time politics, his military training a one-year ROTC stint from college days, Myers ran his presidential race with a crutch under each arm. Bobby, his older brother and a career senator, supplied the practical advice. There was a shit ton of that, I'm guessing. The other crutch was Reverend Carl, the vote supplier, the man people listened to. Anna Myers, pretty and popular, didn't hurt the campaign, although in the end, it hurt her. Plenty.

Our only real hope had been the Supreme Court. But with one empty seat on an already right-leaning bench and two more retirements looming, the Supremes didn't offer much hope. Even now, I'm told it will take months for the handful of restraining orders to make their way through the labyrinthine system. If they make it at all.

Patrick tolerated my absence two winters ago, reheated batches of soup and other one-dish meals, took care of the kids on weekends while

I marched and phoned and wrote and protested. He didn't seem to require explanations or apologies, not like Evan King next door would have if Olivia had suddenly decided to be a poster girl against the administration. Patrick and I had an unspoken understanding of the direction our lives—my life—might steer if I stood silent.

Tolerance didn't extend to those in charge, to the men Patrick works for.

There were rumblings, and they were much louder than mine.

One day, and I can point to it on a calendar (I often did during that first year after the counters went on), when the magnolias were pregnant with white stars, Patrick sent the children to bed early and led me out into the garden, under the canopy of trees.

"I've heard things at the office," he said, holding me close, whispering. "The administration is discussing ways to shut you up."

"Me?"

"All of you. So do me a favor and skip next week's march on the Capitol. Let the other women go if they want, but hang out in your lab, Jean. The work you've done is too important, too—"

I slammed my palm into a nearby trunk, cutting him off. "And what exactly are they planning? Forced laryngectomies? Slicing out our tongues? Think about it, Patrick. You're a scientist yourself. No one can shut half of the population up, not even that bastard you work for."

"Listen, I know more than you do, Jean. Stay home with us this time." Above us, a high wind whisked away the clouds. Patrick's eyes, soft and moist, reflected the naked moon.

I didn't march that weekend. Or any other.

The next day, though, I told my gynecologist, Dr. Claudia, what Patrick had told me. I told Lin and the women in my book club and my yoga instructor—everyone. The more I retold the warning, the more preposterous it sounded, like a bad science fiction tale, the kind of thing you see in movies. All gloom and doom, Dr. Claudia said. "Never gonna happen."

Lin echoed this sentiment one day in her office. "Simple economics," she said. "Imagine cutting the workforce in half"—she snapped her fingers—"just like that. Overnight."

"Maybe we should go away," I said. "Europe is better. I have a passport and I can get Patrick and the kids their own. We could—"

She cut me off. "And what are you going to do in Europe?"

I didn't know. "We'll think of something."

"Look, Jean," Lin said. "I hate the bastard. I hate all of them. But that Reverend Carl, he's a joke. Take a long, hard look around this city. You see anyone who actually believes his bullshit?"

"My neighbor does."

She leaned over her desk, pointing a finger up in the air. "That's a sample of one, Jean. One. You know more about statistics than to hang your hat on a single subject."

Lin was right and wrong at the same time. My neighbor Olivia was an outlier, but she was an outlier only here in Washington. What Lin didn't consider—what none of us considered—was how much of a bubble our city was, how different from the rest of the country with its bearded duck people and Christian communities cropping up like weeds. There was a documentary about one of those places, *Glorytown* or *Gloryville* or something like that, where all the women wore pretty blue dresses with high collars and followed special diets and milked cows. The director, when interviewed, had called it "neat."

Jackie had made the bubble reference first, that snide remark about me in my safe little lab, and followed it with an unhappy-birthday-to-you basket of things that went pop: bubble gum, balloons, sparkling wine. She asked me—it seems like a million years ago now—to think about what I would do to stay free.

What would I do?

Lorenzo has something cooking, I know. Something that costs quite a bit of money, more than he would have stashed away as a wandering academic. I don't dare raise my hopes that it's a ticket out of here, a stolen passport, anything like that. But I'm thinking exactly those things as I drive up our street past Annie Wilson's old house, now inhabited by one man and one boy while Annie works long hours in some no-man's-land.

Extraordinary circumstances require extraordinary actions.

"Mommy, look!" Sonia chirps. "More lights!"

We're even with the Kings' house now, and this time, the ambulance is really an ambulance.

FORTY-FIVE

Julia King wasn't the first girl to find herself a victim of Reverend Carl's fornication police, and Olivia wasn't the first mother who watched her child being taken away in the middle of the night, only to reappear, transformed, on television the following day.

Nor was Olivia the first woman to try her own way out.

I've seen them in Safeway, the regular customers who disappear for a while and come back in a week, a little dopey in the eyes, the bandages on their wrists peeking out from long sleeves when they reach to a high shelf for that elusive can of peas or chicken soup.

And there have been funerals, of course, not all of them for old men and women who died of natural causes.

Evan's car was still in the driveway this morning when I left with Sonia. He'd stayed home, I assumed, to console his wife—not that I believe Evan capable of much consoling. Possibly, he stayed to watch her until the house could be suicide-proofed or Olivia could be doped up enough so she wouldn't be tempted to try anything.

I park, and send Sonia into the house as soon as the gurney emerges on the Kings' front porch. "Go to the den and watch something with your brothers, okay?"

"Why?"

Why? *Because Olivia King's body is on that stretcher.* "Because I said so, baby girl. Now."

Olivia's body is on the stretcher, her face uncovered and serene. Her left arm dangles down beneath the white sheet.

Or what's left of her arm.

The fingers are five charred stubs, black with necrotic tissue that crawls up her palm to her wrist, a wrist now the size of a baby's. I think even one of Sonia's infant bracelets would hang loosely on it, clattering against the exposed bone. An acrid odor fills the air, and stray wisps of smoke billow out their front door.

Oh god.

Our own screen door bangs open, and Patrick catches me in time, just as my knees buckle. "It's okay. Don't look, Jean. Don't look at it."

It. Always *It.*

Inside, he pours me a drink and tells me the kids are watching a video. "No television today. Not after—" He pauses. "I'll tell you about that later. Drink this."

"What happened to her?" My own voice is thin and stringlike. I take a sip of scotch, and it burns.

Patrick pours himself a glass of the same—not his usual afternoon beer—and steadies himself against the kitchen counter. "Evan said he'd thought of everything. Locked up all the knives, anything sharp. Took away whatever she might use as a rope, even shut off the electricity."

"Good thinking," I say. *But he forgot something, didn't he?*

"After lunch, Olivia said she was going to lie down for a while. So he stripped the bed and took everything out of the bedroom that she might, you know, use. Oh Jesus, Jean. I can't." He swallows a long draw of scotch. "Okay. She had this little recorder, see? One of those Dictaphone things, maybe from when she used to work as a secretary—I don't know. Evan heard her talking when he went to check on her, but she didn't say much, only a few words about Julia. Twenty or so words in all. Then she went quiet, and he figured she was sleeping. You don't want to hear the rest, Jean. I swear you don't."

"I have to."

Another draw from his tumbler of Dutch courage, and he continues. "He went out to the garage to find some boxes—I don't know—maybe to pack the knives in or something. He didn't say. He thinks he was gone about ten minutes when he saw the smoke from their bedroom window. They kept it open a crack, even though it's warm. I guess they liked the fresh air. I don't know, Jean." Patrick's voice starts to tremble.

"It's okay," I say, laying a hand on his.

He tips the bottle again. "She made a loop, you see. She recorded twenty words and made a loop out of them on the Dictaphone. Then she put the gizmo out of reach and set it to play. Over and over and over again. If she even knew what she was doing after the first of the charges, she wasn't able to get to the machine and turn it off."

"Oh. Oh no."

Patrick falls onto the counter, head in his hands, still talking, although his voice is muffled. "Evan said when he came into their bedroom, the recording was still playing. Same words, over and over. 'I'm so sorry, Julia,' it said. And all the time, it was burning her, that goddamned metal monster on her wrist, eating into her skin until—until—"

I run a dish towel under the tap, wrap a few ice cubes in it, and lay it over the back of Patrick's neck. "Shh. Be still for a minute."

"When did it get so bad, Jean? We're doing everything we can. But when did it get so fucking bad?"

We.

A moan—no, a low, animal-like sob—comes from the living room. I leave Patrick at the counter, the towel on his motionless head, walk through the dining room, and crane my neck around the corner toward the front window.

Steven is there, watching as the ambulance reverses down the Kings' driveway and takes off, sirens blaring. My son's shoulders undulate in a jerky, arhythmic pattern.

"She'll be all right," I say, coming up to where he stands, but still keeping some distance.

"Nothing's all right," Steven says.

This is not the right time to talk about making beds and lying in them, so I stay silent.

"You have no idea, Mom. You have no idea what they said about her today."

He watched it at school, the broadcast of Julia and Reverend Carl. "About Julia?"

Steven spins around, and his face is a picture of horror, pale and drawn, puffy around the eyes. His nose is running, and he swats at it with a sleeve. "Who do you think?"

All of a sudden, he's five years old again, sniffling and crying about a scratched knee or a palmful of road rash from when he tipped his bike and went skidding to a stop. So much for sullen seventeen-year-olds.

"Want to talk about it?" I say.

"They didn't act like that with the lady down the street. Remember her? Mrs. Wilson? They just yawned while she was on television." Another sniff, another sleeve wipe. "Maybe because she was old or they didn't know her. But they all knew Julia. We all went to school together before . . . before it all changed."

"It," I repeat.

"So her picture came on the screen, and Mr. Gustavson told us she was the kind of girl we all had to watch out for because she had the devil in her and would drag us down. You know, like to hell."

"Jesus, Steven."

He's composing himself now, pulling in deep breaths and steadying his voice. "You know what he said?"

I don't think I want to. "No. What?"

"He said we should never call people ugly things, like whore and slut and harlot. But then he told us that some people deserved to be called that stuff. Like Julia. So he made us scream at her while she was on television. She looked so small, Mom. So helpless. And they cut off all her hair. All of it. Like a marine cut, you know? Mr. Gustavson said that was good. It's what they used to do to heretics during the Spanish Inquisition and witches in Salem." Steven starts laughing, cackling almost. It's a maniac's laugh.

He keeps going.

"It gets worse. He went around the room, smiling, and he handed out a sheet of paper with the foulest garbage written on it. You remember that old thing about seven dirty words? Well, they were there, and about fifty other ones. He wanted us to take out our notebooks and write a letter—one letter from each of us—to Julia King, using as many shitty words as we could. We were supposed to tell her she deserved whatever she got, to have fun breaking her back in the fields."

I don't flinch when Steven says "shitty." Compared to everything else he's telling me, profanity sounds like a goddamned lullaby. "Did you do it?"

"I *had* to, Mom. If I didn't, they'd all think—" He stops short, and a smile creeps up one side of his mouth. "Evil triumphs when good men do nothing. That's what they say, right?"

He's got the essence of Burke's quote, if not the exact words. But I know what he means, and I nod.

Jackie would like that.

FORTY-SIX

This is almost normal, sitting around the table amid boxes of pizza, Sam and Leo arguing about who has the best soccer team, Sonia educating us on the ins and outs of cow milking and stable mucking. If I close my eyes, Patrick isn't slumped in his chair, almost shrunken, and Steven is working his way into a sixth slice, crust and all. There's chatter, and arguing, and interruptions. All that normal family-dinner shit.

Except it isn't.

Patrick had more to drink than he should have. Steven picked off the pepperoni on a single slice and made piles of it on the side of his plate. And me? Tiredness has become an endless song, a never-ending loop of exhaustion running through my head and my limbs, pulling me down.

Then again, this is my chance, and it happened all by itself.

I put Patrick to bed—no small feat given his bulk and my fatigue—and read Sonia a story. She's asleep before Winnie-the-Pooh gets himself stuck in Rabbit's house.

Good for you, kid, I think.

The little clock on her nightstand tells me it's eight—too early for the twins to be in bed, and way too early for Steven. I go to check on the three of them.

Sam and Leo are teaching each other card tricks in the den—also a normal thing. Steven, when I knock on his bedroom door, says he wants to be alone for a while. To tune out, he tells me through the thick walls.

This makes me think of Olivia.

"You sure you're okay?" I say. What I don't say is *Don't do anything stupid, kiddo.*

Maybe he's read my mind; maybe he's got more sense than I'm giving him credit for. "I'm not gonna—you know."

Nothing like having a little pre-bedtime suicide chat with your son, I think, and go find Patrick's keys.

My husband has a nightly ritual: an hour in his study with a beer after dinner, teeth brushing, and—on occasions that have grown rarer over the years and as scarce as hen's teeth in the past twelve months— sex. At some point between his study time and crawling into bed, he locks his keys in a steel safe in his nightstand, the kind of box with a keypad you see in hotel rooms.

Once, he tried to pass off this sequestering as a side effect of his new job, but I know better. I know if he resigned from the advisory position tomorrow and went back to consulting for the AMA, those keys and drawers and boxes would still be here, just like they are in every other house. I saw Evan King going through the same motions last month on a night he forgot to roll the shade down. And Evan's not science adviser to the president of the United States. Evan's a fucking accountant for a grocery chain. There can't be much secrecy in that.

It's *Father Knows Best* now, baby. All the way.

Patrick skipped most of this locking-and-unlocking ritual tonight, but habit forced him to roll over, open the drawer, and punch in the six-digit code he keeps more secret than a mistress. I heard the keys clang into their hiding place, and the electronic pulse of five more numbers before he slid the drawer closed and rolled onto his back, mumbling something about trying hard and needing more time.

I filled a glass with ice water and set it on a coaster within reach, along with three aspirin for the morning. Then I went in to read to Sonia. In between Rabbit and Pooh and Tigger, I thought of those five beeps when Patrick locked the safe.

Five beeps. Not six.

After checking on the boys, I slip off my shoes and pad down the hall to our bedroom. Patrick is snoring softly on his pillow, his chest rising and falling under the thin sheet. In the dim glow of the bedside clock, I feel for the brass drawer handle on his nightstand, hook an unsteady finger under it, and ease the drawer out along its runners. The humidity has made the old wood sticky, and a single finger isn't enough to get it open. My hand curls around the brass and tugs.

Physics is a fascinating thing. I think of the times when I've been out for a drink with friends, in one of those bars where they serve beer in heavy glass mugs, except you find out—just about when the beer hits you in the face—that the mugs aren't made of glass but of plastic, some kind of composite that has the look of glass but not the weight. You calculate the force needed to lift a pound or so of beer mug, and—whoops!—you've got a face full of lager. "Drinking problem," you say, and start wiping.

Well, now I have a pulling problem.

The foot-pounds I exert on the drawer would have been enough to unstick it. Would have, if the brass handle hadn't popped off.

I fly backward, hardware in hand, and my head hits the floor. Patrick stops snoring.

"What you doing, babe?" he mutters.

"Just tripped on the rug. Go back to sleep."

Amazingly, this works, and I wait a full five minutes listening to his breathing become shallower before going to the kitchen in search of a screwdriver.

It's nine o'clock by the time I'm able to pry the nightstand drawer open wide enough to snake my hand inside, feel for the closed but unlocked safe door, and get a fingernail into the crack. The safe swings open, and I palm the cool metal of Patrick's keys before pushing the drawer closed.

Time to send Sam and Leo to bed.

They resist, Sam telling me he's got just one more trick.

"Now," I say, and wait until I hear them settle. Then I walk to the end of the hall, to Patrick's locked office door.

I have the lie already prepared, ready to go, in case Patrick wakes up and finds me sitting behind his desk, rifling through stacks of papers and envelopes. After all, my mother's in a hospital thousands of miles away, the language center of her brain possibly damaged beyond repair. Of course I need to call, even at the late hour. Papà won't be sleeping tonight.

But I'm alone, me and my sticky fingers and Patrick's neatly squared piles arranged like paper soldiers in rows across his desk. Everything looks exactly the same as it did last night, and it would, since no one has been in this room today. Olivia's gruesome self-electrocution left no time for such banalities as paperwork. *Attempted electrocution,* I remind myself, trying to put the image of her burned arm out of my mind.

Everything is exactly as it was, except for the manila envelope and its TOP SECRET stenciling.

By eleven, I've been inside every drawer and cabinet, examined under the two fake Persian rugs, felt along each inch of baseboard molding for a loose board. Finally, I give up and lie back on the hard floor, head still pounding from my earlier fall.

I'm so tired. Like, bone tired. It would be nice to stay here, limbs stretched out and eyes half-closed, until morning.

It would be nice, and it would get me in a shitload of trouble, even with the ruse of trying to FaceTime my father.

I push myself up, willing my legs to take the weight, and go over Patrick's desk one final time, squaring up the stacks of reports and memos with flat palms. If he says anything in the morning, I'll tell him he tried to work while he was drunk.

As the office door key turns in its lock, the other keys jangle together. I close my fist around them to keep them still and silent, and rack my brain for what they might unlock. There are three keys in all: one for the office and two smaller ones. I suppose one of these others fits the lock on the trunk in the attic, where most of my books are. But the smallest, with its round bow, reminds me of Jackie.

We kept a key hanger, a kitschy little job Jackie picked up at a yard sale, on the wall next to our apartment door. She repainted it in a Native American motif, coloring over the paw prints and the text that proclaimed ALL YOU NEED IS LOVE . . . AND A DOG, replacing the lettering with our names, DOOR, and MAIL. I was always misplacing the mailbox key, she said, so from now on the sucker gets hung up on the hook. I can still picture it, that tiny key with its round bow.

When I'm sure Patrick's office is locked, and Steven hasn't emerged from his room in search of a midnight bowl of cereal or a Snickers bar, I slip out the front door. Night air hits my skin, and it prickles, reminding me that I've been sweating.

Next door, the Kings' house is blacked out, not even a porch light on. Of course, Evan had left in the ambulance with Olivia while the sun was still high in the sky. Perhaps he hasn't come back yet. I feel around the inside of the doorjamb for the switch that turns our light off, flip it, and wait for my eyes to adjust to the night. Above me, over the Kings' roof, hangs a sliver of crescent moon. It looks like a hook.

Wiping the sweat from my palms on my skirt, I fumble for the smallest key on the ring. With one trembling hand, I find the lock on our mailbox, the steel container Del Ray peered into only this morning, finding a single envelope. The key turns easily, once I get it into the lock, and I hold my breath.

What the hell are you expecting, Jean? I think. *Top secret government documents in your mailbox?*

And yet, under that fingernail moon that looks as if it might float down and whisk the house next door away, into the night clouds, I see the outline of a manila envelope.

FORTY-SEVEN

As of two minutes ago, my name isn't Jean.

My name is thief.

Or traitor, I think, and wonder for a moment what sort of punishment Reverend Carl and his pack of Pure Men might have set aside for subversives. In a world where women are sent to the Siberia of North Dakota for crimes as petty as fornication, where Jackie serves a life sentence in a concentration camp for homosexuals, surely there must be some fresh horror for women who steal state secrets.

They'll take me away; that's certain. I'll never see my kids again, or Patrick, or Lorenzo.

I try to imagine a life, somewhere on what cons used to call the inside, where I spend every new day watching the mental photographs of everyone fade and silver with time until nothing but the faintest outline is left. Or maybe I won't have to do that. Maybe my last image will be of the inside of a hood as a noose slips around my neck, or the gel-smeared cap of an electric chair is strapped firmly onto my shaved head, or a needle slides into my vein.

No, it wouldn't be a needle. That would be too kind.

The clock inside chimes twelve, counting out my heartbeats. There's no need to count them; I can feel each beat in my ears like a kettledrum.

But I've gone this far, so why not a bit further?

I lock the mailbox after taking out its contents, only the single envelope, and go back into the house. Despite the still, warm air inside, a chill runs up and down my arms, raising the flesh into a braille of goose bumps.

We don't have it as bad as Winston Smith, having to crouch into a blind corner of his one-room flat while Big Brother watches through a screen on the wall, but we do have cameras. There's one at the front door, one at the back, and one over the garage, aimed at the driveway. I watched them being installed a year ago, on the day Sonia and I were fitted with the wrist counters. No one could possibly monitor every household all the time—there isn't enough manpower for constant surveillance; nevertheless, I'm careful to keep the manila envelope flat against my body as I turn from the mailbox and slide back through the front door. Then I walk from living room to dining room and toward the half bath at the side of the kitchen. It seems a private enough place.

Inside, I sit on the floor, my back to the wall, and pry up the prongs on the metal clasp.

The cover sheet is there, the same memo I read last evening. Under it are three separate sets of documents, each paper-clipped to a colored cover page, one white, one gold, and one red. I flip the white cover first, revealing an outline of my team's goals:

Develop, test, and mass-produce anti-Wernicke serum

Behind this page, there are the usual Gantt charts—the project manager's tool of choice—stipulating deadlines for interim reports and clinical trials. The rest of the packet consists of the team's CVs. Nothing new here, but I note Morgan's curriculum vitae is only one page long, while the rest of ours span half a dozen sheets. I flip the pages back, square them, and adjust the paper clip before setting the white batch aside on the bathroom tile.

The gold packet is almost a duplicate of the one for my own team. Under the yellow cover page, the goals read:

Develop, test, and mass-produce Wernicke serum

More Gantt charts and five CVs, all documenting the publication histories and academic positions of various biologists and chemists I don't know, are also in this set, along with Morgan's credentials. So they're doubling up, hedging their bets, it looks like. Hell. It's typical government. Why have one team when you can pay for two?

The gold set goes on the pile next to me, and I move to the Red team's packet, expecting another redundancy, but this one is different.

For one, its goal is singular:

Explore water solubility of Wernicke serum

The team members on the following pages—all six of them—are also scientists, all PhDs. Below each name is a military rank and branch. I squeeze my eyes shut to the harsh light above the bathroom's sink and think back to this afternoon, to all the doors I passed as Poe led me down the fifth-floor corridor toward Morgan's office.

One of the names—Winters—rings a faint, but clear, bell at the same time the clock in the living room chimes the hour. One o'clock.

Carefully, I assemble the packets as they were: white, gold, and red. Before sliding them back into the envelope, I check the Gantt chart in the white set. The timeline, a color-coded horizontal bar chart of tasks, goes back to the previous year, to November 8, the date our lab equipment was requisitioned.

So I was right. The Wernicke project wasn't conceived yesterday. It was started seven months ago.

My legs don't want to stand. They're disobedient limbs, all cramped and prickly with pins and needles from sitting cross-legged on the floor for so long. I lean against the sink and stretch out my hamstrings.

"Jean?"

The voice on the other side of the bathroom door is muffled, but it's unmistakably Patrick's. He knocks once; then the doorknob turns.

I didn't lock it. I didn't think I needed to.

Shit. Shit, shit, shit.

Quickly, I turn on the tap, letting the manila envelope slide into the narrow space between the vanity and the wall. When Patrick opens the door, I'm bathing my face in cold water.

"Holy Christ, babe," he says. "You're a mess."

My reflection agrees. Sweat-smudged mascara circles my eyes, the cotton blouse I put on this morning sticks to me like a thin coat of glue, and my hair is either matted down or sticking out in all the wrong places. I twist the tap and towel off, smiling a little sheepishly at Patrick, who seems much less drunk and much more concerned.

"Didn't feel so hot," I say. "Must have been the pizza."

He holds a hand up to my forehead, a cool, clean doctor's hand, the skin of it pink and scrubbed. For an instant, I think of Lorenzo's hands and how different they are. I think of how Patrick's hands might not be as clean as they seem.

"You never get sick, babe," he says. And then, with a small laugh, "Well, unless you're preggers. You know, with four kids, that amounts to a full year of private bathroom time."

I try to laugh along with him, but my voice sounds hoarse, wrong.

"You're not—" Patrick's eyes dart from my face to my belly, and he frowns. He's not stupid, and he's a doctor. Between the math and his textbook grasp of embryology, he must know it's impossible. Our sex life over the past several months means that I'm either three days pregnant or carrying around a beach ball.

"Of course not," I say. "I really think it was the pizza. Tasted off."

"All right, then. Come on back to bed." He takes my hand and shuts the light in the half bath off, leading me out of my midnight reading room.

"Be there after I get a drink of water," I say. "And I might as well call Papà while I'm up."

When his footsteps fade down the hallway toward our room, I slide the envelope out of its temporary hiding place, backtrack to the front porch, and reverse the process of stealing. I stop in the kitchen for a glass of ice water and suck it down while I dial my father's cell number from memory.

"Pronto," he says, sounding not like my father at all but like a much older man.

"Papà, it's Jean. How's Mamma?"

His voice tells me everything, even before he says the words "brain damage" and "that area that begins with a *W*" and "why can't I talk to her anymore?" "Can't you fix her, Gianna?"

"Of course I can." I pull as much confidence into my voice as possible, hoping it camouflages the telltale jitter I feel in my throat. "Soon, Papà. Real soon."

After one more glass of water, most of which I end up patting onto my face, I walk down the hall to our room.

Patrick is snoring again.

I lay the keys on the carpet, just next to his nightstand, and crawl into bed for six hours of sleep.

FORTY-EIGHT

In my nightmare, the kids are gone.

One by one, I see them taken away from me, their faces darkening and fading. Someone—Olivia, maybe, or possibly a soldier—holds Sonia up amid a flash of camera lights. The twins wave, and Sam flicks a pack of playing cards in the air above Leo's head. "Fifty-two pickup!" he says. Steven smiles a crooked smile and calls, "Later, Mom." He cocks his head to one side, as if to say he's sorry.

And all the while, Patrick watches, saying nothing.

This isn't really how my Saturday starts.

Patrick opens the blinds, letting a blast of morning sun into the bedroom. The twins and Sonia march in with a tray smelling of coffee and warm bagels—smells that on any other day might get my appetite going, but today they bring another wave of nausea. In the middle of one cream-cheese-smeared bagel is a single candle.

"Happy birthday, Mom!" four voices scream.

I nearly forgot that I'm forty-four today.

"Thanks," I croak, trying to look hungry. "Where's Steven?"

"Asleep," Sam says.

The clock next to my bed glows a digital nine-one-one. I told Lin and Lorenzo I'd be in the lab by ten.

"Blow out the candle and make a wish, Mommy," Sonia says.

I do it, dripping wax onto my breakfast, then heave myself out of bed and sprint to the bathroom. "Back in a minute. Get Steven up. I want to talk to him before I leave for work."

The birthday parade reverses and files out. Thirty seconds later, while I'm pouring my undrunk coffee down the sink, Patrick comes in.

"Steven's gone," he says quietly.

I think of "gone" in every other semantic sense. Gone to the store, gone running, gone out for morning pizza, gone crazy. I don't think of it in the simplest of terms. I don't think of "gone" meaning absent, not here, as in my dream. I don't think of it as in gone from this life, dead.

Patrick holds out a sheet of notebook paper. "This was in his room. On his pillow."

It could be worse, I think, reading Steven's scribble. Still, it—that horrible *It*—is enough to take the wind out of me.

Gone to look for Julia. Love you. S.

In four days, everything has changed from lousy to shit.

"Should we call the police?" I say.

Patrick shakes his head as if he knows what I'm thinking. "Probably better not to." He touches my arm and takes the empty coffee mug from my hand without asking *What's the matter with your coffee?* or eyeing the streaks of brown in the sink. What he does say is, "I haven't been a very good husband, have I?"

Then, like magnets, we're together, attached, holding each other up. He touches that soft spot behind my ear with a finger, and I feel my pulse beat a rhythm, syncopated at first, then steady. It's odd to think of love at a time like this, with our son gone and the brown sludge of coffee in the sink, but Patrick's hands roam down from my neck, across my back, and forward to my breasts, which swell in the silk nightie, responding to his touch in that automatic way the flesh has of pricking up, even when the mind tells it not to.

"I can't be late," I say, pulling back from him. I also can't lie under my husband this morning, thinking about the first time, the time we made Steven.

I'm also thinking about what Patrick would have done if, instead of Julia, it was me who Reverend Carl tore from my home and made stand in front of television cameras before shipping me off to a life of silence and servitude. Would he come after me?

Lorenzo would, but not Patrick.

"Where do you think he went?" I say, turning on the shower. "Steven, I mean." Julia might be anywhere—up the coast, inland, across the country in a California orange grove. "Finding her would be like finding a black cat in a coal cellar."

Patrick shakes his head. "I don't think so. Let me show you something." He leaves me in the bathroom and goes to the nightstand on his side of the bed. "What the hell?"

The lie's already prepared, and easier to recite when I'm not looking him in the eyes. "Damn handle came off last night. Don't you remember?"

There's a pause while he thinks this over. Finally, I hear the jangle of keys and a single, perplexed "Huh" from the bedroom before I escape into the shower.

"I'll make you some tea if you want," Patrick calls. "When you're done, come to my office. I think I know where Steven's headed."

I take the quickest shower of my life, comb out unwashed hair, and dress in loose jeans and a linen shirt that I don't have to tuck in. Screw the dress code; I'm hot, rushed, and pregnant. Then I go down the hall into Patrick's study.

Reverend Carl's face fills the screen, and his hands are held up as if in prayer. It's his preferred speaking pose. The news camera trained on him tracks back, opening up the shot to reveal the rest of the stage. Julia King is unrecognizable.

They've shaved her, of course—I expected that. I didn't expect the job to be so half-assed, like an amateur sheepshearing by a blind man with palsy. Clumps of remaining hair stick in rusty patches on her head.

"What did they do, use a dull straight razor?" I say, not taking my eyes off the image on Patrick's laptop. Steven has seen this, was forced to watch and join in his classmates' name-calling.

Reverend Carl calls his audience to prayer and bows his head. "Lord, forgive our wayward daughter, and guide her as she joins her sisters in the Black Hills of South Dakota. Amen." A chorus of shouts and hisses follows the prayer. A few people echo "Amen," but mostly it's a hate-fest. Reverend Carl presses the air under his raised hands and calls for silence, but when he lifts his head toward the cameras, I see the faintest of smiles on his lips.

Now the camera closes in, tight, on Julia's tear-streaked face. Her lips tremble, and her eyes search from left to right, looking for a shred of sympathy among the shouters. Reverend Carl's hand appears on her shoulder, and she shirks away, but the hand seems only to clench more tightly, fingers digging into her clavicle under the gray material. It fits high on her neck and has long sleeves. She must be dying in this heat.

It isn't the first time I think about how much I hate Reverend Carl Corbin, but it is the first time I want to kill him.

f I'd spent my last few minutes at home looking out our front window instead of unknotting my hair, I might have seen the anonymous black SUV parked across the street, its engine running and puffing out streams of exhaust smoke.

But I didn't. By the time I walk out the side door and start my car, it's too late.

Del the mailman is already up the porch steps, courier bag over his shoulder, his key to our mailbox in one hand. He waves to me, and I wave back through the Honda's rear window.

The realization hits me like a tidal wave: keys, an envelope, Del peeking inside the mailbox yesterday and removing a single item, Sharon warning me about an underground organization that's using a mailman as its go-between. And, finally, Patrick's words last night after he told me what Olivia had done to herself, there in her bedroom, with the Dictaphone repeating its endless loop of her own words.

We're doing everything we can.

When the dots connect, I'm left with one terrible, frightening, and at the same time relieving explanation: Patrick isn't working for the government. He's working against it.

I pull halfway out of the driveway, stopping when I'm in line with the porch. Del opens the mailbox, careful to shield his hands from the street and the porch camera. I want to shout at him. *Stop! Stop! Don't open it!*

He slides the manila envelope out, holding it close and hiding it in his courier bag before relocking the mailbox. He won't hear Poe's silent steps behind him, coming up the walk, climbing the porch stairs. He won't hear the quiet click and hum of the black stun gun in Poe's massive right hand, or the crackle as it presses against his ribs, shocking him twice—first in his body, then in his mind.

Poe turns toward me and waves me down the driveway, as if to say *Move along now. Nothing to see here.*

And now two more men rush up to the house from the black car across the street. They lift Del by the armpits, dragging his rag-doll body down the steps, along the path, and to the car while I wait helplessly to see if Poe rings our doorbell and repeats the show with Patrick.

He doesn't; he only walks away from our house, folds himself into the rear seat of the black car next to an unconscious Del, and waits for me to drive away. Then the black car pulls from the curb, following my Honda all the way to Connecticut Avenue, where it turns and heads south. It crosses my mind to reverse course and go to the Rays' farm to warn Sharon, but I shunt the thought aside. I'd be caught or too late or—best case—have Morgan all over my ass for not showing up to work on time.

As I weave through morning traffic, I process the morning's events. Poe must think Del had the envelope all along, that he was about to deliver it, perhaps to some other address.

I don't have an eidetic memory—not even close. But I do have a head for text. In a previous life, or in a future life if I had access to books, I might make a decent editor. Not that I can write worth a shit, but I can process mistakes. And the ones I'm processing as I wind through traffic on my way to meet Lorenzo and Lin are the twin typos I found in the red and gold packets inside a manila envelope.

The errors aren't the only things running through my mind like rabid hamsters on a wheel. The very nature of three distinct teams duplicating one another's work shouldn't merit classified status. And my team was never classified, or if it was, our president declassified it in a press conference three days ago.

I park the Honda in my designated spot, between Lorenzo's Mustang and the space where Lin's Smart car should be but isn't. Inside the building, a soldier waves me through the checkpoint after taking my purse and laying it on the X-ray machine's belt.

"What's this?" I say.

"New security procedures," the soldier says, watching me. This time, there's no smile, no cheery *Have a nice day!*, only a pair of eyes, narrowed into slits, watching me from under the brim of his cap as I collect my bag and walk toward the bank of elevators where Morgan is waiting with crossed arms.

"You're late," he says.

"I was working through the night," I lie, and step into the open elevator.

Morgan follows. "You're not supposed to take work home, Jean. Or did you forget that one simple rule?"

I spin toward him, wishing I'd worn more than a pair of sandals so I could look down at the bastard. Still, our eyes are even. "No, I didn't forget, Morgan. I don't forget things. But I've got a working brain, so unless you want me to leave that locked up in your fucking lab, get off my back and let me do what I need to do, you little prick."

"I won't stand for that kind of talk," he says.

"Then sit. Or lie down. Or crawl in a hole. I don't care. I'm busy."

"I'm writing this up. I'm sending a report to—"

"To who? To the president? Fine. Tell him I'm taking the rest of the month off for bad behavior." I punch the Close Doors button on the elevator before slipping out, leaving Morgan to fester.

"What the hell was that all about?" Lorenzo says. He's in the corridor between the elevator and the lab, dressed casually but smartly in a polo and khakis under his white coat.

"I hate that piece of shit," I say. "Where's Lin?"

"Hasn't come in yet. Guess we have the lab all to ourselves." Mischief lights up his eyes as he closes the gap between us.

A quickie on one of the epoxy resin counters isn't part of my schedule today, but we do need to talk. "Show me what you've been working on," I say, inserting my key card into the main door of the laboratory. Mice and rabbits greet us with a cacophony of squeaks and chatter. I wish Lin were here, not only because I don't want to inject the animals myself.

What I know needs to be shared.

Lorenzo turns on the tap in the biochem lab and starts washing his hands, rubbing soap in between each finger, scrubbing his nails one at a time, inspecting each digit. "Well?"

"The three teams. They're sort of the same, but different." I think back to the goals statements, to the way two of the teams seemed identical in one way, and two others in another. All because of one little word: "anti." At the time, sitting cross-legged on the cool of the bathroom floor, I thought it was a typo.

Lorenzo continues the charade of washing his hands, turning up the water, leaning in closer to the faucet.

"Our team's goal is development of the anti-Wernicke serum," I say. "At first, I thought the Gold team's goal was identical, but then it hit me—there's nothing top secret about what we're doing here, I mean what you and Lin and I are working on."

"You don't advertise classified shit to a press conference," Lorenzo says, agreeing.

"Right. So the Gold team's packet left out one word."

He raises an eyebrow.

"Anti," I whisper. "That team isn't developing an anti-Wernicke serum, and the Red team isn't working on water solubility for an anti-Wernicke serum. The 'anti' was missing there, too."

"Holy shit," he says, staring at his hands. "You're sure it wasn't a typo?"

"No. I'm not sure. I can't be sure. But it makes sense. It's the only thing that explains why the materials are classified, and why Morgan has a single binder labeled 'Project Wernicke.' We'd always called it Anti-Wernicke, or, later, Wernicke-X. Just like you wouldn't be working on a cancer cure and name your study 'Project Cancer.'"

"Not unless you were developing cancer in a lab," he says. "It sounds wrong."

I tell him about Patrick and Del, the locked mailbox, Poe's men coming to take Del away this morning. "They know," I say. "Poe or someone knows there's an underground operation, and they know they've found out what's really going on."

For a long time, we look at each other over the running water, careful to keep our heads bent toward the sink. There isn't anything to say, because we both know our work is being reverse engineered somewhere in this building.

Whether Reverend Carl is behind it, or Morgan or the president or the Pure Movement, doesn't matter. It could be all of them, all working to create a serum that doesn't cure aphasia, but causes it.

FIFTY

Lorenzo and I prep two groups of mice for injections. Each set will receive one of the two neuroproteins he's been formulating, and, with luck, we'll know which direction we need to take by the end of the day, when half of the mice are dead. As I remove the tiny creatures from their cages and shave a square patch of fur from them, one by one, a single word ping-pongs around my brain.

Why?

The answer comes much too easily, also in the form of a single word: *silence.*

Lorenzo reaches over and takes the brown mouse from my shaking hands. "I'll do it," he says, guiding the clippers along its flank. "There. You put Mickey in the Group One cage. And don't worry, I'll take care of the injections."

"I'm that bad?"

"Let's say you're a little unsteady this morning. No big deal." He pats me on the shoulder, and I jump. "One thing at a time, Gianna."

I watch his hands with their long fingers, tipped with calluses from years of fret work and strumming, as he sedates the next mouse, waits for it to relax in his palm, and shaves another square patch. "This one's Group Two," he says, handing its limp body back to me. Another Mickey or Minnie goes into the second cage.

"They're monsters," I say.

Lorenzo nods. He knows I don't mean the mice.

Now it's two winters ago, and I'm back in my own living room sitting next to Olivia King as she sips coffee and watches Jackie go to battle with three Pure Women, their pastel twinsets a quiet contrast to Jackie's red power suit. Olivia is nodding at the twinset women, shaking her head violently every time Jackie opens her mouth.

"Someone should shut that woman up," Olivia says. "Permanently."

Oh, Olivia, I think, *what the hell did you expect?*

They'll start with the women in the camps, I suppose. Jackie, Julia, Annie Wilson from down the street. We won't see any of it televised. Next, Reverend Carl will round up people like Del and Sharon, squelching the last hope of any resistance. Before they take away his voice, though, they'll go to work on Del, maybe use his three daughters as an incentive. And Del, of course, will talk. What father wouldn't?

Patrick will be next in line. I feel my heart stop as I think of the methods they'll use on him, of the threats to Sonia that will encourage him to speak. And so on and so on, until every last member of what must already be a threadbare operation is found, forced to talk, and ultimately silenced.

With my own damnable creation.

I don't believe this will be the end.

Lorenzo touches my shoulder again. "We're all finished for now. You okay?"

I shake my head.

Minus a husband, and plus the wrist counter that goes back on once I've finished my work here, I'll have no means to take care of a house or children. Steven might manage to hold things together for a while, if

Steven ever comes back. If not, with Patrick's parents both dead and mine in Italy, the McClellan clan is finished, extinct.

And then there's my baby. Lorenzo's baby.

I've spent so much of my time thinking about what used to be, how I used to be, but the future always remained a blur. Up until now, that is. Now I see ghosts of years to come, only malformed swirls at first, then coalescing into razor-sharp pictures in full color. Me, babbling nonsense phrases after they inject me with a serum of my own making. Me, bent-backed and gray, pulling at a patch of weeds with hands I no longer recognize. Me, lying on a cot under a thin blanket, shivering in winter. Me, vacant-eyed and, perhaps, teetering on the edge between awareness and insanity, wondering where they all went to. Steven, Sam, Leo, Sonia. Baby.

Only when Lorenzo takes me by the arm and pulls me up do I realize I've been sitting on the lab floor, my back resting against the bottom row of empty wire cages.

"It's all right, Gianna," he says, brushing the tears from my eyes with his fingers. "It's all right."

"It isn't, you know."

"It will be."

I want to bury myself inside him, but I remember the cameras. "I'm fine," I say, straightening myself out. "Let's get on with the injections."

When I first started experiments with lab animals, I had one golden rule: don't name them. In other words, don't think of them as pets; don't think of them as anything other than a way to get from point A to point B. Think of them as test tubes or Petri dishes or microscope slides, nothing more than innate vehicles to fill and observe. While I hold each tiny mouse for Lorenzo to inject with a potion that will either cure it or kill it, all I can think of is the names I've given them:

Jackie. Lin. Jean.

FIFTY-ONE

Lorenzo's idea is risky, but necessary.

After we've called upstairs for an assistant to clean up the lab and filed a report for Morgan, I leave first, retracing my steps through the security checkpoint. There's a new pair of soldiers on guard during the afternoon shift, their uniforms pressed to sharp creases, their boots shined to a high polish that reflects the entry vestibule's fluorescent lights. My purse goes back on the conveyor belt to be scanned while one of the soldiers pats me down, his hands running short, swift arcs over my hips, back, stomach, breasts. Once cleared, I walk out into the May sunshine.

May 31, I think, is my birthday, the day Steven ran off with a wad of cash from Patrick's wallet, and the day I'll meet Lorenzo for another secret rendezvous in a rented Maryland crab shack.

We decided to take opposite routes from the city, so I follow traffic south toward the highway that cuts through Washington, past the fish market that's still there at the waterside. I wonder where the fish come from. Maine? North Carolina? Probably both. I don't wonder who works in the processing factories, gutting and scaling, packing and freezing. Maybe one day, I'll have a job doing the same. Long hours. No pay. Permanent stench of fish in my skin.

Lin was wrong about the economy falling apart. It might not be thriving, but the machine chugs along at a constant, working speed. Our workforce wasn't cut in half, only reassembled and redistributed. Men who performed unskilled labor were replaced with whoever the Pure deemed unworthy of hanging about in society. Industries—and that all-encompassing industry, government—cherry-picked freshly graduated males from the country's top universities to fill the gaps women left: CEOs, doctors, lawyers, engineers.

It was an eminently doable reworking of the system.

I've been pushing Steven out of my mind all day, and now the sadness uncorks itself and spills out of me. There were so many times I wanted to blame him, but I can't. Monsters aren't born, ever. They're made, piece by piece and limb by limb, artificial creations of madmen who, like the misguided Frankenstein, always think they know better.

He won't get far, anyway, even with the cash. Steven will find his way back home. This is one thing I have to believe.

The traffic subsides at the same time my tears run out, just as I pull the Honda onto the exit ramp and turn eastward toward the Chesapeake Bay, that land of William Styron and blue crabs and sailboats skimming over calm waters. It's a long drive, but a quiet one, and it gives me time to think.

If the Wernicke cure works, which I expect it will, I'll ask Morgan to have a dose sent to my mother in the Italian hospital. That small benefit is a single bright ray of sun in an otherwise drab landscape. Not much, but it's something to hold on to.

Lorenzo's car sits in the driveway of the shack, radiating distorting waves of heat from its hood. Of course he's arrived first—you can take the mad Italian driver out of Italy, but you can't take the madness out of him. I drive past it, up to the next lot, which has stood vacant since the time Lorenzo rented our place. The rule is, first one arriving parks at the shack; second, in the empty lot. I've never been first.

He's in the kitchen, or what would be a kitchen if it contained more than a sink, a two-burner stove, and a cube-shaped refrigerator for water and wine. We never wasted time cooking in this place. Not food, anyway.

I had everything planned out during the drive. Get in, talk, and get out. But when he lays a hand on my right cheek, the plans all go to hell. It isn't Lorenzo leading me to the small bedroom off the kitchen, a dark and wood-paneled room with a single window we've never opened. Instead, I take his hand from where it rests on my cheek and lead him.

The last time, there wasn't any talk. I still had my wrist counter on, and Lorenzo stayed silent, perhaps out of solidarity. He didn't whisper my name, as Patrick did, and he had no words of pity. He simply didn't speak as he moved over me and in me. We're still quiet today, our hands and bodies reciting the words for us, but inside me are the clangs and horns of an orchestra playing full out.

After one round of love, we go at it again, this time slowly and unrushed, as if we had days or years, not hours. Not fractions of hours.

When he finally softens—in every sense of the word—Lorenzo lies on top of me, covering me with his body like a shield that blacks out the world.

"I can get you out," he says.

For a moment, I'm not sure what he means, but he reaches over to where his jeans lie with mine, twin puddles of denim on the pine floor, and comes back to me with a slim burgundy booklet in his hand.

I recognize it immediately, the cogwheel and five-pointed star surrounded by branches—olive for peace, oak for strength.

"How did you get this?" I say, leafing through the new passport. Page two has my picture, but another woman's name: Grazia Francesca Rossi. The birthdate matches my age, roughly.

"I have friends," he says. "Well, friends who can be bought."

"Who's Grazia?" Rossi is a common surname in Italy, but the coincidence seems over the top. "Your sister?"

Lorenzo shakes his head. "No. I don't have a sister. Grazia is—was—my wife." He doesn't wait for me to ask before explaining. "She died five years ago."

"Oh," I say, as if he's given me a piece of ordinary news, a weather report, the outcome of the World Series, where the next Winter Olympics will be hosted. I don't ask questions, and he doesn't offer answers. "I can't leave, you know."

There's no argument from him, only his hand running down my body, starting at my collarbone and stopping an inch above my sex. "What if it's a girl, Gianna?"

FIFTY-TWO

What if it is a girl?

I lie on my side, one finger tracing the gold emblem on the front of my passport, this gift that cost Lorenzo the earth, my ticket out of hell. Our ticket out, I think, holding my other hand to my belly. Only an hour ago I was thinking about Styron, and now, here I am, his short-lived Sophie, lying with her man, a terrible, Solomonic choice dangling in the space above us.

Which one? Which one do I save?

"How long do I have to think about it?" I ask, here in the dark of our bedroom.

We both know I don't have long, not once we stage our first trial on Monday.

"We could stall the project," I say. "Buy a few weeks."

"Would that be enough?"

"No."

Suddenly I'm thinking of a beach from more than twenty years ago, not a posh beach, not Cancún or Bermuda or anything—Jackie and I could barely scrape together the cash for a couple of nights in a crappy motel with no ocean view. But we went every summer to Rehoboth, to drink beer and sun ourselves and escape the madness of grad school for a few days. The last time we were there, I told her I'd socked away some money. We could stay another day, maybe two.

"Would that be enough?" Jackie said, sucking on a Corona she'd plucked from the cooler and squeezed a wedge of lime into.

"No." I laughed.

"It all ends, Jeanie. Sooner or later. You can't stay in the vacation bubble forever, you know."

I don't remember whether we stayed the extra day in that motel room, or whether we drove back the following morning. What I do remember is thinking, once we hauled the beach bags and suitcases full of bikinis and suntan lotion into our apartment, that it really didn't matter. Sooner or later, we'd be right there in our Georgetown hovel, throwing leftovers turned science experiments out of the fridge, checking the piled-up mail, losing our tans, diving back into the academic grind.

Jackie, once again, was right. Sooner or later, it all ends.

"It crossed my mind," I tell Lorenzo. "When Reverend Carl first asked me, I thought maybe he'd invented the whole story about the president's brother's head injury. I remember standing in my kitchen, wondering if he'd take my work and reverse engineer it." I flop back on the pillow, wishing it would swallow me whole.

"Not your fault," Lorenzo says.

But it is. And my fault didn't start when I signed Morgan's contract on Thursday. My fault started two decades ago, the first time I didn't vote, the umpteen times I told Jackie I was too busy to go on one of her marches or make posters or call my congressmen.

"Tell me I don't have to leave this bed," I say. "Ever."

Lorenzo checks his watch. "The mice have two more hours to go. It'll take forty-five minutes to drive back to the lab."

"An hour," I say. "For me, at least. Remember, I'm not Mario Andretti."

"So we have an hour."

I say I can't, but I do. And this time, I'm not silent. I scream with my body and my voice, nails digging into the bedclothes or into Lorenzo's skin. I bite and moan and scratch like a feral cat on amphetamines, letting out all the stress and all the fear and all the hate, pouring it from me into him. He takes every last drop of it, then gives some back, pulling my hair, gnawing at my lips and breasts, attacking me with kisses. It's violent, but it's still love, a tandem scream from us to the rest of the world, and all of the world's sins.

FIFTY-THREE

We allow ourselves fifteen minutes to clean up and decide what happens next.

"There's another lab," I say, letting the shower rain over my skin. The hot water stings when it hits an abrasion. I look down and realize I'm a mess. "Oh Christ."

"Your face is fine. Perfect, actually," Lorenzo says, working up a lather in my hair. "And you're right: there has to be another lab. But we won't get inside it."

"We have to."

He rinses off and leaves me to deal with the rat's nest my hair has become. Two minutes later, he's back in the cramped bathroom, leaning one hip on the sink while he talks. "Listen to me, Gianna. Even if we get into their other lab, which we won't, what then? Arson? We'd be caught. Steal their supplies? Sure, and if we weren't caught by those security creeps with an armful of vials on our way out the door—which, by the way, we would be—then what happens? It's the government, honey. It's a machine. They'll only start again. By next year, you and Lin will be picking fish guts out of your nails." Lorenzo pauses, then says, "If you stay."

I consider this. He's right. "So we do nothing?" I step out of the shower and start toweling. "Nothing at all?"

"No. We do something. We get the fuck out of here."

"I have kids, Enzo. Four of them. Even if I could leave Patrick—"

He looks me up and down, pausing at the swell of my belly. "Well. I have one, too. Do I get a say?"

"You could take her—it, him, whatever it is. You could take her away." Even as I speak the words, I know it's impossible. By the time this baby's come to term, who knows what new enforcements will be in place?

"We both know that can't happen," he says, sterner now, decisive. "It's now or never, Gianna."

"No. It's next week or never. I have a test on Monday and should have the results by midweek."

"And?"

And here, in this crab shack that smells of sweat and semen and love, I make my decision.

"If it's a girl, I'll go with you. As soon as you want."

He waits, watching me dress and comb out my hair. He waits an eternity before speaking. Then he pulls me close, whispering into my ear. "Okay, Gianna. Okay." His voice sounds strong, but I know he's praying to a god neither of us believes in that the genetic analysis comes back as a double X. A baby girl.

"Come on," I say. "We need to get back. I'll go first."

The air is cooler now, and the few spare vacation houses cast shadows where, when I arrived at the shack, there were none. I click open the Honda, climb in, and think about what I would pray for—a boy or a girl. Stay or leave. Watch Sonia taken away from me, or, in a marginally more pleasant scenario, watch while some uniformed male nurse, following orders, injects her with a concoction that will take all her words away, forever. I don't think I could stand it either way.

I pray to a god I don't believe in for a girl, so I don't have to witness any of this. And I pray to that same god for a boy, so I never have to leave my Sonia.

FIFTY-FOUR

Lin has not made an appearance today, the soldiers at the security checkpoint tell me as they pat me down for a third time.

"No, ma'am," one says. He's the same spit-polished youngster who frisked me when I left. The name above his left breast pocket is PETROSKI, W.

"I need to see Morgan," I say.

"Who?"

"Dr. LeBron." Calling him "Dr." anything brings a nasty taste of bile to my mouth. He doesn't deserve the title.

Sergeant Spit-and-Polish Petroski checks my bag, even though it's already been X-rayed, and nods to his partner. After two rings, Morgan picks up.

"What?" he says.

The soldier picks up my key card, turning it over in his hands, reading my name. "Dr. McClellan says she needs to see you."

"Tell her I'm busy."

That strident voice, as squeaky as a lab rat's, pierces the air between the soldier and me. It's how I think of Morgan, as a rat, a foul and vicious, but not too bright, creature.

"Tell him we're about to check on the mice," I say to the soldier. "But I want to brief him first."

Again, the squeak, this time tinged with a thin hopefulness, says, "Send her up. With an escort."

Thirty seconds later, I'm in an elevator with a man—no, a boy—not much older than Steven. For no reason I understand, I think of what he might have been like as a college kid, sucking cheap beer through a funnel bong, pledging at a fraternity, dragging himself sleepy-eyed to an early-morning calculus class.

"Did you go to college?" I ask.

"Yes, ma'am."

"What did you major in?" I'm thinking poli-sci or prelaw or history.

He stiffens next to me but doesn't turn. "Philosophy, ma'am."

"They teach you how to fire one of those in Epistemology 101?" I say, nodding to the service piece on his hip. I expect him to clam up, tell me it's none of my business. *Move along now, ma'am. Nothing to see here.*

But he doesn't. Instead, his lower lip trembles slightly, and I see the boy inside Sergeant Petroski's smart uniform.

"No, ma'am," he says.

The old saying goes *Keep a stiff upper lip*, but as I watch his reflection in the polished steel walls of the elevator, I think that it isn't the upper lip we need to worry about. The bottom one gives our terror away. Every single time.

I decide not to torture him with further questions. Petroski's only a boy, after all, a kid who took a wrong turn at a sign somewhere along life's road, not so different from Steven. Although Steven, after a brief detour, turned back. Maybe this one will, too.

"There's still time," I say, not really knowing whether I'm talking to the young soldier or to myself.

The elevator doors slide open into their hidden pockets at the same time a mechanical voice—female, it turns out—says "Floor Five," and the young Petroski turns slightly, extending his arm, showing me out. It's so quick, I almost miss it, the three measured blinks of his eyes.

Blink once for yes, twice for no.

Or three times for Not Pure.

I bat my eyes at him, a gesture that the cameras might pick up, or not, but if they do, I can make something up. A bug in my eye, a stray lash, strain.

"Let's go," I say.

On Saturday afternoon, the fifth-floor corridor should be a ghost town, all those generals and admirals out golfing or batting tennis balls or playing Axis and Allies in their basements. But every office door is open, and behind every door is a man at a desk, busy and focused.

The third door on my right after we've left the elevator bank has a brass nameplate with WINTERS, J. on it. Inside, the man behind the desk looks up from his work, scowls, and returns to reading. He's the same one I saw yesterday afternoon, and the same name I read on the Gold team's list last night.

"Here we are," Sergeant Petroski says. He knocks—three sharp military raps—at Morgan's closed door.

"Enter."

Petroski turns on one polished heel. "Good luck, ma'am. On the project, I mean. I'll take you back down when you're ready."

Morgan stands when I enter, offers me a seat, and punches a button on his desk phone. "Andy, bring coffee for two." He looks at me. "Milk? Sugar?"

"Black," I say, returning the smile. If he's feeling magnanimous, why not join the party, even if his eyes do remind me of the lab mice Lorenzo injected this morning?

He relays the order to Andy, his assistant, and sits in the chair behind his desk, the chair that he's ratcheted up so that he looks larger. It must be painful, I think, to sit like that without your feet touching the floor.

"So, progress?"

I check the clock above Morgan's head. "We'll know in about thirty minutes. Where's Lin?"

The non sequitur slows him, as if someone has just offered him ice cream, then given him a choice between anchovy and tuna. As he processes what I've said, the corners of his mouth turn, first down, then straight, then up again. "That's terrific. Think we'll be ready to roll tomorrow?"

"Our first subject is scheduled for Monday."

"Change it to tomorrow," he says. Then, "If you can, Jean. Only if you can."

I take the cue to play nice. He wants something; I want something. "Absolutely."

Morgan relaxes now, and Andy knocks softly before bringing in a tray.

"Let me," I say, tipping the carafe over two white mugs with a blue *P* emblem. "Listen. I'm sorry I yelled at you earlier."

"We're all under a great deal of stress, Jean. Peace."

Sure. Peace. I almost remind Morgan that the word for "peace" and the word for "submission" are virtually identical in some languages, but there's no point in confusing him. I need the bastard too much.

"I have a small favor to ask. My mother's suffered a burst aneurysm. Left hemisphere. Wernicke's area."

Morgan's eyes narrow, but he says nothing.

It's hard to tell whether these eyes convey concern or sympathy or distrust, so I press on, feeling my way one step at a time. "I was wondering, since we're starting the clinical trials anyway, could we put her on the subject list?"

"Of course we can. Bring her in tomorrow and set it up."

"Well," I say, "that's going to be difficult. She's in Italy."

He sits back, one elbow on each of the chair's armrests, his right ankle resting on his left knee, as if he's trying to occupy as much space as possible. "Italy," he repeats.

"Yes. You know, land of pizza and ass-kicking coffee." *Unlike the crap Andy brought in,* I think.

"I have a problem with that, Jean. Relations between us and Europe are"—he searches for a word—"not good."

Just like Morgan. Of all the English terms he has to pick from—"tenuous," "strained," "problematic," "tense," "adverse," "hostile," "unpropitious"—Morgan chooses "not good."

He continues, his eyes moving slightly up and to the left, a sure sign he's creating a lie, or holding back, but I don't think Morgan's aware of the subconscious tic; most liars aren't. "You understand, don't you, Jean? I mean, we can't just send a valuable product like this over to Europe. Not with the current climate."

My coffee tastes more bitter with each sip. "What if you sent me? I could administer the serum and—"

"Ha!" The single syllable is more bark than word. "You know the travel rules," he says, softening, but only slightly. "No way."

How could I have forgotten? "All right, then. Lorenzo. He can travel."

Morgan shakes his head, as if he's about to explain a difficult mathematical construct to a child, a concept so far outside my capacity to understand that he thinks breaking it down would be useless. "He's Italian, Jean. A European citizen."

"He's one of us," I say.

"Not really."

"So that's it?"

He starts shuffling papers on his desk, Morgan's classic this-meeting-is-now-over tell. "Sorry, Jean. Call me when the mice are ready, okay?"

"Sure." I turn to leave his office. "By the way, where's Lin?"

"No idea," he says, and his eyes move up and to the left.

FIFTY-FIVE

As I ride the elevator down to the basement, a series of horrible vignettes flashes through my mind.

Doctors in France, their brains intact in all but one place, are unable to process the instructions on a bottle of hand sanitizer, let alone talk to their patients, write prescriptions, perform surgery. German stockbrokers will happily tell their clients to *Dig!* instead of *Buy*, and *Fork!* instead of *Sell*. An airline pilot in Spain, charged with the safe delivery of two hundred passengers, interprets the warnings of an air traffic controller as a raunchy joke, and laughs as her craft dives into Mediterranean waters. And so on, and so on, until an entire continent is drowning in a languageless chaos, ripe to be taken over.

"You let me know if you need anything," Sergeant Petroski says when the elevator reaches the first floor. He steps out, not looking back, and takes his post at the checkout point as five men file in through the main doors.

So. Lorenzo and I aren't the only ones working today. *Quelle* fucking surprise.

I continue down to the basement, every second feeling like another step on a journey to hell. Inside the lab, Lorenzo is sitting before two cages of mice, studying paperwork.

"Group One," he says quietly.

He doesn't need to say anything. The cage labeled ONE is a circus of frisky rodents, chattering and squeaking, milling about their little mouse community as if they're at a church social. The second cage holds a dozen lifeless creatures, their furry bodies already stiffening with rigor.

I hate myself for giving them names.

Mice don't have the capacity for language, but we didn't need them to, not for this final test. Because of Lin's previous work—thankfully—I didn't have to take part in the ape experiments of two years ago; we already isolated the neurolinguistic components of our serum. The mice today serve a single purpose: to test the two neuroproteins Lorenzo developed. None of us wants to inject a human subject with a toxin.

But, of course, this is exactly what will happen.

I sit next to Lorenzo and slide one of the blank lab reports from his pile toward me. In small letters, I write one word in the top corner of the sheet, covering it over with my other hand:

Bioweapon.

As soon as he's read it, I crumple the page and take it through the internal door to the biochem lab. Lorenzo follows, and together we watch the paper turn yellow, then black, as it disintegrates in the blue flame of a Bunsen burner.

"You're sure?" he says, twisting the sink tap open and staring at the ashes.

"No, but it makes sense." I tell him about my conversation with Morgan upstairs. "Think about it, Enzo. Project Anti-Wernicke, Project Wernicke, and Project Water Solubility. Injections take time—rounding people up, training the medical techs. That would give them a chance to escape. Spike a city's water supply, though, and you might as well drop a neutron bomb." I snap my fingers. "Bang. But without the sound."

"That's insane," Lorenzo says.

"So is Reverend Carl. And by the way," I say, wiping down the epoxy resin counter, getting rid of all traces of burned paper before we call Morgan downstairs, "our fearless leader wants the trials scheduled for tomorrow."

"They're moving fast."

"Yes. They are."

I let Lorenzo call Morgan on the intercom so I don't have to talk to the son of a bitch any more than absolutely necessary. Meanwhile, I prep vials of the first neuroprotein serum and fill out the day's report. The mice—the dead ones—I lock inside a freezer so Lin can work her post-mortem magic on them when she gets here.

If Lin ever gets here.

"She didn't say anything to you yesterday, did she?" I ask when Lorenzo is off the intercom.

He shakes his head. "Only that she was going to meet a friend for dinner."

"Which friend?"

"You remember Isabel?"

"How could I forget?" I say.

Isabel Gerber used to hang about our department when she wasn't teaching advanced Spanish conversation. Argentine, but of Swiss descent, she stood a foot taller than Lin, wore her hair in a blond waterfall down her back, and spoke with a slight and charming lisp. The two women were poster girls for polar opposites, but they clicked in every way a couple can click.

Until last year, when they cut it off, canceled their engagement, and did what every gay man and woman had to do to avoid being shipped off to a camp: they never spoke to each other again. Not that there was a hell of a lot to talk about once Lin's and Isabel's wrist counters went on.

"I hope they're being careful," I say. The thought of Lin, big brained and small bodied, working off her sins of the flesh with her bare hands, makes me cringe. Jackie could deal with that shit. But Lin's not Jackie. And then another, more sinister, thought weasels its way in: *what if we're all being followed?*

I shake the question from my head—there's no room for any more thoughts, not one single neuron left to spare—and wash dead mouse off my hands while we wait for Morgan.

"So. Monday," Lorenzo says. He's not talking about work.

"Monday. Afternoon."

The clock on the lab wall says five. I have less than forty-eight hours to make what I know will be an irreversible decision.

My parents, this baby the size of an orange inside me, and Lorenzo balance on one side of the scale. Patrick and the kids, on the other. Two seemingly inevitable but different fates hang over each choice like storm clouds. Stay and wait for Reverend Carl to ratchet up his terrible game, or go and watch Europe crumble to its knees, close-up, front row, best seats in the house.

Next to me, Lorenzo inches closer, enough so that our hands touch. It's a solid feeling, those fingers of his brushing mine.

But it's not enough.

FIFTY-SIX

It's nearly seven o'clock by the time I pull my Honda into the driveway. The sky is still light enough that I can't imagine winter or the darkness it brings. At this time of year, I always fool myself into thinking winter won't come.

But it will. It always does.

Patrick has told Sonia and the twins a white lie, although I'm not sure how white it is, which explains why they're in the middle of three simultaneous board games instead of moping about Steven's absence. Sonia breaks away from her brothers to hug me. "I'm winning!" she says. "Again!"

I raise an eyebrow at Patrick.

"I said he went to stay with a friend for a couple of days," he tells me, then glances over at the kids and their forest of plastic pieces. "Sam, Leo, watch your sister. Your mom and I are going outside for a few minutes."

"We are?" I say.

"We are. Here, Jean." He hands me the bottle of beer he's just popped the cap off of. "You might need this."

Jean. Not "babe" or "hon," but "Jean." Patrick's in business mode. Or he's pissed off, which makes sense. In the past twenty-four hours, I've committed two crimes. Maybe more, if I throw in tampering with the mail.

"Come on." He opens the back door and leads me as far from the house as possible. "Got anything you want to tell me?"

I swallow, not sure which is worse—stealing the project envelope and reading it, or spending half of the afternoon with Lorenzo. Or, I think, being two and a half months pregnant. *Don't forget that one, Jean.*

He brushes a stray lock of hair from his forehead. "Look. I know you were in my office."

"I wanted to FaceTime my father," I lie.

"Nice try, babe, but no. I checked the call log on the kitchen phone."

Well. If nothing else, we're back to "babe."

He sits down on one side of the bench, pulling me to join him. I back away. "I'm not going to bite, you know," he says.

Automatically, my right hand moves up to my collar, and I tug the material closer around my neck. Just in case I've brought home any souvenirs from the crab shack. "Okay," I say, and sit next to him.

"I saw a man executed once," he says, staring straight ahead into the thicket of azaleas now past their late-spring flush of color. "It was last September. September first, actually. At two twenty-three in the afternoon."

I don't know what to say, so I ask the first question that pops into mind. "You remember the time? The exact time?"

"Yeah. I never saw a man—or woman—die before that. Hell, I never saw an animal die. Kinda sticks in your brain, you know? Anyway, he was from my office. One of the junior scientists, worked on liaisons between the administration and the other organizations, National Science Foundation, Centers for Disease Control, NIMH, stuff like that. He was always throwing out those acronyms, Jimbo was. His name was Jim Borden, but we all called him Jimbo. Good guy. Had a young wife and a girl about Sonia's age, maybe a year younger. He liked to tell jokes. That's what I remember about him. Isn't that funny, Jean?"

It isn't, but I say it is.

Patrick takes a swallow of beer and smacks his lips. "The other funny thing, Jimbo was always blinking. I mean, like the way you blink when you've got a stray eyelash or a fleck of dust. He would do it in threes. Blink, blink, blink. Not to everyone, but I'd catch him at it every so often. Ever see anyone do that?"

I nod.

"Yeah. So, Jimbo kept his head down most of the time, shuffling around papers and making copies. Every afternoon, around three, he'd leave the office saying he had a meeting with some guy across town. He'd pack up his briefcase and walk right out the door. I don't know if anyone noticed, not at first, but when he came back, that briefcase seemed lighter. You could tell by watching the way he swung it. I never said anything about that. Not to anyone."

My beer is warm now, and I don't want it. I set the bottle down on the flagstone and turn back to Patrick. "But someone caught him."

"Someone always catches them, babe. Always. Sooner or later, you fuck up." There's a pause, and then: "I don't mean you. I mean 'you,' like, in the general sense." He pats my hand, and all I notice is how clean his hands are. "He must have seen it coming. Jimbo, that is. Because the week before they shot him, he came to me. Asked if I was as pure as the rest of them." Patrick laughs lightly, but there's no humor in it. "Guess I don't look like a bad guy, eh?"

"No. You don't." I've never thought of Patrick as a bad guy, only a keep-your-head-down-and-shut-up kind of guy. But I don't say this. I know where the conversation is going.

"Jimbo left something for me, before they took him out of the office in handcuffs. Just a name and a number. Said it was my decision whether to make contact or not, and that he hoped I would but wouldn't hold it against me if I stepped aside. That's how I got in touch with Del. You saw what happened to Del this morning."

"Yeah."

"They'll shoot him, you know. Like they shot Jim Borden. They put us in a bus, Jean. Well, two buses. Drove us up to Fort Meade, not saying a word about where we were headed. Some team-building exercise was the rumor. I can still see him. I see him every single day at two twenty-three in the afternoon. Jimbo there, cuffed to a post, staring out at all of us as Reverend Carl read the scripture. Glory, glory fucking hallelujah, we've got a fox in the henhouse, men, and there's only one way to deal with a prying fox. Thomas—you remember Thomas—well, it was that son of a bitch who did the shooting. No trial, no jury of peers, no last request. They just fucking shot him, there in the rifle range of Fort Meade. I watched Jimbo go down, slump down the pole he was cuffed to, watched him bleed out life onto a patch of sand that was already stained red."

Patrick leans over, picks up my beer, and swallows it down in one long gulp. "Anyway, that's why I didn't tell you. When they come for me, it's better if you don't know anything." *When. Not if.*

"But I do now," I say.

"I guess you do, babe. I guess you do."

"Steven?" I don't want to ask the question, but I can't help myself. "If he makes it up to North Dakota and they find him—"

Instead of answering, Patrick folds himself forward, head buried in his hands.

FIFTY-SEVEN

There's no love tonight, but there is.

We put three children to bed and silently make a wish for Steven, that he turns back before it's too late. Then Patrick takes me to bed, wrapping himself around me.

"You need to get out," he says. "Any way you can."

"I can't," I say, even though I can.

"You know someone, don't you? That Italian who worked in your department."

So this is what it's like, having my own husband sanction my affair.

I get out of bed and take Patrick's hand. "Let's have a drink."

On the way to the kitchen, I still haven't fleshed out the story, not the whole story, not the end of the story, but I know how it begins. And it might as well begin with the truth. I take out two glasses and pour an inch of neat scotch into Patrick's, a full measure of water into mine.

"No grappa tonight?" he says.

Everything is about to spill out: that first day in Lorenzo's office with the music box, when I watched his long musician's fingers and imagined them playing over my skin. The oldness I felt seeing Steven, only a baby yesterday, rush into his teens. Boredom after so many years of the same man, the same sex. Finally, my anger at Patrick's passiveness, the meeting with Lorenzo after bumping into him at Eastern Market. The baby. My new passport.

Except, before I talk, I think.

I think all of these things, imagining the words bouncing off the tiled walls of our kitchen. In reality, there is no perpetual motion; all energy eventually gets absorbed, morphs into a different shape, changes state. But these words that I'm about to unleash, they'll never be absorbed. Each syllable, each morpheme, each individual sound, will bounce and ricochet forever in this house. We'll carry them with us like that cartoon character who's always surrounded by his own dirt cloud. Patrick will feel them prick like invisible, poisonous darts.

The way things turn out, I don't have to say anything at all.

"I think you should go with him," Patrick says at last, as if he's seen the whole story in my eyes. "With the Italian."

I should be relieved, I think, that I didn't have to say the words. Instead, I'm sick from having to hear Patrick say them, sick realizing his knowledge of who I am comes not from prying, but from years of intimacy. His voice is cold; an artificial chill sharpens its edges. I reach out and lay my hand on his arm, and two things happen.

His own hand covers mine. He also turns away.

We stand there, a middle-aged married couple in a kitchen, a frying pan from dinner soaking in the sink, the coffee maker ready to go into action when morning comes. Everything about this tableau is normal, the simple routine of a life together.

Finally, he breaks away. It's nothing, really, only Patrick turning to busy himself by wiping a stray crumb from the counter or by checking the soaking pan. And at the same time, that break is everything. When he turns back to me, the V in his forehead seems deeper, almost branded onto his skin.

"Take Sonia," he says quietly. "I'll stay with the boys and figure out something."

"Patrick, I'm—"

Now it's his turn to console, and the hand he lays on me feels like a weight. "Don't, Jean. I'd rather leave things"—he sighs—"I don't know. I guess I'd rather we not go into it all. It's bad enough knowing. Okay?"

I have no idea what to say to this, so I push all the pain somewhere dark, to be taken out and dealt with later, to feel the sting on my own, in my private time. For now, Patrick doesn't need to know about the baby. "What will you do?"

"I said I'll figure out something." The V that I didn't think could deepen further does just that.

"Like what? You know what they're planning, don't you? A new serum, a goddamned water-soluble serum. How long do you think we'll last in Italy—or anywhere—before the whole goddamned world turns Pure Blue?"

He doesn't have an answer.

But I do. I don't need Patrick and his political insight to tell me what I already know. All those smiles and nods and *How about some coffee, Jean?* in Morgan's office aren't fooling me. I'm as disposable as an empty lipstick tube, or I will be the moment we test the new serum. The lab will keep me on, for a while, until we've established a successful track record, until they're sure I'm no longer needed. It will happen like this:

I'll be in my office, maybe seated at the desk with no phone, maybe standing at the wall that should have a window but doesn't. Morgan will knock at the door, only a perfunctory little rap, because I can't prevent him from entering, from penetrating my space. My office door is lacking a lock.

"Dr. McClellan," Morgan will say, possibly stressing the title, either because he's tired of having to use it or because he's relieved he won't have to use it anymore. "Would you please come with me?"

This will not be an invitation.

We'll walk down the corridor of offices, Morgan stretching his short legs to keep one pace in front of me. Whether this is a gesture of leadership, or whether he doesn't want to look me in the eye, I won't know, but I'll guess it has something to do with both.

I'll ask Morgan where we're going. Another meeting? Did he find a flaw in the serum? What I'll want to say, but won't, is *I'm next, aren't I?*

If I leave now with Lorenzo, I'll become Grazia Francesca Rossi. I'll shop in fruit markets and at butchers', visit my parents, make love to a man who's my husband on paper only. One day, maybe in a few weeks or months, after I've come back from a pleasant walk around the streets of old Rome, I'll have a glass of water in my own kitchen, as I'm doing now.

Jackie's words come back to me, trite but true.

It all ends, Jeanie. Sooner or later.

"Water," I say to Patrick.

He pours me another glass, misunderstanding. But then, I've only just figured it out myself.

"What would you do to get rid of all of them?" I say. "To go back to the way things were."

Again, I hear Jackie:

Think about what you need to do to stay free.

Patrick swallows the last of his scotch, considers the bottle, and pours another finger. I have to take it from him before whisky spills all over the counter—that's how badly his normally steady hands are shaking.

"Anything," he says after a long gulp. "Absolutely anything."

"Anything" is a funny little word, overused and rarely literal. *I'd do anything to get a date with her. I'll pay anything to get front-row seats to the concert. Anything you want. I don't need anything.* "Anything" never covers the whole gamut of existence.

I lean over the counter, close enough to smell the sweetness of scotch on his breath, until our noses are almost touching.

"Would you kill?" I say.

Patrick doesn't blink. For a moment, I wonder if he's still breathing. He's that still.

I have to remind myself of who and what Patrick is. The quiet guy. The one who doesn't want to get involved, who would rather talk theory than practice. The man Jackie called a cerebral pussy all those years ago in our crappy Georgetown flat with the rat-eaten secondhand sofa and the Ikea furniture whose veneer fell off a year after we'd assembled it. Also, he's a man who once swore to tread carefully in matters of life and death, who recited the promise *I must not play God.*

When he speaks, he says one word:

"Yes."

The kitchen, stuffy and still, turns cold.

Then he says, "But you know we don't have to."

"Exactly," I say.

All we need to do is take away their voices.

FIFTY-EIGHT

They say there's no rest for the wicked, so neither of us sleeps to-night. Instead, I go back into the rec room and retrieve my folder, the one with the red *X* I hid from Morgan only two days ago, and take it to Patrick's office.

He's waiting for me in the dark but flicks on his desk lamp when I come in.

Page by page, Patrick goes through the data. He stops at the section containing formulas written in Lorenzo's neat, continental hand. "You did this?"

I shake my head, then realize he can't see me. "No. Lorenzo."

"Huh."

"What?" I say, straining to read in the faint light.

"It's some kind of beautiful."

I understood, and still understand, little of Lorenzo's work, but Patrick's got the biochemistry background to process it. He reads every notation, every scribbled comment, his lips moving as he goes from page to page. When he reaches the bottom of the fourth sheet, he turns it, laying the paper flat on the others, facedown.

I'm not quick enough.

Patrick's head moves a hair to the left, away from page five of Lorenzo's notes, and his eyes settle on the back of the previous page.

We work differently, Patrick and I. My desks have always been cluttered with non-necessities: a framed photograph, a pack of gum, hand cream, more pens and pencils than I need. As a consequence, I move through loose paperwork by taking the top sheet and putting it at the back of the stack. Patrick, with a desk as sterile as a hospital floor, lays the stack down and makes two piles, one read, one unread, turning each finished page over and placing it to his left.

Which is why I've never seen what Lorenzo wrote on the back of page four.

It looks like a poem, but not a very structured one. The verse is chopped here and there, one word on a line, then a break, then a phrase. The upside-down text is impossible to read from where I sit opposite Patrick, but I make out the title clearly enough.

A Gianna.

To Gianna.

"Oh," Patrick says. His Italian is on a par with his Swahili, so I know he won't understand a thing. But there are certain words that will give it all away: *amore, vita,* my name. He takes off his reading glasses and looks across the desk at me. The light from the desk lamp shows every crease on his face. "He's very much in love with you."

"Yes."

"Is it mutual?"

I hesitate, and I suppose that's what gives me away, there in the dark, even though my own face must be nothing more than a vague outline.

"All right," he says. "All right."

As if it were.

"How about you put some coffee on, babe?" he says.

"Sure." I know he needs a minute, maybe several of them. In the kitchen, I measure out five scoops of high-test, fill the reservoir with water, and watch the coffee maker as it drips black tears into the empty carafe. When it's ready—when I'm ready—I load a tray with mugs and sugar and milk from a carton that is almost full, an awful reminder that Steven is gone. And I go back into the office.

Whether Patrick cried or not, I can't tell. He's all business now, making notes and looking up forgotten stoichiometric symbols in a chemistry text he's opened on the desk.

"Well?" I say.

He shakes his head. "It looks reversible, even easy, but I can't do it. For one, I don't have a lab. Second, it's been twenty years since I've worked in one. What about your—" He pauses, correcting himself. "What about Lorenzo? It's his brain baby anyway, right?"

At the word "baby," my coffee goes down the wrong way. "Right. What about the water-solubility problem?"

Patrick actually beams. "That's the brilliant part. It's already water soluble, at least for our purposes. Assuming you don't care about unwanted side effects." He points to Lorenzo's final work, the cognitive key that, when turned in the lock of cells in the superior temporal gyrus of the brain's left hemisphere, will open the door to repair. Or, in the case of the anti-serum, create a room full of word chaos.

I know what Patrick means, and I don't care about whatever ancillary problems might result from systemic application of the drug, not when we're talking about Reverend Carl Corbin's system. Or the president's.

"Think he can get to it by Monday morning?" Patrick says.

"That's soon."

"That's when the next all-staff meeting is scheduled for Project Wernicke. Your entire building will be at the White House."

"What about Reverend Carl?"

Patrick nods. "Him too."

Okay, I think. *Monday.* The clock on Patrick's desk glows six four one.

FIFTY-NINE

Wicked or not, I sleep, and for three sweet, dreamless hours I don't think about the plan, or Patrick, or Lorenzo. I don't think about where Steven might be, or whether Del the mailman turned spy is sitting in a locked room deciding whether to talk or watch his daughters beg while Thomas works them over. I don't think about Olivia King's burnt stump where her hand used to be, or whether Lin and Isabel have been caught and are now on their way to a prison.

Sleep is a fantastic eraser, as long as it lasts.

With nothing but coffee in my stomach, I leave for the lab, Patrick's notes folded up inside the powder compact I keep in my purse.

Lorenzo is in his office, making coffee.

"Want some?" he says.

"No way." I can already feel one ulcer burning through my stomach lining. I take out the compact, open it, quickly palm the paper, and slide it across his desk. "I'll go set things up for Mrs. Ray. Meet me downstairs when you're ready."

My own office is empty and dark, exactly the way I left it yesterday. I know Lin hasn't come back. Worse, I'm sure she's not going to come back.

So I have a plan. Hope, not so much.

In the elevator, my reflection stares back at me from three sides. From the front, I don't look so bad, a little puffy under the eyes, hair misbehaving as usual, face drawn somewhat from my recent diet of coffee and water. The side views show a different me than I'm accustomed to. I remind myself to straighten my shoulders and pick my chin up; there's no sense in letting Mrs. Ray see me beaten down; she'd only worry. I try sucking in my belly, but it's no use. The irregular bulge under my blouse reminds me I had to leave the top button of my jeans undone.

Christ, I hope Patrick didn't notice when he kissed me goodbye this morning.

Inside the lab, I say hello to the remaining rodents and rabbits, ignore the freezer where the dozen dead mice wait to be dissected, and prep one of the side rooms for Mrs. Ray. It's sparse and sterile, not exactly what I had in mind for her first moments rejoining the land of language, but I can make it better.

I head back into the room of cages and pick a snow-white rabbit from the top row, placing him in a plexiglass cube with airholes high on each side, adding a bed of wood chips, a water tube, and a scattering of food pellets from the storage container. I know they're alfalfa, but they smell like crap.

"There you go, Thumper," I tell him. "Got a new friend for you to meet."

Morgan walks in.

"What's that, Jean?" he says. "I thought you were finished with the animal tests."

Again, my brain tells my body to stand up straight. "He's for Mrs. Ray. I thought she might like to see something besides a white wall."

He shrugs, as if our first subject is nothing more than another lab animal. Which, I think, she is, in Morgan's mind.

"You coming down for the trial?" I say, carrying Thumper's plastic house closer to the room where I'll inject our first human subject.

"Wouldn't miss it."

I open the refrigerated cabinet, the one Lorenzo stored the vials of our anti-aphasia serum in. He's labeled the second group of vials—the ones that killed the mice—with a bright red *X* and segregated them on a different shelf. Where the six glass tubes should be, there's only one.

"Did you take these?" I ask Morgan.

"What?" His eyes move up and to the left as he dodges the question. He turns to leave, and I have an idea.

"Morgan, how plugged-in are you?"

His eyes narrow and his face hardens, suspicious and fearful at the same time.

"Oh," I say, forcing a girlish smile, "I was just wondering if you've ever been inside—you know—the White House."

Like a game fish after a chum line, he takes the bait I've thrown out, and relaxes.

Go on, little fishie, I think. *Go on and grab it. Sink your teeth in.*

"As a matter of fact," Morgan says and puffs himself up, once again trying to fill more space than he possibly can, "I'm an invited guest on Monday. All thanks to you, Jean. You're a real team player."

The smile stays plastered on my face, but this time I don't need to force it. "That's just wonderful, Morgan. Really wonderful. Listen, we need to get ready, so—"

He cuts me off. "Absolutely, Jean. Whatever you need. We'll bring Mrs. Ray down when the—when she arrives." He sticks his index finger into the rabbit's cage, wiggling it. "Hi there, little bunny."

"Not a good idea, Morgan," I say. "They're territorial."

"Nah. Just a cute little bunny rabbit." His hand shoots back as if he's touched fire. "Fuck! He bit me!" It's all I can do to stifle a laugh. "Fucking beast."

"Good for only one thing, right?" I say, watching the blood on Morgan's finger bubble. "Hang on. You won't die."

While I'm bandaging Morgan's rabbit wound, Lorenzo walks in.

"What happened?" he says.

"Rabbit-inflicted wound," I tell him, pouring more iodine than necessary over the puncture on Morgan's finger.

Lorenzo smiles. "Not the *Sylvilagus floridanus*, Dr. McClellan? Were they tested for rabies?" He leans over and inspects the wound, shaking his head. "Could be bad."

Morgan's face moves through the spectrum, from pink to green to the sickly shade of wallpaper paste. He doesn't see Lorenzo wink at me over his head.

"You'll be fine," I say, finishing the bandaging job and ushering him out of the lab. "See you in an hour or so." Then, turning to Lorenzo: "I wonder who's bringing Mrs. Ray in."

It won't be Del; I know that. Sharon is just as unlikely an escort— by now, she'll be in custody along with her husband. I picture Poe and his gang of thugs in business suits and black SUVs and dark sunglasses driving up the dirt road to the Rays' farm, tearing through barns and stables until they find Del's workshop. It's an ugly mental image.

"So?" I say to Lorenzo.

He nods. "Biochem lab." Then, in Italian, he whispers, "I'll need to work through the night, and all day tomorrow, but I can do it."

I put Thumper's plexiglass house into the room where Mrs. Ray will be and consider filling Lorenzo in on my early-morning activities and conversations. The poem. The defeated, but somehow accepting, tiredness in Patrick's eyes. Instead, as we cross the white tile of the main lab to the locked door at the other side, I switch gears.

"Morgan's going to the White House on Monday morning," I say, putting the necessary awe into my voice. "Big meeting. Think we'll ever see the inside of that place?" Then I add, "Patrick will be there."

Understanding lights up Lorenzo's face, but he says nothing.

I'll tell him the rest once we get inside the biochem lab.

Or not.

He slides his key card into the slot, and this time, instead of the light turning green, instead of the soft ping and click of electronics and mechanics, there's a sharp buzz and a flashing red light. I try mine, with the same result.

We're locked out.

SIXTY

I'm on the intercom to Morgan before Lorenzo can stop me.

"We need access to the biochem lab," I say. Then, hearing the fury in my own voice: "There must be a mistake, Morgan. Can you—"

He cuts me off. "No, you don't. And no, I can't."

"What?" The word comes out as if I've just spit, which is exactly what I'd like to do, right in Morgan's ratlike face.

"Jean, Jean, Jean," he says, and I prepare myself for his impatient-kindergarten-teacher lecture. "If the Ray woman's trial is successful, you're done here. You and Lorenzo have nothing more to work on."

Oh yes, we do, I think.

"And Lin," I say, fishing. "Or is Lin not on the team anymore?"

"Of course. I meant you and Lorenzo and Lin. The whole team."

Lorenzo, who's been listening in, his head so close to mine I can feel the bristle of unshaved cheek, interrupts. "Morgan, we need the lab for propagation. We've got a limited quantity of serum. You know that."

Silence, then: "That's being dealt with. By another team. The propagation, I mean."

Right. And the reverse engineering. The Gold team must be as busy as a hive today.

I nod to Lorenzo and point toward the storage refrigerator behind him, then wedge the intercom's handset between my ear and shoulder, leaving my hands free. I hold up six fingers, then only one.

"Nice," Lorenzo says after opening the refrigerator and counting the vials. He mouths, "Morgan?"

I shrug, as if to say, *Who else?*

"Jean? Did you hear me? I said Mrs. Ray is here. We're bringing her down in a few minutes."

"Yeah, Morgan. I heard you." And I hang up.

Last night, or this morning, I asked Patrick about the viability of reversing the serum, turning our cure into a weapon using only the product.

"It's doable without Lorenzo's formulas," he said in the darkness of his study. "If they have the right type of chemists on the Gold team." He looked over the notes, this time using my method—top page to bottom—instead of turning the pages over and laying them to the side as he finished. Of course he didn't want to see the poem again. Getting slapped in the face once was enough. "Definitely doable, but slower. See, they need to break down the product and—"

Everything else Patrick said was a blur. I'm no chemist.

"Lorenzo," I say, taking the single vial of serum from the fridge and two packets of sterile syringes from the cabinet next to it. I pretend to study them, and lower my voice to the barest of whispers. "The notes I have are the only copies, right?"

He slaps the counter with the palm of his hand and sprints toward the rodent and rabbit room. I hear the main door of the lab hiss open and closed.

SIXTY-ONE

Lin, even absent, guides me through the setup. Her notes are pristine, as detailed as a set of blueprints. If she were here, I wouldn't be handling the injection, and that injection wouldn't deliver a concoction of proteins and stem cells into Mrs. Ray's bloodstream. Lin would take care of that, through a strategically placed borehole in our subject's skull—not an operation I was keen on trying myself.

As if she anticipated her own sudden disappearance, Lin assembled two separate procedures. I put the instructions for direct-to-brain delivery aside, wincing at the photographs of skulls and immobilizing frames and boring instruments, wondering what sort of nutcase one had to be to try this on himself. Or herself, I think, remembering the woman who took an electric drill to her own head sometime in the 1970s. She said it opened up her mind.

Right.

What I'm about to do is easier, since Mrs. Ray will have already been prepped with a catheter before leaving the nursing home where she now spends her days. I suppose she'll be returning there once the trial is over; she has no home to go to with Del out of the picture. *Some favor I'm doing her,* I think, and wonder if the old woman who planted my gardens might be better off in her current state. At least she won't understand what's going on when some bureaucrat in a suit informs her what's happened to her son and daughter-in-law.

And her grandchildren.

Lorenzo's offer is still on the table, but how can I even debate it with myself? What brand of monster would hop on a flight with a forged passport and leave four children behind? Then again, how fucked-up would I have to be to stay, knowing exactly what will become of this next baby?

Super fucked-up, I decide. Either way, I lose.

The main door hisses open and shut again, and footsteps echo through the empty lab. The mice squeak at the intrusion into their space.

"Enzo?"

But it isn't Lorenzo. The intruder is Morgan, and behind him a young man dressed in orderly's scrubs wheels Mrs. Ray into the room.

She looks much older than the last time I saw her.

Steven, now on a fool's mission to find his girl, was still struggling with multiplication tables when Delilah Ray came to the house with her plans for my garden. America's first black president had taken the keys, and Mrs. Ray was in high form, all talk of politics and hope and how "it was about time, darlin', this country got on the right track." She always called me "darlin'" in that sweet Southern way of hers.

Until she had the stroke.

It happened not long before the hopeful president handed over his keys to a new man, the one Mrs. Ray would never refer to as a darlin' or hopeful or charismatic, or anything else on the positive end of her rich vocabulary's spectrum.

When I called that day to ask about a problem with one of my rosebushes, her son answered and gave me the news. I can still hear the hope in his voice, feel the breathless, wordless optimism hanging between us like a storm cloud as I outlined my research.

"What if it doesn't work?" Del said. "What if my mother still speaks in riddles and nonwords?"

"Then we'll try again," I said. "And we'll keep trying."

That was when he mentioned money. I told him not even to think about it; there would be no fee.

I turn to my first human subject now, an old woman in a wheelchair gazing around the white emptiness of the lab. "How are you, Mrs. Ray?" I say, knowing she won't interpret this as anything but a string of unfamiliar words.

Delilah Ray, the botanist who designed my garden and talked politics and pie recipes, looks up at me through a veil of confusion and noncomprehension. "Fine twinkles, today. Cookie for your thoughts and when the Red Sox gossiping and galloping, I don't know. There's going to be hypertension!" Her speech is fluid and unencumbered and meaningless.

I hope to change this.

Looking back, I can never recall whether I expected success or failure, but in my dreams I've always imagined the old woman's first words that would hold real meaning since her stroke. As I fill the syringe with fluid from the single vial, I realize my hands are shaking.

"Here. Let me." It's Lorenzo. I was so lost in my memories, I didn't hear him come into the lab.

He takes the vial and syringe from me and expertly draws out the prescribed quantity of serum, according to Lin's instructions. He taps it twice with the knuckle of his first finger and holds it up to the light.

I look a question at him.

Lorenzo nods to Morgan, signaling that it's time. As the orderly wheels Mrs. Ray into the room I've prepared, Lorenzo takes my arm. And he shakes his head no.

The Gold team—whoever they are—have the serum and the formulas.

"All right," I say. "Let's get to it."

"I have tickets," he says quietly.

"Tickets for what?" Morgan has poked his nose out of Mrs. Ray's room.

"For the symphony next weekend," Lorenzo lies. "Beethoven, you know. Hard to get if you're not on the A-list."

"Well, I don't care about your A-list or your symphony," Morgan says. "We're waiting in here, and I have other meetings."

"Sure you do, Morgan. Big wheel like you," Lorenzo says. He's almost snarling.

I put away thoughts of flight, at least for now, and walk into the sterile room with Lorenzo close behind me. Mrs. Ray is regarding Thumper with a quizzical look, as if she's remembering something.

"Beauty is as beauty does and crops of corn. So silly," she says.

The orderly reaches down and gives her a reassuring pat on the back. Morgan smirks. Lorenzo and I exchange a look.

I know what he's thinking: an entire city, country, continent, of this. A modern-day Tower of Babel, except instead of being caused by some invisible deity, the confusion will happen at the hand of a very visible man, one who enjoys being on television and who has tasted the power that comes with millions of blind followers but still wants more. One who has no idea of the hell he's about to unleash.

Reverend Carl Corbin must be insane, truly insane. Has he thought ahead to the inevitable outcome? Does he realize the havoc, not only in Europe, but everywhere, his plot will wreak? Supply chains—gone. Banks and stock markets—gone. Mass transit, any transit, really, other than foot traffic and the occasional horse—gone. Factories—gone. Within weeks, most of the world's population will die of hunger or dehydration or violence. The ones who are left will be eking life out in a twisted *Little House on the Prairie* existence, building from the ground up, one haystack and corn silo at a time.

Maybe that's what he wants, though. Maybe Carl Corbin and his

Pure Blue followers aren't as insane as all that. They certainly aren't too insane to wield the strings from which President Myers dances.

"We're ready, Jean," Lorenzo says, holding out the syringe. "You do the honors."

I take it from him, inspect the fluid for any remaining bubbles of air—such a necessary substance, unless it happens to work its way into Mrs. Ray's cerebral circulation—and remove the plastic cap.

Morgan licks his lips as I insert the needle into the catheter, holding my breath, and steadily depress the plunger.

"You'll be fine, Mrs. Ray," I say.

The room has become a sauna, heavy and hot and airless.

Beside me, Lorenzo starts a stopwatch, and we wait, all eyes on the woman in the wheelchair.

It seems hours, but I'm told only ten minutes have passed when Delilah Ray checks the catheter, rubs at a spot on the left side of her graying head, and turns to the plexiglass box holding Thumper. "What a lovely rabbit that is," she says. "A cottontail. Used to have a whole warren full of them when I was a girl."

The air in the room clears like the tropics after a monsoon.

feel like celebrating. Or dancing. Or turning cartwheels down the empty hall of the lab. I feel like champagne and chocolate and fireworks.

I feel, just a little, like a god.

Also, I feel my life may be over.

Morgan leaves us after a brief conversation on his phone, most of which involves references to "my team" and "my project" and "my work." He's still smirking as he walks past us and out the lab's main doors, calling for the orderly to pick up his pace and take Mrs. Ray back to her nursing home. Morgan, of course, has more work to do.

"So," I say, turning to Lorenzo, "I guess that's it."

"Not necessarily." His eyes move to the refrigerated cabinet where six vials, all labeled with the red *X* of death, remain.

"No way," I whisper.

"It's the only way," he says, and the very words I spoke to Patrick last night play over in my head, a broken record of *Would you kill?*

"We'll never get them out of here."

He opens the refrigerator door and slides out the tray with the deadly neuroproteins, the poison that, even in the smallest of quantities, killed a dozen mice. "We only need one, Gianna."

I check the clock on the lab wall. Both hands point straight up. When I came in this morning, Sergeant Petroski was on duty at the security station. He yawned, said hello, and yawned again. If he was up all night, the only ally I have in this building will be at home, sleeping off a graveyard shift.

All right. On to plan B.

Except I don't have a plan B.

Or maybe I do.

There's a closet-sized washroom off the main lab, nothing more than a five-by-five square of tile with a toilet, a sink, and one of those hand dryers that roar like twin jet engines and make the skin on your hands stretch into a taut, science-fiction special effect. I lean over the fridge, pluck one of the vials from its tray, and wedge it into the front of my bra, then take a single surgical glove—the kind with no powder—from the dispenser on the counter.

"Be right back," I say, blowing air into the glove. After considering what I'm about to do, I take two more and head in the direction of the washroom.

Lorenzo raises an eyebrow.

"Six vials, right?" I say, and hear a cabinet opening behind me, followed by the running of water from the lab sink's tap.

The soldiers never check us over thoroughly when we enter the building in the morning or when we leave it at night. They're men, after all. Perhaps, after a year of not having to worry about mouthy women and girl power and female wiles, perhaps after so long in their men's world, they've forgotten our secrets, our ways of hiding small cylindrical objects. Perhaps, after all this time of our silence, even their suspicions have lapsed into nothing.

I check the vial's stopper five times before I'm satisfied it's secure, then fit the tube inside the latex finger of one glove, tie a knot before trimming the excess bulk, and repeat the process with the next two gloves. The end result is a wad of blue latex, not exactly cylindrical anymore, and not small, but likely leakproof. *What the hell,* I think. I've had four baby heads the size of Nerf balls pass through me. I can stand some minor discomfort for the next hour.

Once I've straightened myself out and blown my hands dry, I rejoin Lorenzo in the lab. He gives me a single warning look, and Poe steps toward me. For some reason, he seems even larger when I'm standing up.

"Problem, Dr. McClellan?" Poe says.

"Only if you lower my daily quota on bathroom visits."

Poe has no response to this, but after checking each room in the lab and stopping to regard Thumper in his plexiglass cage, he turns to us. "Follow me."

"We're not done here," I say. "Are we, Enzo?" The look I give him is hard and unmistakably a different question.

"We're done," he says.

Poe snoops around for another five minutes, and I hold my breath as he opens the storage refrigerator and spends more time than I think is necessary counting the vials. Then he leads us through the lab doors and down the corridor and presses the up button on the elevator. "Key cards, please." He holds out one meaty hand.

"That's it?" I say, pulling the lanyard over my head. It gets stuck in my hair, and Poe reaches over to untangle it. His hand brushes my temple and sends a shiver through me. He's ice-cold.

I think of Del again, and Sharon, and their three girls. For the oddest of reasons, I wonder who's feeding the animals on the Rays' farm.

Once, when he was more child than man, Steven asked me if animals had language.

"No," I said.

"Do they think?"

"No."

He'd read a book about bees in school and showed it to me one afternoon in the kitchen. That was when Steven, not Sonia, wanted hot cocoa every day at four o'clock.

"It says that bees can go find pollen and then come back to the hive and tell the other bees where the pollen is." He read part of the chapter aloud. "The bee dance is like a language. So there."

I checked over the book, examining the bio of one of the authors. She was an apiarist with a long line of credentials, none of which had much to do with linguistics. "So there, nothing," I said. "Yes, the bees dance. They do a little 'Hey, guys! Here's the good pollen!' sort of a jig. But that's it, kiddo. Tie their wings down and make them walk back to the hive, and they're giving directions to the nearest rock. What bees have is communication, and only a specialized form of it. That's not language. Only humans have language."

"What about Koko the gorilla?" His book was cowritten by a team of animal experts.

"Koko's terrific and she knows a few hundred signs, but she still doesn't do what your brothers can." Sam and Leo were four at the time. Koko was forty-five.

Steven took his textbook and went to his room to sulk. Another bubble burst, I thought. It's pleasant to imagine our four- and two-legged friends have a linguistic mechanism of their own. Maybe that's why people keep searching for proof. But it isn't true.

Here, in the elevator, I find myself wishing it were.

"That's it," Poe says when we reach the first floor. "You can collect your laptops. They've been scrubbed."

Lorenzo and I collect our bags. He's allowed to take his coffee maker, but nothing else, from his office before Poe closes the door and leads us out to security. Everything is the same: two soldiers, one X-ray machine for our bags, and zero smiles now that Sergeant Petroski is off duty. One by one, we're frisked, our pockets are searched, and the soldier working me over spends an unpleasant amount of extra time on my crotch and cleavage. From the look on Lorenzo's face, he's getting the same treatment down below.

Every possibility runs through my mind now. Full-body search. Anonymous hands—*only obeying orders, ma'am*—roaming over me, sliding into places they don't belong, finding the latex-wrapped vial. *What's this, Jean?* Morgan will say. I see myself on a thousand television screens, a surprise performance interrupting a news segment, a documentary on Bengal tigers, a cartoon. Me, next to Reverend Carl as he reads off another chapter and verse, as camera flashes blind me, as my scalp burns from the sting of a sloppy razor job. I see the horror in Patrick's eyes as he's bused to Fort Meade and forced to stand at attention while my blood mixes with the remains of Jimbo and Del and Sharon and god knows who else. Maybe my own son.

Instead, we're shown the door.

"Nothing like a little *Here's your hat—what's your hurry?*" I say when we're out in the late-afternoon light.

Poe watches us walk toward our cars. If he hears what I've said, I don't know, but he calls out after us. "Leave. And don't come back here." He disappears inside the building, hands stuffed into his pockets. I think I see him sigh.

use Lorenzo's phone to call Patrick and tell him I'm on my way home. Lorenzo, of course, still has a cell phone; I don't.

You would if you were in Italy, kiddo, I tell myself, but push the thought out of my head. I can't think about that right now. I can't think about anything except getting into my car and getting this poison out of my body.

"So," Lorenzo says, taking hold of my left wrist, stroking the old burn with his thumb. "I have to get out, you know. While there's still time."

"I know."

He breaks away and opens the passenger door of his car. From the glove compartment, he removes a slim envelope and hands it to me. "This is for you."

It feels like a passport, and something else, something flat and hard. A smartphone is my best guess.

"Give me a second," I say.

I pull the door closed and hitch up my skirt, ridding myself of the latex-wrapped package and stowing it in one of Sonia's pastel sippy cups. She's outgrown them, but juice in a plastic cup has always been a happy alternative to juice all over the Honda's windshield. The lid snaps closed and I breathe easily again.

"Jean!" Morgan is running toward us, arms out, frantic. The soldier behind him takes measured strides, arms relaxed—except for the slight crook at the left elbow and the splayed hand poised too close to his service weapon. He's a picture of military discipline. It's a good thing for Morgan he wasn't around during the draft era. The kid would probably die in his first foxhole. If, that is, his platoon didn't get to him first.

Lorenzo's envelope goes under my car seat, as if someone else's hand is obeying instructions from a foreign brain. I don't think about it, only reach down automatically, sliding the evidence out of sight before Morgan, now at my window, catches me with the passport of Lorenzo's dead wife. I don't know what the penalty is for carrying forged identification, and I'm not at all eager to find out.

The serum, unfortunately, has to stay where it is for a while longer.

"We need you back inside," Morgan says.

"Why?" I say, starting the Honda's engine and faking ignorance. "If I forgot something, I'll get it tomorrow. I haven't seen my kids all weekend." Only then does it occur to me why I'm wanted back inside. The project's over, and so is my reprieve from silence.

Morgan reaches into my window with one small pink hand. At the same time, Lorenzo steps in between us. "Let her go," Lorenzo says.

The soldier hasn't moved, except to draw his service weapon. I know shit about guns, but I know enough to understand where this could end up if I don't take some control. Fast.

"Enzo. You need to leave," I say, seeing in his eyes that he's got zero intention of moving from his position between the steadiness of that steel barrel and my open window. He proves my point.

"Neither of you is leaving," Morgan says.

The clock on my dashboard takes an eternity to turn from one thirty-six to one thirty-seven.

"Okay." I take my hands off the steering wheel. "Okay. I'm turning the car off." With my left hand still in the air, I kill the Honda's engine with my right. "Okay? Can I get out now?"

Morgan, who has squirmed as far from the line of fire as possible, signals to the soldier, and the gun moves down slightly. It does not go back into its holster as I open the car door.

Morgan leads our four-person parade across the parking lot. I take little comfort in knowing Lorenzo is a few paces behind me, a vulnerable shield between several rounds of ammunition and my own body. We're waved through the security checkpoint and herded into an elevator. This time, instead of hitting the button for the basement floor, Morgan inserts his key card and presses SB. Sub-basement.

I meet Lorenzo's eyes, my own filled with questions mixed with fear mixed with defeat, as the door slides open. He puts a hand on the small of my back, steadying me, and we follow Morgan out the door, the soldier still and quiet, but very definitely present, behind us.

SIXTY-FOUR

If our own lab and office floors were lonely tombs, the sub-basement is a buzzing hive of activity. Cubicles housing two men each sit crammed side by side, their flimsy shoulder-height walls allowing no privacy, only constant observation by the uniformed guards patrolling the corridors. I count twelve of them, each as devoid of any outward signs of jocularity as the man now walking behind me, close enough for me to get a whiff of some sickeningly sweet aftershave, tobacco, and burnt coffee. Not a single cubicle occupant raises his head as we move by; their heads are down, poring over stacks of Excel charts and handwritten formulas, or staring blankly at computer screens.

There must be fifty people in this windowless, airless room. Some of them—most of them—are young, barely out of college.

I pause and peer into one of the cubicles, thinking I recognize Lin's handwriting. Morgan snaps his fingers in front of my face. "Eyes ahead, Jean."

The aftershave, tobacco, and coffee mixture is hot on the back of my neck. Lorenzo's hand brushes against mine, lingering, reminding me I'm not alone in this.

We pass through the bank of cubicles and reach the far end of the hive. Morgan inserts his key card into another slot, and double doors open to a room not different from the rodent and rabbit den one floor above us. Here, instead of squeaking mice and sniffing cottontails, the cages house primates. Great apes, to be specific. Three rows of wire doors line the walls to my right and left, each labeled with an identification number and four rows of data: age, species, date of experiment, overseeing technician. The hoots and grunts of chimpanzees as we enter are deafening.

But this isn't what bothers me.

Three-quarters of the cages are empty. Labels remain on their doors: BONOBO, GORILLA, ORANGUTAN—three of the five great apes. The screeching chimpanzees make four, and half of them are already gone.

I swallow drily and look over at Lorenzo, who is pale enough to blend in with the lab's white walls. Of course he is; he's thinking the same thought I am.

They're working their way through the apes, one species at a time, and they've saved the chimps, the closest human relative, for last.

Or next to last. There's a fifth great ape not in the cages, not yet, one they haven't gotten around to. All the blood in my veins chills to ice.

The fifth species of great ape is us. Human.

My knees buckle, and I stumble to my left, hurtling into the cage of Experiment Number 412, a male chimpanzee that must outweigh me by seventy-five pounds. Lin's repeated warnings sound in my head like a klaxon.

"Never, Jean, and I mean never, get close to them. We have techs and handlers for that. Don't feed them, don't try to pet them, don't even get within spitting distance of the cages. Stay in the middle. These guys have a reach of three feet, and, believe me, they're not cute," Lin said on our first tour of the lab, a few months after her grant funding came through and allowed us to purchase two chimps.

"They look cute," I said. "Check that one out." Mason, a four-foot-tall diaper-clad male, was sucking on a Popsicle in a nearby cage.

"Wait until he bares his canines, honey," Lin said. "These guys are time bombs with no set timer. A pro wrestler couldn't hold one still if he tried. You ever hear of Charla Nash?"

I shook my head. "Do I want to?"

"No. Tell you what, you think about that Hannibal Lecter dude. Think about what he did to that nice nurse when they forgot to put the weird hockey mask on him. Compared to a chimp, Lecter's harmless as a kitten under anesthesia. And you'll never know what hit you."

What hits me now is a swat to the face and the bitter taste of iron on my lips. Part of my scalp—the part Number 412 is pulling with the force of a monster truck in a redneck tractor-pull contest—has been either set on fire or pierced with the ugly end of a pickax. My knees sing high C when bone meets tile as two opposing forces act on me: gravity drawing me down, the chimp trying to heave me up by my hair.

Lorenzo's voice, faint and far away, calls out. "Do something, for fuck's sake. Do something!"

Is he talking to me? I reach up to the fire on my head, and a hand that's not a hand but a claw grabs it with a vise grip. *Charla Nash, Charla Nash, Charla Nash,* I think, the name screaming inside me along with pictures of her missing eyes, her hands that looked as if they'd been fed into a meat grinder, the gash in her face where a mouth should be.

A single shot buzzes in the air over my head, and I float down.

SIXTY-FIVE

I'm not unconscious. If I were, I wouldn't feel fingers working their way through my tangled hair, putting out the fire of pain. I wouldn't be adding zoos and safaris and childhood fantasies of Jane Goodall to my list of things never to think about again. I wouldn't hear Morgan yelling like a petulant child who has just had his pacifier plucked from his mouth.

"What the hell did you do that for?" he says.

I open my eyes and see the soldier, gun hand still trembling after what might have been his first kill, looking from me to Lorenzo to Morgan to the dead Number 412 in the cage above me. Before he can answer, Morgan opens his mouth again.

"That's just terrific. Just great. You idiot. I should put you in one of these cages, except you don't have enough of a brain for me to work with. Do you know how much these animals cost?"

"Apparently more than I do, Morgan," I say.

"Christ." He turns to Lorenzo. "What's the damage?"

Lorenzo has unworked the chimp's fingers from my hair and lays me on the tiled floor as he inspects the gash on my face. A trickle of hot blood runs into my mouth. "Does that hurt?" he says, prodding at a spot near my temple.

Hurt? No. It feels like I've been dragged across coarse sandpaper. It *burns.* "Yeah," I say, moving my hand up to the injury.

"No, you don't. I need to clean this. Morgan, get me a first aid kit."

"How am I supposed to know where they keep the first aid crap? I'm a project manager."

"You're a shit project manager, Morgan," Lorenzo says. "You're a lousy scientist and a poor researcher and if I ever get you alone, I'm going to tear you apart one bone at a time. For now, start looking. Try the cabinet in the corner marked with a red cross." Under his breath, he says, "Asshole."

"Am I okay?" I say, wanting to touch my face, make sure everything is still where it's supposed to be.

"Better than okay," Lorenzo says. "And, Morgan, when you find that kit, call a doctor."

Morgan's shoes cross back until they're so close I can almost see my reflection in them. "No can do. This is a secure facility, in case you missed that."

Lorenzo ignores him as he bathes the right side of my face with peroxide and fixes a clean bandage over the wound that runs from my hairline to the corner of my mouth. "Surface scratches, mostly. Can you stand?"

"I think so." The lab, with its remaining chimps, comes into focus. "What's going on, Morgan?" I say.

He's all business now, my near brush as the victim of a rogue primate forgotten. "We need you back to work."

"Doing what? You said we were done. That hired thug called Poe said we were done. You scrubbed our files."

I wait while Morgan studies his shoelaces.

"Follow me," he says.

We leave the animal containment room and go through another set of doors. Inside, a replica of the basement lab hums with activity. No one, apparently, heard my screams. Or the shot.

Or maybe they did, and don't care.

It takes a few seconds before I see the gold emblems on their lab coats and the small gold squares on the key cards that hang around all the men's necks. Here, as in the cubicle-cramped room outside, everyone keeps his head down and soldiers patrol the aisles.

"Welcome to the Gold team," Morgan says, sounding more like a game show host than a scientist. No surprise—the man can't find a first aid kit when it's staring him in the face. He leads us to four square feet of unoccupied lab top and pauses, waiting for us to sit.

"Okay, Morgan. I'll bite," I say. "What the hell is this?"

"This is your new team." He stretches an arm out. *And you can win all these prizes,* I hear him say.

"I don't get it."

"You will." Morgan nods to somewhere behind me.

A man with bifocals as thick as glass brick appears and sets two thick binders on the counter in front of us, each one labeled TOP SECRET in gold lettering. Inside them are most of the data I had on my laptop. Before the bifocal man leaves, I catch another glint of gold on his left fourth finger. Morgan turns to the soldier who shot the chimp—*with no time to spare,* I think—and issues instructions I can't make out.

"Gianna," Lorenzo says, nudging my elbow. He doesn't look at me; his eyes are roaming the lab. Then he taps the ring finger on his left hand.

The stool I'm sitting on is one of those adjustable numbers with a lever below the seat. I reach down and raise it until I can see most of the lab. Men are scratching their heads, twirling mechanical pencils, rubbing tired eyes. Every left hand I can see has a gold wedding band on its fourth finger.

And every pair of eyes holds fear.

"They're not volunteers, Enzo, are they?"

He shakes his head.

"Oh Christ." Every single man inside this complex is married, maybe has children. "Some incentive," I say.

Morgan, now finished lecturing the poor soldier, who looks like he's seen his last paycheck, comes back to us. "I need a formula, people. By tonight. By tomorrow morning, I need a working serum."

"We just gave you the working serum," I say. "And you have the vials. All five of them." I steel myself for the *Jean, Jean, Jean* routine that he does, and grip the edge of the counter with both hands. Better to keep them gripping anything, since what they want to do right now is close around Morgan's neck. Tight.

He smiles. "You gave me *a* working serum, Jean. I want another one."

I feign complete ignorance.

Morgan claps his hands together. "All right. Let me explain this in simple terms. We have an anti-Wernicke process. It works. We all saw Mrs. What's Her Face make the leap from babbling idiot to bunny-rabbit enthusiast."

"Mrs. Ray," I say. "She has a name."

"Whatever. Now we want the same thing, but different."

Lorenzo rolls his eyes. "You want semantic opposites, Morgan?"

If this jab bothers our boss, he doesn't show it. Maybe he doesn't get the joke. Morgan never was a shining star in the linguistics universe. "I want the opposite of what you've already given me. I want a neuro-protein that induces Wernicke's aphasia, and I want it by tomorrow. So get to work."

Lorenzo speaks first. "What did they promise you, Morgan? A life-time membership to Washington's finest girlie club? I didn't know you could get it up."

"Just give me what I want."

Every pair of eyes in the lab is now looking at us.

"No," I say.

Morgan leans over until his nose almost touches mine. "Excuse me? I didn't hear you."

"I said, 'No.' It's a negative, Morgan. A denial to your request. The opposite of agreement."

For the first time since I've known him, Morgan laughs. It's a titter of a laugh, breathy and hollow. "It isn't a request, Jean." He checks his watch, sighs as if this business is taking up more of his valuable time than he anticipated, and calls one of the patrolling soldiers over to our corner of the lab. "Corporal, take these two to Room One and show them what's inside. When they've had a good look, bring them back here."

Room 1 is on the other side of the lab, through a set of locked doors, which might hold anything. I try not to think of Orwellian possibilities like rats and snakes. In any case, they're not my worst fears. My worst fears walk on two legs and have names like Sam and Leo and Sonia. My worst fears are my kids.

The corporal, dressed in camouflage and combat boots, leads us to the steel doors. With his left hand—he also wears a ring, I notice—he slides a card into the electronic reader and stands aside as the doors slide open, revealing a vestibule and an additional door that remains closed as we leave the lab behind us. Only when the entry slides closed do I realize this space is like a tomb.

I hate confined spaces, always have.

Lorenzo reaches over for my hand. His own skin is hot; the entire room is a furnace, and sweat trickles down my face in what has to be rivers of salt, burning me underneath the bandage on my cheek. But I don't feel warm at all. I feel as if an ice sheet has wrapped itself around me as the corporal steps forward and unlocks the next door.

Inside, seated on the only furnishing in the room other than a lidless toilet, are three people.

I think of the great apes, the hominoids. Gorillas and orangutans, bonobos and chimpanzees. And, of course, humans.

The human on the left speaks my name, my old name, a name I haven't heard for twenty years. By the second syllable in "Jeanie," a jolt of pain knocks her back into the steel wall. The sickening thud echoes in the room.

It sounds like the muffled shot of a gun.

lunge forward on unsteady feet, but Lorenzo catches me by the arm. His grip is firm, almost bruising.

"No," he says. "If she speaks again, the current will—"

He's stronger than I am, but I break away, flinging myself at the woman on the bench, whose body sags like a lifeless doll under the harsh overhead lights. She's not how I remember her, not in low-riding jeans and a crazily printed paisley blouse, not smiling from under a fringe of color-of-the-week hair while she brewed herbal tea in a crappy Georgetown apartment and cursed at the Ikea table instructions that defied minds with multiple degrees. She's in a gray tunic that matches her hair and the color of her skin, except for the palms of her hands, which have been rubbed as raw as fresh meat from a year of labor that would make even the most stalwart farmer turn his back on the land and find a job pushing paper across a desk. She's wearing a single black band on her left wrist where a charm bracelet of Chinese horoscope animals used to be.

"Jacko," I say, placing one hand over her chapped lips. "Jacko, don't say anything else. Don't let them make it worse for you."

Jackie Juarez, once the woman who I thought would stop the world, slumps wordlessly into my arms, and sobs.

The door behind me slides closed, then opens again. I don't need to turn to check who it is. I can smell the bastard.

"Morgan," I say. Then I hear the slap, the surprised whine, the metallic click of a firearm being cocked.

This is another thing I know about guns: you don't cock and aim unless you're ready to kill.

"Careful, Morgan," I say, still holding on to Jackie. "You need him. You need his formula."

He doesn't, of course; Morgan already has Lorenzo's notes. I'm only buying time.

And then it hits me: Lorenzo, dashing out of the upstairs lab to check his office, coming back and shaking his head to tell me the papers weren't there. Morgan demanding a formula by tomorrow.

"Soldier," Morgan says, "put it away."

I turn from Jackie toward Lorenzo, who stands stock-still, ready to take a bullet in exchange for a slap, and I realize Morgan can't possibly have taken the notes.

So, who the hell did?

The question stays in my mind, but I tuck it back in a quiet corner for later as I turn to the other women in the cell.

Lin looks at me, then at Lorenzo. Next to her is the Argentine-Swiss beauty who used to hang out in our department. She's still a knockout, even without the blond waterfall of hair streaming down her back.

Isabel Gerber.

The two of them are in the same drab gray as Jackie, sitting hip to hip, hands folded in their laps. Twin black bands circle their wrists.

"Caught them making out in a car," Morgan says. "Fucking dykes."

Lin opens her mouth to speak, then rethinks and closes it. The decision process takes all of a second, but it's there, in her eyes.

Over my shoulder, I catch Lorenzo's hands curling into fists. "Don't do it, Enzo. He's not worth it."

Suddenly I wish I hadn't left the vial in my car. I'd take it out right now and shove the entire thing down Morgan's throat, glass and all. Or, better yet, I savor the image of Jackie, Lin, and Isabel locked in a small room with the bastard. A soundproof room, with no windows.

"So. Ready to work now, people?" Morgan says. "Or do I send one of them up to Fort Meade?"

The expressions on the women's faces tell me Morgan has already filled them in, one vivid picture at a time.

Time, I think. Everything comes down to time in one form or another: The time I didn't have twenty years ago, when textbooks and orals and qualifying papers were more important than Jackie's marches and Planned Parenthood tea parties. The twenty-four hours I'll wait before I find out whether the creature inside me is a boy or a girl. Lorenzo needing to leave "while there's still time," although I'm not sure there is still time anymore, not for either of us. Morgan's hard deadlines. The morning meeting in only eighteen hours.

The time I slapped Steven. And all the moments I'll spend wishing I could take it back.

Morgan steps forward and takes three identical pink booklets from the inside breast pocket of his suit coat. He passes them out like playing cards, first to Isabel, then Lin, then Jackie.

"Don't forget to read your manifestos, girls," he says. There's a nasty emphasis on "girls."

"Really, Morgan?" I say.

"Hey, Jean, I don't make the rules. Take it up with Reverend Carl if you don't like it." He looks at my wrist and laughs a hollow chuckle. "Better hurry before your bracelet goes back on."

Jackie, whose eyes are dry, and look like they have been this whole time, picks up the booklet from the bench next to her, and, without so much as a glance at it, flings it at Morgan. It hits him square in the forehead with a satisfying thwack.

He doesn't stoop to pick it up, but kicks it across the small room. "You'll learn," he says, and motions to the corporal to open the inner door.

Lorenzo takes my hand, helping me up from where I'm kneeling next to Jackie.

"Stay cool, Jacko," I say. "Promise?"

She nods.

"I'll do everything I can."

Everything I should have done, I think, as I follow Morgan out of the room and back into the hive of the lab.

SIXTY-SEVEN

There's a television in the lab, a flat-screen the size of a football field. A reasonable size, I suppose, given that the kinds of men who buy these things spend most of their weekends watching other men toss a piece of pig around a hundred-yard-long swath of Astroturf.

When Reverend Carl appears on it, dressed in his usual funereal style, it's impossible not to look at him. Also, someone has turned the volume up to a low roar.

"Friends," he says, opening his arms in that trademark way he has, as if he's Rio's very own Christ the Redeemer. "Friends, I have some unfortunate news."

"I'll bet you do," I whisper to Lorenzo beside me. He's been busy at the stoichiometry again, a language as foreign to me as the words coming from the television.

"Settle down, please, settle down." Reverend Carl's hands press the air around him down, and the murmur in the audience dulls. It's difficult to tell where he is, but the crowd is too large for the White House press room. And he's on a stage. The Kennedy Center, maybe. Or the Arena Stage in southwest DC. More than a year has passed since I've seen anything that passes for live entertainment. Plays—the few that are performed—are either family-friendly drivel, censored down to unrecognizability, or off-limits to most of us.

He continues on, reading out the Pure's manifesto, line by line, affirmation by affirmation, belief by belief. His current theme is suffering. It's one of his favorites.

"Friends, my dear friends, suffering is an inevitable reality in our earthly world. We are called to suffer for doing what is good, at times, and no one suffers more than I at this moment." A lengthy pause now, for effect. Reverend Carl likes to draw things out, suffering or not. "We have here a lost sheep." The camera pulls in close to his face, smiling and tear streaked, then pulls back to show him extend his right arm and wave toward the wing of the stage. "That's it. Come on, now."

A lone figure emerges from stage right. I don't know whom I expect. Del Ray, most likely. Or another Julia King. Anyone.

I don't expect my own son.

The gasp of the televised crowd—if there is a crowd at all; it could be canned—is drowned out by the intakes of fifty breaths in the lab. Blinking under the floodlights, Steven shuffles shyly toward center stage, toward Reverend Carl's outstretched arms.

"He's seventeen," I whisper to Lorenzo. "Only seventeen."

There's no need to explain; Lorenzo has seen pictures of my children. Once upon a time, those pictures littered my office.

"Caught," Reverend Carl says. "Caught in a place no man or boy should be." He turns to Steven. "Isn't that right, son?"

Steven starts to speak, then only nods. Rage boils inside me, through every vein and artery, until the pressure builds to a trapped scream.

I miss most of the remaining speech. I can't hear anything except the sound of my own heart, deafening in my ears. The few words that make it through settle in my gut like lead weights: "fornicator," "traitor," "example," "trial."

Reverend Carl calls the audience to join him in prayer, bows his head, and takes Steven by the hand. Another close shot pulls in, showing their intertwined fingers. Carl's are wrapped like tenacious constrictors; Steven's are limp, five helpless digits having the life squeezed out of them. A few inches up from my son's hand is a wide metal band circling his wrist.

A million years ago—it was only twenty, but it feels like a million, it feels like tens of millions, like all the lifetimes of the entire world—Jackie asked me what I would do to stay free. Last night, over a kitchen counter that seems as distant as that Georgetown apartment, I asked Patrick if he would do anything, if he would kill.

Right now, with a half-baked formula on the table and Reverend Carl scolding Steven on the television, I put all the questions together and come up with a single answer.

Yes, I would do anything. I would kill.

The woman who thinks these words doesn't sound like me at all.

Or maybe she does.

In any case, I sort of like her, this new Jean. I like her a hell of a lot more when I catch Morgan smiling up at the flat-screen.

SIXTY-EIGHT

At five o'clock on Sunday afternoon, on what should be a bright pre-summer evening full of barbecue smells and june bugs, Morgan informs us no one will be going home.

"Cafeteria's on the third floor, people. Dorms on the sixth and seventh. If you need to make a call, see Sergeant Petroski." Morgan nods to a makeshift security station at the entrance to the lab. "Nightie-night, folks," he says before turning tail and striding out.

"Stay close to the cages on your way through the chimp room," I call after him. The thought of Morgan having his face shredded by a few angry lab animals brings a satisfying tingle. I turn to Lorenzo.

"Petroski's the key," I say. "How's the work coming?"

He leans against the back of his lab stool, smiling broadly. "It's done."

"What?"

Lorenzo runs me through the chemistry. "I need your eyes on this, Gianna." He points to a set of correlations between the old neuroprotein we tested on Mrs. Ray and semantic fluency, then moves a finger down the page to the notes he's been working on this afternoon. "Look good?"

It looks terrific. It also looks as if we've unleashed the very devil. "With this quantity, Enzo, we're taking about total contamination, flat-out disruption of"—I check the numbers against my data a second time—"of more than three-quarters of the superior temporal gyrus. Forget Mrs. Ray's disfluency; this thing would turn Henry Kissinger into a mute. In about five seconds."

The grin hasn't left his face. "Yeah. It's beautiful, isn't it?"

Depending on what your idea of beauty is, I think. And I have a delicious idea that must be all over my face, because Lorenzo raises an eyebrow. "I can cook this up in a few hours, I think. Got a first subject in mind?"

"What do you think?" I say, scanning the lab. No one seems to be listening to us. What little chatter there is focuses on Reverend Carl and "that poor kid—I wonder what he's done."

"I think," Lorenzo says, twitching one eyebrow and then the other, "great minds think alike."

"And sometimes we do, too," I finish. "Anyway, better Morgan than one of the women in there," I say, and point my chin to the locked doors on the opposite end of the lab. "You saw how many chimps are left. When they run out, Morgan's going to want to climb up the great ape food chain."

Lorenzo stops chewing on the end of his pen and taps it lightly against his teeth. It's an old habit, one I haven't seen him do in more than a year. "There's one hitch," he says.

"What? It turns people blue?"

I watch the humor leave his face.

"No, not blue."

"Oh Christ. Lethal?" I say.

"Could be." He points to a series of formulas on the notepad between us.

"They don't look anything like your old ones." As I read further, Lorenzo's work becomes clear. "This isn't water soluble. Or injectable into the bloodstream."

"Correct. Try that, and you'll fry half his brain. This needs to be administered locally. In situ, as Caesar would say. It's one thing to repair cells. Overshoot the target and, okay, no big deal, you've got a few extra happy neurons. Destroying them is a different pile of wax."

"Ball of wax." The correction comes naturally to me, so naturally I don't hear it over the single word screaming inside my brain: *Trepanation.* "No way, Enzo. We'll never pull it off." Not only that, but the thought of wielding an electric drill within a mile of a human skull—even Morgan's—makes me ill.

"Maybe not." He checks around the lab, counting heads with the ink end of his pen. "Fifty people in here, not counting our boys in blue. A few of them look like they've been recruited young, straight out of school. But they're not *that* young, Gianna. Grad students, at the least. How about we take a walk around and read ID cards?" He points toward the lab entrance. "You take that end; I'll take the back. Nothing thorough, just a quick survey of titles, okay? Anyone asks, you're on your way to the security desk to call your husband. About the car."

Of course I need to call Patrick, since it doesn't look as if I'll be getting out of this building soon. He'll need the Honda, or, at least, what I left inside the Honda. I leave my four-foot-square work space and start walking down the nearest aisle toward Sergeant Petroski's desk. Slowly.

"I need to make a call," I say. "To let my husband know I'm not coming home tonight."

Petroski smiles. "Sure, ma'am. Number?"

"I'll dial it."

"Afraid I have to do that for you."

Of course he does. He probably has to speak for me, too.

I'm right about this. Petroski asks for the message and hands me a blank sheet of notepaper and a pen. "Just write it all down here, and I'll convey it. Word for word."

The note's short. *Pick up car, get Sonia's sippy cup. She'll have a meltdown if she has to go to bed without it.* It isn't really a lie, not if you put some of the verbs in the past tense. I hand it over to Petroski and blink three times.

He blinks back.

"Anything else, Dr. McClellan?" he says.

I remember a different soldier sitting at this desk when Lorenzo and I came in, so Petroski must have arrived recently. "You're on duty tonight?"

"Yes, ma'am. Another graveyard shift."

My eyes move to his left hand. "You're married," I say.

Of course he is.

"Yes, ma'am. Two years this month." His mouth curls into an embarrassed smile. "We were high school sweethearts."

"I got married young," I say. I omit the fact that it might not have been one of the smartest relationship moves. "Had kids young, too. You got kids?"

Petroski hesitates, and the shy smile fades. "One. A girl. She turned a year old in April." More quietly, he says, "One year. Can I ask you a question?"

"Sure."

"Look, I'm no scientist or anything. I got a high school degree and some community college hours; then I joined up. Figured the army would give me a steady paycheck and all that. Plus, you know, if you make it twenty years you get a pension. Insurance and all that."

"They do make it sound good," I say.

He leans forward. "But I know something about kids. I'm the oldest, see. Have five brothers. Youngest one born when I was fifteen. Danny's his name. Good kid."

I nod. Sergeant Salt-of-the-Earth keeps going. "Danny knew what 'no' meant by the time he was five months old. Before he was one, he could say 'Mama' and 'Dada' and 'Boo.' Boo was the name of our dog. He didn't make much sense, but he was talking. And then"—Petroski slaps the desk with the palm of his hand—"bang! Two words, questions, stuff like 'Where Boo?' and 'Want juice.' It was like some kinda miracle, you know?"

I do know. I watched four babies go through all those stages. Prelinguistic babbling, one-word holophrases, two-word sentences—usually nothing more than a subject and a predicate. Then, in Petroski's words, *bang*. It all started happening. At three, Steven would make demands: *Take me to school* in the morning; *Please make chocolate* in the afternoon.

I also know the flip side, and so does Petroski.

"I saw this documentary once, ma'am," he says. "Couldn't watch the whole thing—too gruesome. These people, see, they kept their little girl locked up in a room and didn't talk to her for something like twelve years. Twelve *years*, ma'am. You imagine?"

I shake my head, even though I can imagine. It's happened in rare cases.

Petroski goes on, an armchair linguist who doesn't realize how right he is. "So you take a kid—any kid—and if you let them talk, they do it. If you don't"—another palm slam on the table between us: *bang*—"that's it. Like they have some kinda clock inside 'em."

"They do." No need to mention critical period hypotheses, also known as the use-it-or-lose-it theory, to Sergeant Petroski. He gets the vibe without all the fancy jargon.

"So my question is," he says, looking straight into my eyes. His own are calm and blue, but there's pain behind them. "My question is what's gonna happen to my own little girl if she doesn't ever get to talk? Is she gonna turn out like that Genie woman? End up in some kinda home?"

I have a thousand answers for him, and none. Genie, the child in the documentary, never did learn to talk. After years of poking and prodding by linguists with more interest in the next big book than in Genie herself, the girl ended up exactly where Petroski suggested. In some kinda home.

When I've put the finishing touches on my message to Patrick, I hand it back to Petroski. He grabs my hand.

"Can you help? You're a doctor, right?"

I nod. Sort of.

"Can you help?" He stops, looks down at the triple stripes on his sleeve, and says, "I took an oath, you know. Maybe we should ride it out. This Pure thing can't last forever."

Time to throw a log on the fire. "You're right. It can't. It probably won't. Another few years and Reverend Carl will be another footnote in a history book. Of course, he might stick around longer."

"Yeah." Petroski's on the fence.

"You know, Sergeant," I say, making it up as I go, hating myself a little as I stoke the flames, "I read an article a few years back. We used to think kids had until thirteen or fourteen to—you know, for that *bang* thing to happen. But I'll tell you, as an expert, they have a lot less time than that. Three, four years, maybe. Afterward, their brains sort of"—I search for the right word—"click off."

His face pales, and I wince despite the fact that it's the reaction I'm going for.

"Well, I'd better get back to work," I say. Better, I think, to give him a few minutes to mull things over while I work out the details with Lorenzo.

Leaving him, and the key to the Honda, at his desk, I walk back to my corner of the lab, this time along a different route. Half the ID cards are turned the wrong way, but I read a dozen of them, keeping in mind Lorenzo's advice to worry about the titles and nothing else.

SIXTY-NINE

pproximately two percent of the population holds a doctorate. If you ignore the PhDs in English, the percentage is less. Much less.

"I count nine," I say. "Out of about twelve."

Lorenzo must have been luckier than I with the ID cards. "I got fifteen out of twenty."

Two-thirds, three-quarters, it doesn't matter. We're sitting in a lab filled with experts. Given enough time, you could get a monkey to type out Shakespeare. In a lab like this, you could build a rocket to Mars in a hell of a lot less time. A brain-scrambling neurotoxin? I'd estimate overnight.

Which is just in time for the morning meeting Patrick will be attending tomorrow.

I check the room again. Eyes are exhausted, but busy. Lorenzo gives them until morning to come up with something that might satisfy Morgan.

"I think I've found us an ally," I say.

"Yeah?"

"Over there. At the security desk."

Lorenzo stretches his neck to see over the rest of the crowd. "You're kidding."

Petroski might not be the brightest bulb in the box, but he's got two qualities I want: he's scared as shit for his daughter, and he's strong. That he wears a uniform and carries a ring of keys on his belt doesn't hurt.

"Take a look around, Enzo," I say. "These guys have been working around the clock. They're dead tired." As I say this, three men, each of them looking to be in his forties, file out of the lab, escorted by a single soldier.

"Haven't seen my kids in a week," one complains.

"Kids?" another says. "My kids are okay with it. My wife, on the other hand—"

"If I don't get some food and some z's, I'm gonna be toast tomorrow." The third man looks as if he's about to fall asleep on his feet.

"See what I mean?" I say, as another five worker bees signal they're ready to hit the hay. "All we need to do is wait."

"Wrong, Gianna." Lorenzo looks me over. "What you need to do is get some sleep. At least for a couple of hours."

I have as much chance of sleeping as I do of winning a Nobel Prize, but he's right. I've run into the fatigue wall at full speed, and my next lab task requires absolute alertness. "Two hours. Max. Assuming Morgan is staying the night."

"He will be. Check with your new pal on the way out." Lorenzo cracks a smile. "And don't flirt too much. I'm the jealous type." From the shelf behind him, he takes one of the tablets, swipes and taps a few times with those absurdly long, but elegant, fingers, and hands it to me. "A little light reading for you."

I read the title on the screen. "*Comparative Neuroanatomy of Primates*? You call this light?"

"In the literal sense. The iPad weighs less than a pound."

"How much does the book weigh?"

"It's about five hundred pages. You want chapters seven and eight." He must see the unspoken questions in my eyes, because he keeps going. "Look, I'd do it, but I'd be starting from zero. Besides, I can't read that shit and set up everything down here at the same time. So brush up on your brain science, okay?" He turns to the computer behind him, pulls out the keyboard, and starts filling in a lab animal requisition form after consulting a chart of available subjects. In the space for the identification number, he types *413*, then moves down the page to an empty block and starts hunting and pecking again. I watch him type *Sedation, trepanation, and intracranial injection of experimental serum Wernicke 5.2.*

"Oh man," I say, picturing myself with a drill in one hand and an iPad open to a set of step-by-step instructions in the other. This is so not what I signed up for. "I'm not really the hands-on type, Enzo."

"You're all I've got." In the blank space where the requisition form says **Technician**, he writes **Dr. Jean McClellan**.

"We have to, don't we?" I say.

"Either that or end up with a dead Morgan." Lorenzo's mouth turns up at one corner. "Unless that's what you want."

Of course it's what I want. But there's no sense in being greedy. A mute Morgan will work just as well.

"All right," I say. "I'm heading upstairs. Send someone to get me if I'm not back down here by ten. Okay?"

"Deal."

I don't stop by Petroski's desk for an escort. Instead, I head toward the soldier closest to him and speak loudly enough for my voice to carry. "I need some shut-eye. Can you take me up to the dorms?"

While my escort calls out to the now half-filled lab asking if anyone else wants the cafeteria or a bed, Petroski motions me to him with a slight nod of his head.

"I made your call," he says.

"Great. Thanks." I don't want to ask him for help—better if the request comes from him.

It does.

"Anything I can do?"

"As a matter of fact, Sergeant, yes. There is."

His face, smooth and whiskerless and innocent as a child's, lights up as I explain, in detail, exactly what I need him to do.

SEVENTY

While Lorenzo is eight floors down sedating chimpanzee Number 4-unlucky-13 and setting up the equipment we'll need, I'm sitting up in a narrow bed, fully clothed, digesting a stale sandwich from the cafeteria and chapter seven of the primate neuroanatomy text, also known as detailed brain maps of our closest relative, the chimp. My squeamishness has fallen aside for now, mostly thanks to this afternoon's near mauling by 413's compatriot.

I swipe a new window onto the iPad, check the database of medical journals for articles on craniotomy and trepanation procedures, and take a long, last look at the uneaten half of my sandwich. It's not the optimal companion for my bedtime reading, so I put the cheese on wheat aside while I review the components of my new friend, the Cushing perforator drill.

When I think there's no way I can bore a hole into an ape's skull, let alone a human's, I remember Jackie and Lin and Isabel.

Steel up, Jean.

And I keep reading until my eyelids succumb to gravity and the iPad slips from my hands.

The knock on my door seems to come at the exact moment I fall asleep.

"Dr. McClellan?" The voice is muffled, cloudy.

"Yeah."

"Time to go. Dr. Rossi says he needs you in the lab."

Everyone needs something. I need about a week's worth of uninterrupted nap time. "Okay. Coming." I peel myself off the bed, smooth down my clothes—by the looks of them, I've slept hard, if not for very long—and open the door. It's Petroski, and he seems to have aged a decade since I left him down in the sub-basement.

"Have a good rest, ma'am?"

My mouth makes the sounds of "yes"; my pounding head argues. One foot follows the other down the hall, automatic marching orders telling them to take it up a notch, and I get into the elevator with Petroski.

"All set," he says. "Everything's exactly like you asked."

"Good. Now, listen, Sergeant. Your job's done. The last thing you know is that Dr. LeBron accessed the lab at— What time is it now?"

"Ten oh five, ma'am," he says, holding out his left wrist for me to see.

"Okay. LeBron entered the sub-basement lab at nine fifty. He told you he had a headache. That's all you know."

In unsurprising military fashion, Petroski responds with a terse "Yes, ma'am," and holds the Open Doors button as I exit the elevator. At the entrance to the lab, he pauses.

Please don't get cold feet now. I can't be sure whether I'm talking to Petroski or to myself.

He slides his key card into the socket and waits for the green light, and I'm in. We pass the remaining chimpanzees, still hooting in their cages, and I note that chimp Number 413's holding pen is empty.

As is the main lab.

Petroski's first job was to evacuate the sub-basement, which, judging by the unoccupied stools and the chaos of paperwork left on every flat surface, he did well. All it took was Lorenzo, a Bunsen burner, some foil, and a mixture of sugar and potassium nitrate. The biochem lab must have looked like a bomb went off.

Well. That was the idea.

I leave the sergeant at his security desk and walk back through the detritus of notebooks and calculators and reading glasses to where Lorenzo is waiting, half standing, half sitting on the counter where I left him two hours ago. He's the picture of cool, and I wish he didn't make it so easy to be in love with him.

"Worked like a charm, Gianna. Silent, smoky, and nondeadly. First thing I ever made when I got a chemistry kit was a smoke bomb. Ruined my mother's best pasta pot." A devilish and boyish mischief flashes in his eyes.

Boys, I think. They love to blow shit up. Or at least make it look like they've blown shit up.

He swings a leg off the counter. "You ready?"

"I don't know if I can do this," I say, feeling the cheese on wheat work its way in a direction it shouldn't be going. "Where are they?"

"In here." He opens the door to a side room. It's vacant, except for two gurneys and a rolling surgical table covered in an array of stainless steel implements I've seen only in pictures—pickups, retractors, forceps, something that looks like a melon baller. On the stretcher closest to me lies a four-foot-tall female chimpanzee, her scalp partially shaved on the left side. On the other stretcher is a five-foot-six life-form of a slightly lower order. Both are heavily sedated, their chests rising and falling in a steady rhythm.

Petroski succeeded in getting Morgan to the lab; Lorenzo finished the job.

"I think I like him better this way," I say. "Which one first?"

Lorenzo points to the chimp.

"All right. Bad joke." But I need the humor to get through this. As soon as I see the craniotomy drill with its irregular steel bit, a little like a malformed tooth, I rethink. I don't need humor to get through this. I need a goddamned neurosurgeon.

"Gianna?" Lorenzo says. He checks his watch. "They're not going to be out forever."

I pick up the perforating drill and turn it on. It makes a low hum as the bit whirs around. There's no way this tiny contraption is going to bust through skull bone.

"I can't," I say, putting the drill down. So much for being willing to do anything.

SEVENTY-ONE

I don't know how many times I've said "I could kill him" in my forty-odd years. Maybe a few thousand.

I could kill him for leaving the clothes in the washing machine. I could kill him for not calling to say he'd be late. I could kill him for breaking Mamma's majolica vase. Could, could, could. Kill, kill, kill. Of course I never meant it. The words are as semantically vacuous as "I love you to death" and "I'm hungry enough to eat a horse" and "I'd bet my life the Sox are going to take a bath in this year's series." No one dies from love outside of a Brontë novel or eats entire horses or lays his life on the line for a baseball game. No one. But we say this garbage all the time.

The fact is, I don't know whether I could have put down chimp Number 412, even while he was going apeshit.

I do know that I'm not taking a skull drill anywhere near either of the two sleeping hominoids on these gurneys.

And I don't have to.

"Get Petroski," I say to Lorenzo.

He stares at me.

"No. I'm not asking him to do it. I need the keys to Room One."

Again, the stare.

"To get Lin out. And the others. Tell the kid I'll say we doped him up and stole his keys, if it comes to that. But I think he'll play." I explain about the daughter.

"I would," Lorenzo says. "Play, I mean. If she were mine." His eyes wander down my body, stopping at the slight swell where my waist used to be. "I wouldn't have left without you, Gianna. Never."

"Really?"

"Really." He does a quick tour around the room, searching for anything that might be a camera, and kisses me. "Never."

"Now you know how I feel about Sonia. And the boys." Sonia, mostly, though. Nothing is as bad as the idea of leaving her behind while everything goes to hell. Nothing except bringing another girl into the inferno. I push the thought out of my mind for the next twelve hours. "Go on—get Petroski to do a little jail-breaking."

Five minutes later, Lorenzo comes back with Lin. When she sees the two gurneys, she turns to me, openmouthed and wide-eyed. I ask Lorenzo to explain while I see to Jackie and Isabel. They don't need to be in here for what we're about to do. Hell. I don't want to be in here for it.

Lorenzo informs me I don't have a choice. Lin makes a thumbs-up sign with her right hand and thumps her left palm.

"She needs you to assist," he says.

I look at Lin's black bracelet. "How'd she manage to say that?"

Lin rolls her eyes, waves both hands back and forth in front of her chest, then sets the index and middle fingers of each hand together and points them at me, shaking them.

"She says never mind and hurry up," Lorenzo tells me. "I'll translate."

"You both know American Sign Language?" I say. "Why?"

He shrugs. "You speak some Vietnamese, right?"

"Yeah."

"Why?"

"Okay. Point taken."

Through Lorenzo, I hear each of Lin's instructions while we scrub ourselves up to the elbows in one of the biochem lab's sinks. It's like Brain Surgery for Dummies. *Monitor vitals at all times. Pass me the tools handle first. Stay the hell out of my light.* And, in true Lin form, *For fuck's sake, don't pass out.*

The first three I can handle. I'm not so sure about number four.

Back in the white room, it takes Lin two full minutes to retract the skin on the chimp's head and another thirty seconds to bore a hole the size of a dime. She turns off the drill, passes it to me along with a hunk of chimpanzee skull, and signs to Lorenzo.

"She says to think about it like the plug in a sink drain," he says, passing along this gem of advice.

"Easy for you, Lin," I say. "I was always more interested in the linguistics half of neurolinguistics."

She laughs, but her hands are too busy for chatter as she palpates the soft tissue inside the chimp's skull. It's stomach turning and fascinating and miraculous, all at the same time. How the hell could people like Reverend Carl and Morgan LeBron want to take this woman and throw her away? How could anyone think that makes sense?

"Okay. Here we go." Lorenzo draws two full syringes of clear liquid from a vial on the surgical table. It looks as harmless as water. He sets one down on the table between the gurneys and holds out the other to Lin.

I watch her calm hands as she inserts the fine point of the needle a few millimeters into the chimp's cortical tissue and squeezes the plunger, glancing at the readouts. She nods, apparently satisfied she hasn't killed her patient, and injects the remaining serum before replacing the round piece of skull—*plug, Jean, it's only a plug*—and stitching up her work. The entire process has taken five minutes.

A good thing, really, since both the chimpanzee and Morgan have begun to stir.

SEVENTY-TWO

One close-up and personal encounter with an angry primate was enough for me. I don't care to relive the experience.

"We need to get her out of here, Enzo. Now," I say, watching with horror as the chimp's chest begins to rise and fall more deeply. "Lin? How much time do we have before she comes out?"

Lin shakes her head back and forth, holds up four fingers, then two.

There's no need for Lorenzo to translate.

"Six minutes?" I say hopefully.

She shakes her head again, holding up two fingers, thrusting them toward me.

I look around for something—anything—we can use as restraints, and find only suturing thread on the surgical table. Not good. "Okay. Okay." No time to spare. "Lin—you make sure the cage is open. Enzo, you and I wheel this baby back where she belongs." My own heartbeat marks every passing second as Lin races out of the makeshift operating room and follows the noise of the remaining hooting chimps toward the front of the lab.

Chimpanzee Number 413, eyes filled with puzzlement, reaches a long and hairy arm up to her head. Then she turns her face toward mine.

"Enzo? Push!" I yell. The gurney slams into a pair of lab stools, knocking them across the floor. Lorenzo catches one before it careers into two more, barely preventing a domino effect of rolling furniture that might block our path. Jackie and Isabel stand in the center of the lab, horrified and helpless.

"Don't say anything, Jacko," I plead. "Don't say anything. Take Isabel somewhere else. Lock yourselves into a closet if you have to." Every mental image I have is of the mauled woman, Charla Nash, missing everything on her face save the skin on her forehead.

"Petroski!" I yell into the empty white space of the lab as Lorenzo pushes the gurney past countertops of flying paper, eyeglasses, a fucking slide rule. "Petroski!"

Petroski comes running from his station. The chimp utters a low moan, not a hoot, not a screech, but a woeful, hollow moan.

Don't look at her, Jean. Don't you dare look at her.

But, of course, I do.

Fury shimmers in her soft brown eyes as we reach the open cage.

Petroski draws his service weapon. His hand shakes as he clicks something with a thumb. The safety, maybe. What the hell do I know?

"Don't shoot her unless you have to," I say. "All right, Enzo. On my count. One . . ."

The chimp's paw leaves her head and reaches toward me.

"Two," I pant.

Iodine from the wound fills my nostrils as she extends.

"Three!" With every ounce of strength, I heave the beast off the gurney with Lorenzo taking most of her weight. A claw brushes my lips as chimp Number 413 rolls into the cage. Lorenzo slams it shut and steps back to the centerline of the cage room, taking me with him. One furry paw shoots between the bars, clawed fingers splayed, then retracts. The chimp goes back to massaging one side of her head.

It almost looks as if she's trying to remember something.

"Oh god, Enzo. Morgan. Where's Morgan?"

Based on the tour, I know there's only one way in and out of the lab, and Morgan hasn't come through. Lorenzo is back across the room in four long strides, as I yell to him to get Jackie and Isabel out of the way. I don't know if he hears me.

Lin signs something I can't understand, points to me, then to the caged chimp.

"Close one," I say, unsure of whether this is what she means.

She nods.

"Go see about Jackie and Isabel," I say. "I'm going to help Lorenzo."

Another nod.

I don't know whether it hits me while I'm still in the primate room, or whether I think it as I walk through the lab with its tilted stools and scattered papers, but it hits all the same. It hits like a fucking grand piano dropped from a high floor. Morgan. A syringe. Lorenzo.

This isn't water soluble. Or injectable into the bloodstream.

Try that, and you'll fry half his brain.

My legs seem to move on their own.

SEVENTY-THREE

Morgan LeBron stands five foot six and might tip the scales at 150, after someone wet him down with a fire hose. Lorenzo can pick me up with one arm tied behind his back. It's no match at all, unless the smaller of the two has an edge.

Morgan does.

He has an edge with twenty cc's of poison and one hell of a sharp needle.

And he's presently holding it to Lorenzo's neck, in that soft spot an inch behind the ear.

"Get out," someone says. I can't tell whether this is Lorenzo or Morgan yelling in the bright white room with one gurney and a table on wheels. It's only a voice. Only two words that have no other purpose than to terrify me.

"Morgan—," I start.

He doesn't allow me to finish.

"You fucking bitch. Fucking *cunt*."

Lorenzo's jaw tightens, but the words don't bother me. The syringe, yes, but everything else Morgan has to push is nothing more than jumbled fricatives and velars. I can divorce myself from those.

But that goddamned syringe. That's real.

I take a step forward, very slowly, a sort of time-warp step from an old sci-fi movie.

"Gianna. No." Lorenzo sounds as rock steady as his body looks.

"Gianna? Who the fuck is Gianna?" And as he says my name—my other name—Morgan's eyes flicker. "Oh. I get it. You two have a little something going on. Man, talk about two birds with one stone." He's bordering on giddy now. "Oh man, this is too sweet. The poor, star-crossed, moon-eyed lovers. Tell me, Lorenzo, is she good? Looks kind of old from where I stand. But maybe you like your bitches run hard and put away wet."

The muscles in Lorenzo's left arm tense, and his hand curls into a fist.

"Ah, ah, ah, Dr. Rossi." Morgan pushes the needle's point harder against flesh.

A pinprick of a red spot appears at the contact point, and a single drop of clear fluid rolls down the side of Lorenzo's neck. It's impossible to tell whether it's sweat or serum.

"You know," Morgan says, his voice syrup sweet but still menacing, "I'm not much of a scientist. All that poring over data and running the same fucking experiments over and over again. I hate that shit. But I'm a good reader. A good people reader. And I can read other things. Like that little bottle over there that says 'Local injection only.'" He knocks his chin toward the spilled contents of the surgical tray without moving his eyes off me. "I saw that, and I had to ask, why? Why local only? What would happen if I pushed this needle in like so—" The needle buries itself a millimeter or two into Lorenzo's neck, far too close to the jugular vein. "What would happen if I just started pushing down on the plunger? Any ideas?"

"Go ahead, Morgan," Lorenzo says. "Gianna, get the hell out of here. There's a spare key under my car's fender. Take it and go."

"Don't be so fucking brave." Morgan's eyes—those nasty rat eyes—bore into mine. "You move, bitch, and I'll start pushing the stuff into him." The eyes shift slightly to the left, over my shoulder. "Go back into the lab."

It takes a moment before I realize he's not talking to me. A firm grip, not as strong as a man's, but strong enough, tightens on my elbow, turning me slightly.

Jackie.

Her head moves in one sharp, defined jerk. *Let's go,* it says. In her free hand are Petroski's keys. They sound like tiny metallic bells in the still of a room where everyone seems to be holding his or her breath.

"Get Petroski," I say. "Let's get this over with." It takes every part of my human brain to ward off the reptilian instinct to flee.

"Don't do anything stupid, Jean," Morgan threatens.

"Listen. If you have a human bone left in you, Morgan, you'll do this right. Have Petroski shoot him. Make it clean. You can always call it an accident later on."

There's a pause while Morgan considers this.

"Self-defense?" I suggest. "The serum's going to be harder to explain. We're talking about a reputable biochemist here, not some schmuck you recruited from grad school. Think about it. Think what you're going to say when Lorenzo Rossi walks out of this building speaking in tongues. Then think about what the Italian embassy's going to say."

Morgan's thinking takes an eternity. I spend half of it thinking about guns.

Like any mechanism, they have parts. The part you put a bullet in, the part the bullet comes out of, and the part that makes the bullet go from one place to another. Easy. Simple. Unchanged for centuries. Lock, stock, and barrel. In one order or another.

During the other half of Morgan's thinking time, I consider Sergeant

Petroski, the philosophy major turned soldier. Husband. Father. A man whose hand shakes when he draws his service pistol. A man who knows where the safety is and how to disengage it.

Jackie yanks on my arm again, and I turn to her.

"What would you do to be free, Jacko? Because right now, I'd do just about anything."

She doesn't say a word, but she does smile.

"Petroski!" Morgan yells.

Heavy boots echo through the lab. Under them, paper rustles. A sharp crack marks the end of a wayward pair of glasses. The entire world slows as Sergeant Petroski approaches the open door behind me.

"Sir!" Petroski barks.

It all happens in the blink of an eye, but I know my mind is recording each image, each still frame of the movie. Maybe one day I'll be able to slow these images down, replay them in real time. Right now, the sequence is haphazard and choppy, the soundtrack garbled.

"Shoot this man," Morgan says.

Petroski draws his service pistol. The gun is close enough to my ear that I can feel small perturbations in the air beside me, see the shimmer of Petroski's hand as it tries to steady itself.

"Safety off?" I say.

The click is like a shot, automatic and deafening.

"Now, Jackie."

She's on him. Petroski's hand slackens. Later, I'll never know whether he cooperated or whether he was taken by surprise, but I make the move I planned, close my fingers around the grip, and aim a few inches below the blue pin glinting on Morgan's collar.

And I squeeze.

SEVENTY-FOUR

Morgan falls, and I fall with him, my ears screaming a note in the coloratura style as Jackie tries to catch me under the arms before I hit the ground. She's strong, or she was once, but gravity wins this game. I hit the floor with a thud I can feel but can't hear, and realize I'm holding something.

Lorenzo is at my side, his breath hot in my face. I see his mouth moving as he pries apart my fingers, disentangling the bulky steel from my grip.

"Relax," he says. The word comes out like he's talking underwater, but I can see the individual sounds. He reengages Petroski's pistol with the flick of his thumb, uses his shirt to wipe the grip and trigger, and hands it back to the soldier, who is leaning over Morgan and watching the blood bloom from his chest. A sickly scarlet puddle stains the white tile floor.

"Where'd you learn to do that?" I say to Lorenzo. It sounds like *Wa ya la ta da tha?*

"Two years in the Italian army." Then, more seriously: "Can you hear me?"

I nod. "A little."

"You'll have some ringing in your ears for a while. Maybe an hour. It'll get better, trust me."

"I hurt him, didn't I?"

Lorenzo checks over his shoulder to where Morgan lies. "Yeah. You could say that." The words are still muffled but slightly more intelligible.

"We need to move him," I say.

Jackie's already thought of this. She's standing in the doorway with Lin, Isabel, and an armful of suit jackets and lab coats—anything left by the men when they evacuated. She touches my arm, then gestures to the floor where Morgan is lying, points to herself, and makes circling motions with a finger. It's less elegant than the structured sign language Lin and Lorenzo use, but I get the point. Jackie will take care of the bloody thing in the corner.

Petroski, slightly recovered from the shock—although I wonder if he'll ever truly recover—helps Lin and Isabel roll Morgan and swaddle him in cloth while Jackie starts working on wiping down the room. It's a scene from a slasher movie, blood on the floor and ugly Rorschach-like splatter on the wall behind where Morgan stood, holding Lorenzo at needle point. Lorenzo sees the look on my face and explains.

"Forty-five caliber, Gianna. You blew a hole in him the size of Virginia."

"I killed him, didn't I?" It's not really a question, more of a processing aid. I killed him. I killed a human being.

"Yeah," he says softly. "And we need to go. All of us."

Lorenzo and Petroski drag the lifeless body of Morgan LeBron onto the gurney and wheel him out. I watch as the doors of Room 1 slide open, then closed. A minute later they're back in the main lab, minus one rolling stretcher. The six of us work in silence with bleach and rags, erasing the gore on the walls and floor of the room, tossing one blood-and-bleach-soaked rag after another into a thick plastic bag Lin procured from a storage cabinet. From time to time, she and Isabel sign to each other. I can't understand it, but what they say looks comforting, hopeful.

When nothing remains save the stinging odor of chlorine, we file out and scrub what's left of Morgan from our skin. Lin disappears and comes back with six clean lab coats, which she hands out. It doesn't take more than a glance down at my own clothes to realize why I need to cover up. Everyone else looks much the same.

I turn to Petroski. "Can you get us out of here and past security?"

None of the six pairs of ears has heard the intruder, the giant of a man who now stands between us and the exit.

Oh shit, I think. Maybe I say it out loud, maybe I don't, but I hear it, clear as a klaxon.

The man who has silently come into the lab is the last person I want to see, and the one I've kept seeing all this week, always when I don't expect to, as if his sole task is to watch us.

Poe.

Now I realize maybe that was his task all along.

"Leave everything and come with me," he says.

Petroski's hand goes to the .45 on his hip, and I follow Lorenzo's eyes as he tracks the motion.

"Don't be stupid, Dr. Rossi," Poe says.

I open my mouth to speak. Nothing comes out.

Poe looks over the soldier standing between him and the rest of us. It seems as if one eye stays trained on the gun while the other surveys our little cadre of rebels. He steps forward, slides the .45 from its holster, and racks the slide. "Better if I have this for now." Nodding to Petroski, he says, "You first. Then Dr. Rossi. Ladies, single file, just like in school. And don't say a word."

We line up, and Poe takes the rear, following us through the chimp room. At the doors, he instructs Petroski to open them, and we walk the short distance from the lab to the nearby service elevator.

It's already open.

And inside is a face I recognize like a mother recognizes her own child.

SEVENTY-FIVE

The elevator doors might as well be the very mouth of hell, complete with their ominous *Abandon all hope* warning inscribed where the lighted numbers should be. Still, I step inside, following the others. Hope be damned.

This is my son.

Steven slumps toward me, suddenly more boy than man. In two days, he's grown leaner, and the rippled bones of his ribs rise and fall under my hands as I draw him close. Wherever Poe is taking us, we're on this trip together.

Poe interrupts, gently breaking this mother-child embrace. "Time for that later, Dr. McClellan. When we get to the main floor, don't look up and don't speak." He takes three black bands from his hip pocket and passes them to Lorenzo, Petroski, and me. "Put these on."

"No way," Lorenzo says. "No fucking way."

Petroski blanches, shaking his head.

"They're plastic," Poe says. "Just do it. Sergeant Petroski can't get you out of here. But I can. As long as you do what I tell you."

I snap the band around my wrist as the elevator doors hiss closed. The men do the same.

I look a question at Poe.

"Go ahead."

"What's going on?" I say, bracing myself for the familiar jolt of pain. Nothing happens.

"Trust me," Poe says. "Keep your heads down and—I don't know—try to look tired until we get past security."

Not one of the people in the elevator—including me, I note, as I catch my reflection in the polished steel wall—needs to be told to look tired. I check Lorenzo's watch and see that it's two in the morning, but an entire year might as well have passed since Morgan brought us back here yesterday afternoon.

Poe presses the button for the main floor. "When we get out, you stay in line and get into the back of the van."

The ride up seems to take an hour.

"Okay," Poe says. "Ladies first."

We file out, Lin, Isabel, Jackie, then me. I feel something press against my back as I leave the elevator, and for a brief irrational moment, I think it's the barrel of Petroski's .45, but it's warm and reassuring. Lorenzo's hand.

"I'm right here, Gianna," he whispers.

Where there were two soldiers, I now count ten pairs of shined boots. One pair steps forward smartly.

"Can't let them leave, sir," a voice says. "Dr. LeBron's orders."

I'm itching to tell him Dr. LeBron isn't going to be ordering anything in the near or distant future, although he may be putting in a few requisitions for ice while he burns in hell. I find myself smiling and bite the insides of my cheeks.

Poe, directly in front of me, waves a familiar-looking envelope. In the upper-right-hand corner is the presidential seal. In the left corner, where a return address would normally go, is a silver embossed capital *P*.

"Tell him," Poe says, handing over the envelope.

There's an anxious rustle of paper as it's torn open and the letter inside is unfolded.

"Fort Meade," the soldier says. "I see. All right, then, you know where to go." Then, in a gruffer voice, "Stand aside, men. Let them through."

Whispers circulate around me. "Isn't that the doctor?" "Hey—he's the kid on television last night." "I think I know her from somewhere." "Damn, seven today."

Burke's quote comes back to me, the same one Steven paraphrased when the men came for Julia King: "The only thing necessary for the triumph of evil is for good men to do nothing."

As we pass by the rows of boots, as I hear the whispers and murmurs of these men, I can't decide whether I feel disgust or pity.

Maybe it's a mixture of both.

Lorenzo is the last to climb into the van and takes a place next to me on the bench. Before Poe closes us in, I note an uncomfortable absence of windows, or of an interior handle on the rear doors. Terror creeps under my skin as the engine fires up, and I wonder if I've—we've—just been played.

"Everyone okay?" a voice says. It's male, soft, and low. I recognize it but can't place the timbre. "Turning lights on now, Christopher."

That voice. It's so damned familiar.

When the lights flicker on, illuminating not seven, but nine faces, I see why. Del and Sharon are in the back of the van with us. I reach out to take Sharon's hand, squeezing it. She squeezes back and I almost want to fling myself into the arms of this woman I barely know.

"Time for that later," she says.

"Sharon, honey, you get to work on those bracelets," Del says, pointing to Jackie's, Lin's, and Isabel's wrists. "You remember how to do it?"

Sharon rolls her eyes. "I did our girls, didn't I?" Then, addressing me, she adds, "Men. They all think they're the only experts." She plants a kiss full on her husband's lips. "Don't you worry, honey. I'll love you 'til you're dead. Maybe a while after that."

She works with the same steadiness on Jackie's counter as Lin did when trepanning the chimpanzee. "You might get a little buzz, girl, but don't say a word unless you want both of us knocked on our asses. Del's good, but his key isn't the same one those goons who put this on you used. Okay. Ready?"

Jackie nods, then looks directly at me.

"There!" Sharon says, a note of triumph in her voice, and moves on to Lin.

The first words out of Jackie's mouth are exactly what I expect.

"Holy fuck. That was worse than that fucking meditation retreat I went on twenty years ago."

Same old Jacko, I think, and talk to her—really talk to her—for the first time in two decades.

SEVENTY-SIX

B y the time we turn in to the Rays' dirt track that passes for a driveway, Del and Sharon have sketched out everything: Poe's successful
undercover work, Del's staged arrest, and Steven's rescue.

"That part was easy," Sharon says. "He was one floor below the lab.
Along with a few army guys who thought they could take over the building. Didn't work. Those boys have more brawn than brains." She looks
over at Petroski, who's staring blankly at the air in front of him. "Sorry.
I don't mean you, soldier."

By the way her eyes move up and to the left, it's clear this is exactly
what she means.

"He did just fine, Sharon," I say, watching a glimmer of confidence
brighten Petroski's eyes.

Poe cuts the engine and circles around to let us out. When he helps
Lin down, her tiny hand disappears into his. The two of them together
make a ridiculous sort of King Kong tableau. Lorenzo hops out and
reaches up for me with both arms.

"Jean?"

Patrick's voice cuts through the still night air at the same time I let myself fall against Lorenzo. I break away and walk across the dirt road to my husband, feeling a pull in both directions, sensing that I'm being ripped in two.

"Thank god, babe," Patrick says, folding himself around me. When Steven appears, the three of us stand in a three-way embrace until Poe has to break it up.

"Later," Poe says. "Some of us have a long night."

My long night begins with a quick check on the three sleeping bodies tucked up on an air mattress in Sharon Ray's living room. It ends with me collapsing face-first on the empty space beside Sonia. The last thing I feel before sleep hits is her tiny chest rising and falling under my arm. The last thing I hear is Poe, in the Rays' kitchen, laying out the plans for my escape.

SEVENTY-SEVEN

Here is how it happens on this last day.

Patrick kisses us goodbye—first the twins, then Sonia, then me, and finally Steven. He pays extra attention to Steven. You never forget your firstborn, I guess. You don't love them more, but the bond is different, primal. As he drives away with the single vial hidden in his briefcase, I'm glad we don't have a dog anymore. We did once, a silly mix of collie and beagle and shepherd that sat morosely on the doormat from the moment Patrick left in the morning until he came home at sunset. I don't think I could bear watching that dog wait.

It's bad enough for me.

Everything after his car disappears, taillights glowing in the pre-dawn, is a construct, a video I play while the kids fight over the last brownie Sharon puts out, while Sonia tells her brothers in no uncertain terms that she *knows* they're trying to cheat at cards, while Patrick's half-empty coffee mug sits on a stranger's kitchen counter, the liquid in it evaporating and condensing into a thick brown sludge. It still smells like shit, this American coffee, but I savor it all the same.

"Just going to lie down for a minute," I tell Sharon, who's making breakfast for a dozen hungry people. She waves me off with an all-too-somber understanding, telling me to use her room if I like. I retreat with the rest of my coffee to an unfamiliar place with still-drawn blinds and a ceiling fan humming a monotonous lullaby.

I see Patrick slowing and stopping at the security gate, holding out his identification card to the Secret Service agent, a man who wears a white squiggle in his ear instead of an embroidered SS patch on his arm. He parks, and I think he looks at the sky, maybe toward that patch in the east where the sun presses through the darkness.

The meeting is held over breakfast, but to Patrick it must feel like the Last Supper, and he's the Judas in the crowd, passing a poisoned cup.

That was the plan, to put it in the water. Or the coffee. Or the champagne that will be popped open and poured out into delicate crystal flutes for twelve distinguished guests to sip while they congratulate one another.

One is President Myers. Another is Bobby Myers, miraculously recovered from his six-day journey into the land of aphasia. I'll never know whether the brain damage was real or fabricated, but if I had to bet, I know where my chips would fall. There's Reverend Carl and Thomas the Intimidator. Six members of the Joint Chiefs of Staff are present, also the attorney general and chief justice, both notorious adherents to the Pure Movement.

Patrick is number thirteen. The Judas Iscariot of the Oval Office.

As I lie here in bed, numbed by the spin of the ceiling fan, these religious coincidences strike me as funny. Water, wine, thirteen men. Reverend Carl and his insanity. They say Christ was one of three things: a lunatic, a liar, or a lord. Mad, bad, or God, as the saying goes. I can't believe Carl Corbin is a god—even if I believed in such divine entities.

Gods may or may not play dice, but they sure as shit don't load them with mind-altering poisons.

My coffee has grown cold, but I drink it anyway.

Sunday night—was it only just twelve hours ago?—Patrick decided he would dose the water and the coffee first. Then, whatever was left in the vial he would keep aside for himself, should the need arise. I shudder when I think of this way out, the Judas escape, but Poe tells me Patrick insisted on it. So many well-laid plans go wrong.

This is all I can see. Maybe my imagination isn't up to the task. Maybe it's too up to the task, Technicolor vivid and laser sharp. After all, who wants to daydream about her husband dying?

I check the clock on Sharon's nightstand. Its hands say this is the time.

don't sleep. I can't. Instead, I walk with the kids to the horse barn, watching Sonia as she leads her brothers on a tour. She's all words now, a geyser of them.

"This," she says, patting the roan with one hand and stroking it between the eyes with her other, "is Aristotle. She's a girl horse. Even though Aristotle was a guy. She's also my favorite. Sharon says she's super smart."

As Sonia passes around thick hunks of carrot, instructing the boys *exactly* how to hold their palms flat and let the horse take the carrot without taking off a few fingers with it, I pull Sharon's mobile phone from my pocket and dial a number.

The receptionist is not thrilled with my sudden change of plans.

"Mrs. McClellan," he says, his voice as nasal and pinched as Morgan's was.

"Dr. McClellan," I correct.

He doesn't apologize, only goes on with his lecture. "We schedule these tests in advance for a reason. You were supposed to be here an hour ago. I don't know if we can fit you in until—" I hear papers rustling over the phone. "Until next week at the earliest."

"Never mind. I'm not coming in for the test," I say, and end the call.

"Come *on*, Mommy," Sonia says. "It's your turn to feed Aristotle."

"If Aristotle eats any more carrots, Miss Sharon's going to have a mess on her hands. And guess who she'll ask to clean out the stable?" I say.

"It's called mucking, Mommy." Sonia looks absolutely ecstatic at the idea of spending an afternoon raking horse manure. *Good for her,* I think.

"Can I be a vet when I grow up?" she says.

"Maybe. Lots of school, though. You up for that?"

"You did it, Mom," Steven says.

I think my heart might explode, and I know I made the right decision. "I'm going back to the house, okay?" I say, and leave, wiping my cheeks with the backs of my hands. The left side burns, although not nearly as much since Lin went to work redoing the bandaging. Still, the salt stings.

Lorenzo is sitting on the rear bumper of the van, looking out toward the road, waiting.

"Well?" he says when I join him.

"I can't go without the kids."

"Poe says you have to. Even if"—he pauses, as if he doesn't want to say my husband's name—"even if Patrick succeeds, nothing's going to change overnight. They have our names. They've got pictures. We need to get out of the country."

"Where is Poe, anyway?" I say, changing the subject. My mind's made up—I need six passports, not one.

"He left with your husband," Lorenzo says. Then, looking up: "Speak of the devil."

Patrick's car comes at us like a runaway train, skidding to a stop next to the van. A dust cloud rolls over the ground as the driver's-side door swings open, and Poe climbs out.

The passenger door does not swing open.

"Where's Patrick?" I say. "Where the hell is he?"

Poe responds by yelling at Lorenzo. I hear every other word: Go. Lin. Stop. Bleeding. Tried. Help. No. Time.

My brain fills in the rest, and I jerk the rear door open, hitting the side of the van. The noise is a dull thud. Inside me, there's screaming, one long and final scream that draws itself out and finally breaks into nothing.

"What happened to him?" I say, but I don't need to ask.

SEVENTY-NINE

I planned Patrick's funeral as a quiet affair, but looking around at the crowd of men and women at the Rays' small farm, I realize my efforts were in vain. Neighbors I didn't think cared are here, including Olivia and Evan King. Julia, too, of course. She and Steven are talking with the tentative air of frightened children, which, I know, is what they are. A few old friends have driven in from the West Coast, since air travel has temporarily come to a halt.

The entire country is in a state of chaotic transition, thanks to Patrick. In many ways, I still love him. In many ways, I'm sorry he's gone.

Radios and televisions have stayed quiet these first few days, and newspapers are running already-told stories. Washington, DC, is locked down tighter than a bank vault. The hurricane of terror may be over, but we all know a storm will linger. We all know we're still not safe.

Del and Sharon have decided to remain, though, and Jackie's staying on at the farm to help with the resistance, to clear out the rubble and rebuild.

"I'll stay, too," I tell her after we put Patrick in the ground. "I want to."

She treats me with the same heavy hand she always did, back when we were young and stupid. Or back when I was stupid. I don't think Jackie ever was.

"You need to go," Jackie says. "Right the hell now." When I try to protest, she puts a hand to my belly. "You know you do, Jeanie."

She's right, of course. Jackie's always been right about some things. She takes me in her arms, now lithe and sinewy from physical work, and in the hug I feel everything. Gratitude. Pride. Forgiveness. No more bubble around me.

"Go on, girl. Your man is waiting," she says, and breaks the embrace.

My man.

It seems too soon to think of Lorenzo as my man, as my lover. But I feel his hand on the small of my back as he leads me toward the farmhouse. The gesture is so simple, and complex at the same time. Part of me wants to turn back, run toward the fresh mound of earth where Patrick is buried, but I don't. I stay with Lorenzo and gather the kids, telling them to start packing.

Maybe, though, a small piece of me will remain here at this farm. To keep Patrick company.

Chris Poe shook his head when I asked him what happened downtown. I insisted, though. It's nice to be able to insist once again, even if the information I demanded was hard to hear.

Life throws little ironies at us. So the fact that Morgan LeBron, the incompetent little shit I took care of only a few days ago, was the cause of Patrick's death held less surprise than it might have.

"I wasn't inside," Poe said, his eyes studying some lump of clay between his shoes. "And Dr.—Patrick—came running out the side door like a wild boar that smells fresh blood."

I nodded, letting him know it was okay to keep going.

"Yeah." Poe ground his boot into the clay, swiveling the toe until there wasn't anything left but dust. "All I heard was 'Lockdown! Lockdown!' and something about Morgan's memo. Well, that's not true." Another clay ball suffered under the toe of Poe's left boot. "I heard shots. You know how they always have those guys on the roof of the White House? The ones no one ever sees?"

"I know."

"Well, I guess that's who fired. I don't know any more to tell you, Dr. McClellan."

"Jean," I said, taking his hand. "Jean is fine."

He turned to leave, shoulders low and fists shoved deep in his pockets. Then he looked back. "I do know one more thing, Jean. When your husband took that bullet, I swear he was smiling."

"Thanks," I said. "That's good enough for me."

And it still is.

anada was warm all through June and July while we waded through the red tape and waited as six passport applications wormed their way around Montreal offices. I would have liked to stay, if only through the summer months. Something about the lakes and rivers as heat-drenched days morphed into cool, calm nights was soothing. But home called, and French never came easily to me. Also, I needed to see my mother.

The south coast of Italy, by contrast, is anything but calm. Tourists have invaded our sleepy town, and more will come in August. Still, it's the place I want to be.

Lorenzo has been working on his project day and night since we arrived on Monday. He says he'll have the serum ready by the weekend, thanks to the notes Poe stole from his office back in Washington. He's promised to take the kids hiking on Capri when he's finished. He's good with them, I think, and Steven, although leery at first, has grown to treat him like an older brother.

I'll take that.

We've kept up with the news since we crossed the border from Maine into Canada, and then the Atlantic from Canada to here.

The radios and televisions came to life again; the presses started to roll out newspapers. Women marched in silence until their wrists and words were freed. Jackie seems to be at the head of every march. She writes that, when she's ready, she'll visit us.

I don't think we'll return to the States right away, not even now that my second country has returned to what it should have been for the past year, not even now that a new president has taken the keys from the old one, stating in the simplest of terms that he will never see America repeat the damage it wreaked over the past twelve months. With the first eleven men in the line of succession, well, not quite what they were before their own aphasia serum went to work, the charge of rebuilding went to, of all people, the secretary of health and human services. A funny thing, really, when I think that might have been Patrick's next job.

Jackie's also volunteering as a campaign coordinator. Her letter from last week told me all about the midterm elections, how Congress will be back to normal—maybe even better—with all the women running for office. *Imagine, Jeanie,* she wrote. *Twenty-five percent in the Senate and the House. Twenty-five! You should come back and get in on it.*

Maybe next year, I wrote back. And I meant it.

For now, though, Jackie has my financial and moral support. I'm not ready to get into politics, not just yet. The boys love the sun and air of Italy, Sonia's second language is on its way to being as expressive as her first, and everyone is excited about the baby coming.

Also, I enjoy watching the women here. They talk with their hands and their bodies and their souls, and they sing.

ACKNOWLEDGEMENTS

A man named Stephen King once said, "No one writes a long novel alone." I was ten or so when I first read those words at the beginning of *'Salem's Lot*. They still ring true today.

VOX was born of multiple mothers and fathers, and I owe thanks to all of them:

To my agent, Laura Bradford, for her honesty and clarity and cheerleading. No writer could wish for a better champion of her work.

To my US editor, Cindy Hwang at Berkley; my UK editor, Charlotte Mursell at HQ HarperCollins; and the entire teams at both publishers for their fierce enthusiasm.

To my early readers, Stephanie Hutton and Caleb Echterling, for speed-reading a novel written in two months and helping to make it shine.

To Joanne Merriam at Upper Rubber Boot Books. Without her original call for submissions to the *Broad Knowledge: 35 Women Up to No Good* anthology, Dr. Jean McClellan's tale might never have happened.

To Ellen Bryson, Kayla Pongrac, and Sophie van Llewynn, who critiqued the short story with keen eyes and told me to keep going.

To the amazingly supportive crowd of flash fiction writers and editors who have sung out my short work over the years. Y'all know who you are.

To you, dear reader, who will ultimately judge this story. I do hope you enjoy it. Most of all, I hope it makes you a little bit angry. I hope it makes you think.

And finally, to my husband, Bruce, who supports almost everything I do. And who never, ever tells me not to talk so much.

ONE PLACE. MANY STORIES

Bold, innovative and
empowering publishing.

FOLLOW US ON:

@HQStories